W9-BEM-993

TO THE BRINK

BOOK THREE IN THE BODYGUARDS SERIES

Cindy Gerard

St. Martin's Paperbacks

This is a work of fiction. All of the characters, organizations and events portrayed in this novel are either products of the author's imagination or are used fictitiously.

TO THE BRINK

Copyright © 2006 by Cindy Gerard.
Excerpt from *Into the Dark* copyright © 2007 by Cindy Gerard.

ISBN: 0-312-94858-1
EAN: 9780312-94858-0

Printed in the United States of America

St. Martin's Paperbacks edition / January 2006

St. Martin's Paperbacks are published by St. Martin's Press, 175 Fifth Avenue, New York, NY 10010.

10 9 8 7 6 5

This book is dedicated to the brave men and women of the United States military who defend, on a daily basis, all that we hold dear.

And to my sister, Wanda Burrows. I love you, Sis, for all you do, for all you are.

ACKNOWLEDGMENTS

I received an extraordinary amount of assistance from some equally extraordinary people who kindly provided me with relative details and countless hours of their time. I am blessed to call them friends.

Very special thanks go out to:

SSG Ian Trammell, USAREC, for his expertise and generosity of time and for being such a nice guy and stand-up soldier.

2nd. Lt., Ret. (Canadian Armed Forces) Darryl Hadfield, who didn't know me from Adam when I accosted him in cyberspace, and was still giving of his time and knowledge, and for his wonderful Web site: www.Rotorhead.org.

SG Jorge Sanchez, U.S. Army, 1-15th IN, my "adopted" son, provider of a wealth of information, and brave defender. Stay safe. Stay strong.

Catherine Mann, amazing author, and her foxy flyboy hubby, Lt. Col. Robert Mann, USAF, for filling in some critical blanks.

Rhodora (Doddie) Householder and Ana Angelica for their invaluable information on the beautiful Philippine Islands. Ladies, your gracious giving of time and detail is so very much appreciated. Thanks also to Marie Nicole Ryan and Sherry Weddle from the KOD/CNN loop for putting me in touch with these wonderful women.

Once again to Cynthia Clark, Psy.D., forensic psycho-pathologist, for her expert assistance in medical issues.

Jim Newberry, Jet Aviation international planning office, for developing the "critical" flight plan.

Jim Connell, all-around great guy, pilot extraordinaire, and my go-to guy concerning luxury jets and air travel regula-tions. Plus, he's a super proofreader!

Susan Connell, dear friend and my source on all things Peru. Someday we will go there together. Heck, maybe we'll even take the guys along.

Leanne Banks, my book buddy. Thanks for the lift when I needed it most.

Kylie Brant and Roxanne Rustand, talented authors both and my conference roommates for life. Thanks for the grins and giggles and support but mostly for not posting certain New York City photos for all to see.

Any mistakes are mine and mine alone and would have been legions had it not been for the assistance of these wonderful people.

SPECIAL FORCES MOTTO:

DE OPPRESSO LIBER—TO LIBERATE THE OPPRESSED

I

"ETHAN. UM. HI. IT'S . . . DARCY."

Darcy Prescott had known this call would be hard. She hadn't talked to Ethan Garrett in the five years since their divorce. So yeah, dialing his number had been good and hard; saying his name—even into his answering machine—was painful. Emotions strong with it made her voice break.

Gripping the receiver with both hands, she dug deep for a steadying breath. "Look. I . . . I think I might be in some trouble here."

The admission was as difficult to make as the phone call. Saying the words out loud gave them credence. It did horrible things to the rhythm of her heart, which had been getting a helluva workout in the past few hours.

That would show those misinformed souls who wondered in admiration and awe over her seemingly unflappable control.

If they could only see me now.

"Maybe some bad trouble," she confessed, still reluctant to believe it as she dragged a hand through her hair. "It's . . . it's almost midnight here in Zamboanga. I can't . . . I can't think, you know, how that equates to

West Palm Beach time. Maybe one in the afternoon? Two? I'm not sure."

She paused again when she heard a thread of hysteria creep back into her voice. She blinked up at the white ceiling of her hotel room.

God. This is great. Piggybacked with her current state of mind—which was only a little to the left of full-blown terror—she felt like she was spiraling out of control.

Okay. That soaked it. She'd never dreamed *hysteria* would be a part of her vocabulary. Not in this lifetime—*which may not be all that long,* she reminded herself with a grim compression of her lips.

"Okay, look," she said, if not steadier, at least resolved to calm herself down. She absently repositioned the base of the phone on the rich mahogany nightstand sitting beside her bed. "I'm at the Garden Orchid Hotel. It's on . . . let me think. Governor Camins Avenue. Here's the phone number.

"Can you . . . can you call me, please? As soon as possible, okay?" Darcy slowly closed her eyes, forced them open again. "I'm in Room 333. If . . . if I don't answer when you call, well, try again, okay?

"Look, Ethan. I—" She cut herself off as a tear surprised her and trickled down her cheek. She brushed it angrily away with the back of her hand. "Just call. And hurry."

She hung up the phone. For a long moment she sat motionless, staring at the cradled receiver. And praying that he would get her message.

Before it was too late.

It probably should have bothered her that her ex was the first person Darcy thought to call the moment she'd realized she had a problem. And it *might* have if she could function on a level separate from the fear. So far that wasn't happening.

This morning, she hadn't been afraid. This morning, she'd had her usual busy day in the Consulate office at the U.S. Embassy in Manila. But this morning, Amanda Stover had still been alive. When a coworker had called Darcy on her cell phone an hour ago and told her about Amanda's death, a cold chill had swept her from head to foot.

"How?" she'd asked, sinking down, in shock, on the hotel bed.

"Hit-and-run."

It had to be an accident, she had told herself over and over, her heart hammering as she'd scrambled for her briefcase and dug out the envelope Amanda had given her just before Darcy had left the embassy to catch her flight to Zamboanga.

Darcy stared at the envelope she had promised Amanda she'd open as soon as she had time. The envelope she'd ripped open only moments ago.

The minute she'd read the note tucked inside, Darcy had known. The car that had killed Amanda hadn't done so by accident. Amanda had been murdered. And because Darcy suspected that she was now in possession of the reason Amanda had been killed . . . she was also certain that she would be targeted as the next person to die.

With trembling fingers, she picked up the padded manila envelope she'd resealed as tight as Fort Knox. Then she addressed it and slapped on enough postage to send it to the moon. All the while she fought to gain the upper hand over a damnable rising panic.

Panic wasn't going to help her get out of this alive. Clear thinking was.

On a serrated breath she stood and walked across
the room, her sandals sinking into the plush cream-
colored carpeting. Slowly, she opened her hotel room
door. She looked up and down the empty hall. Reason-
ably certain it was safe, she slipped outside and headed
for the elevator.

"Good evening, Miss Prescott."

Rudy Mar startled her as she hit the ground floor
and stepped out of the elevator into a lobby done in
soft tropical colors and more mahogany wood so deep
reddish brown it was almost purple. She paused to see
the night clerk standing at his post behind the polished
registration desk where the older man appeared to be
reading the *Manila Bulletin.*

She forced a smile. "Good evening, Rudy Mar."

She always stayed at the Orchid when her duties
took her from Manila to Zamboanga. She knew many
of the staff on a first-name basis. Had learned that the
Zamboangueños were warm and friendly. As a rule,
she enjoyed a little pleasant banter with Rudy Mar,
whose chocolate brown eyes and salt-and-pepper hair
made him look grandfatherly and kind.

Tonight, however, the rules had changed.

"Going out so late, miss?" Rudy Mar's wide smile
was tempered with concern.

"Actually, I need to mail a letter."

Rudy Mar laid the newspaper on the granite top of
the registration desk. Darcy thought of the headlines that
would appear on tomorrow's edition: *U.S. Embassy Employee Victim of Hit-and-Run,* and her blood ran cold.

"Miss?"

Her gaze snapped to back to Rudy Mar. His expec-
tant look made her realize she'd completely tuned out

something he'd said. She forced a smile. "I'm sorry . . . what?"

"I said I'd be happy to take care of that for you. The letter," he clarified with a nod toward the envelope.

Involuntary reflexes had her clutching the envelope in question tighter. "Oh. Thank you, but I . . . I want to take a walk anyway, get a little air. I'll just drop it at the post office while I'm out."

She smiled in what she hoped was a credible impersonation of a woman who wasn't about to jump out of her skin.

"As you wish, Miss Prescott. Enjoy your walk. But stay on the main streets, all right?"

"Thank you. I will. I'll be back in a few minutes."

As she walked out the hotel door, Darcy understood both Rudy Mar's concern and his puzzlement over her actions. American embassy staff were often targets of terrorists in the Philippines and she was not employing hazardous-duty procedure. Normally she followed protocol to the letter—she buried her route to work in the mornings, alternated modes of transportation, and when out of Manila, as she was now, she would normally phone for a car and driver if she needed to go out.

Tonight, there wasn't time. She had to get the envelope out of her possession, in the mail, and get back to her room before Ethan called back. And the bigger problem: she no longer knew whom she could trust.

She cut a seemingly meandering path along the main streets, checking often to see if anyone was following her, hoping she'd spot a motorcab or a jeepney and could hitch a ride. One or the other would provide some cover and a little anonymity at the least and make her less of a target with a big bull's-eye on her back.

Tonight, however, both were as scarce as taxis. So she walked. Fast.

It was a typical Philippine evening. Close, hot, tropical. The sidewalks had sucked in the sun's rays during the day and now breathed them back out like heat from a cooling oven. Darcy had dressed for the sweltering night in a white short-sleeve cotton T-shirt and khaki shorts. Still, her back was damp with perspiration. In her espadrille sandals, the soles of her feet were damp as well.

Another night, another time, she'd have enjoyed an evening stroll as she had many times in this beautiful place that was heralded as the city of flowers and reminded her of southern Florida. But this wasn't just any other night.

She caught a glimpse of herself in a storefront window and realized how tense she appeared. Determined not to draw attention to herself, she made her shoulders relax, deliberately slowed her pace in the face of a warning voice that cautioned her to hurry.

Hurry; hurry!

Struggling to ignore it, she walked on past a towering old cathedral rich with Spanish influence, past a more modern gift shop. The streets were, for the most part, deserted, but should anyone see her, they would see an American of average height, a little on the slim side, out for an evening stroll. No one special. Nothing remarkable. Except, maybe, for the auburn hair she'd cut to shoulder length a year ago when she'd started her Permanent Change of Station with the embassy in Manila.

Tonight more than ever before, she regretted the bureaucratic snafu that had restationed her from Mexico City to Manila. As she'd always done when her rotation was drawing to a close, she'd filled out her dream sheet requesting a PSC in Paris. *Paris, Philippines—*

easy to get the two mixed up, she thought sourly, then sucked in her breath on a gasp when a cat sprang out of an alley and, yowling, ran in front of her.

When her heart dropped back into her chest, she made another quick visual search around her. Only after she was satisfied that no one was following her did she walk across Corcuera Street toward the post office she'd intentionally bypassed the first time she'd strolled past, playing tourist again, staring at the Mayor's office.

Without breaking stride, she walked behind the Mayor's office where the post office was located, fished the padded envelope out of her purse, and dropped it in the after-hours mail slot.

For the first time in an hour, she felt a tentative sense of relief. If anyone was watching her, they'd never have noticed what she'd done. And if anything happened to her, at least now there was a chance someone would eventually discover the envelope and know the reason why.

Now all she had to do was make it back to her room and wait for Ethan to call and tell her what to do to get out of this fix.

Everything was going to be fine.

And then she noticed the van.

Her heart did that ricochet thing again and she faltered, barely catching herself before she stumbled.

A quick glance over her shoulder told her the vehicle was long and black and beat-up; the windows were tinted so dark she couldn't see inside. Even as she told herself it was nothing to worry about, her pulse ratcheted up several beats.

But when the van crept up and kept pace beside her, her heart damn near jumped out of her chest.

Adrenaline fueled by apprehension rushed through

her system so fast it made her nauseous. She told herself that just because a van was the most commonly used abduction vehicle in the islands it didn't mean that's what this one was about. But when it pulled up to the curb a few feet ahead of her and the side door slid open, the apprehension churning through her chest shifted to flat-out panic.

"Don't stop; don't stop; don't stop." She repeated the command like a mantra.

When the gruff voice belching out from the murky black interior of the van ordered her to do just that, she broke into a dead run.

She was three blocks from the hotel. So close she could see the sign—GARDEN ORCHID HOTEL—ahead.

She pushed herself harder. Pushed until her lungs burned with the effort.

Almost there. Almost—

Something slammed into her from behind. She fell face-first onto the pocked concrete walk. And pain momentarily edged out the panic as the fall knocked the air out of her lungs.

She couldn't breathe, couldn't scream, as the leaden weight of a man who smelled like smoke and sweat and mean sandwiched her between him and the sidewalk.

The white-hot abrasion of her skin scraping against concrete seared her knees; her palms, where she connected with the paving to break her fall, burned like fire.

Her breath finally rushed back on a gasp. She tried to scream, but a filthy hand clamped over her mouth. Something jabbed into her ribs, hard.

Oh God. He has a gun.

"Come with me or die here, Miss Prescott. You decide."

She went limp, prayed for a miracle—the *pulis,* police, an off-duty Special Ops soldier. Anyone who might help her.

No one did.

Her attacker stood, made sure he stayed behind her so she couldn't see his face, and hauled her roughly to her feet. With the gun still buried in her ribs, he pushed her toward the van, then shoved her, hard, into the backseat.

Her head hit the opposite window with a crack. She groaned, fighting through the dizzying pain. She was still seeing stars when her abductor climbed in behind her. Before he'd even slammed the door behind him, the van shot off through the Zamboanga streets with a squeal of tires.

Coarse hands wrenched her arms behind her back; he tied her wrists so tightly that she bit back a cry when the rope dug into her skin. Then he blindfolded her.

She fought it, but there was no escaping the dirty rag that he pressed over her mouth and nose.

Panic outdistanced pain.

Loss of consciousness was terrifying and fast.

Her last coherent thought was of Ethan. His name broke on a sob just before everything faded but the truth: not even Ethan could save her now.

MANILA, PHILIPPINES
PRESENT

"Charles. Charles!"

He could feel an irritating nudge at his ribs. Hear the ring of his alarm. And his wife gnawing away at the edge of his consciousness.

"Charles, for God's sake. Wake up and answer the phone."

Phone?

The cobwebs started to thin.

The phone. Not the alarm.

He dragged a hand across his face, shook his head to clear the sludge, and reached for the phone on his bed-side table.

"What?" he said in a tone that said much more than the four-letter word suggested.

"I am sorry to bother you at this late hour, sir." The man on the other end of the line recognized anger when he heard it, and this was the last person he wanted to piss off.

"Then why are you?" Charles growled, and glanced at the alarm. It was the fucking middle of the night.

"You said to notify you when it was done, sir."

Charles lay back on a pillow cased in fine Egyptian linen. He stared at the dark ceiling. Ah. Yes. He had asked to be notified.

So it was done.

Well. He hadn't expected to feel remorse. Frustration over the need for it all, yes. Relief that his little problem was solved, absolutely. But not remorse.

He exhaled a deep breath. Couldn't be helped.

"And you're certain of this?" he asked finally, relieved to hear Marion's deep breaths beside him, telling him she'd fallen back asleep.

"Yes, sir. It is done."

Without another word, he hung up the phone.

Darcy Prescott's pretty face flashed before him in the night. It wouldn't be pretty now.

It was a shame. A waste to lose her.

Amanda Stover had been no great loss. She had been a blond airhead. *Yet she'd been smart enough to run to Ms. Prescott when she'd discovered what she'd gotten ahold of, hadn't she?* a niggling voice reminded him.

He plumped his pillow, cursing his own carelessness.

It was water under the bridge now. Everything was taken care of. Everything was fine.

And what was done was done.

He rolled over and went back to sleep.

2

HE'D KILLED FOR DARCY PRESCOTT ONCE. And as the *whump, whump, whump* of the Huey's rotor blades chopped through the murky Philippine night at six hundred feet, Ethan Garrett accepted that he was about to kill for her again.

I think I might be in some trouble here. . . . Maybe some bad trouble.

Face grim, Ethan remembered the tremulous sound of his ex-wife's voice on his answering machine almost thirty-six hours ago. Like an automaton, he punched a cherry Life Saver out of a half-eaten roll and slipped it into his mouth. He barely noticed that his fingers smelled like the oil he'd used to clean his M-4 assault rifle. What he did notice, in the muted cockpit light while the chopper spit out a full-bore attack of noise that his radio headset couldn't block, was the faces and the demeanor of the other occupants on board the bird.

The three other men were also in combat mode. And as they neared the target zone among the seven thousand plus islands making up the Philippines, Ethan prayed to God that he'd not only get Darcy out alive, but also that the men who were risking their lives for her, at his request, came out the same way.

He stared at the instrument panel; it was a blur of tiny green lights in the darkness. Familiar ground. Once he'd climbed into the Huey, it was if he'd never left the service. It was Groundhog Day. Muscle memory and combat instincts resurfaced and took control as they had hundreds of times on hundreds of ops. Instincts as ingrained in his psyche as breathing made the years since he'd made his last land assault as a Special Forces soldier fall away on a welcome adrenaline spike.

Yeah. He'd been here before.

The stench of jet fuel. The swelling heat from the tarmac just before takeoff. Chopper engines revved until the earth shook. Rivers of sweat running beneath his flak vest, and the clutch in his gut as the bird lifted off and up into parts unknown.

It could have been yesterday that he'd made that last op. Only it wasn't. It had been three years. And this op was entirely different. He didn't have the might of the U.S. military behind him now as he had then. In fact, if the Army knew what he was about, *they'd* probably shoot him out of the sky long before the bad guys got a bead on him. A little matter of international diplomacy. To which he said: *Screw it.*

The Huey shuddered and Ethan longed for a shiny new Blackhawk like the ones he'd spotted at the recently reopened Clark Air Base that were used and maintained by the Special Ops guys and their support personnel stationed in the islands. As long as he was wishing in one hand and spitting in the other, he wished like hell he was going into this op with a couple of Ranger chalks and an ODA—a twelve-man Special Forces operational detachment A-team—on point. But beggars couldn't be choosers and he'd trust these three men—two who were his brothers and one who was like a brother—to pull off the impossible. Which, according to his father, was exactly what the probability was of getting Darcy out alive.

Impossible was a word Ethan had never accepted—except when it came to their marriage. And that was old, old news.

On a deep breath, he smeared camo paint on his face and reviewed the extraction plan in his head. They would start their search for Darcy on Jolo. The tadpole-shaped island was 960 kilometers south of Manila. The AO they were targeting was pure, rugged jungle spread out over thousands of acres of hills and gorges at the base of Bud Tumangtangis Mountain and far from Jolo City. It was also home to any number of belly crawlers, both the cold-blooded and the human kind. Ethan was only interested in the human kind—a ragtag cadre of murderous Abu Sayyaf terrorists. This particular cell of guerrillas and their larger counterpart on Basilan Island specialized in kidnapping. All indications were that the bastards had Darcy.

They had Darcy.

The grim truth replayed through his mind like a bad dream. It had been five years since the divorce, but Darcy *had* been his once. A part of his life. A part of his family. And he took care of his own.

He *would* get her back.

And the motherfuckers would pay if they so much as put a bruise on her.

He closed his eyes, thought of what they could do to

her creamy white skin, and fought a churning clot of nausea. This was gut-check time. He needed to keep his head on straight. His mind clear. So did his brothers and his brother in spirit, Manolo Ortega.

Ethan bit down on the Life Saver; the rush of adrenaline coupled with the tart, sweet taste of cherry that flooded his mouth settled him as he quietly observed each man on board.

His youngest brother, Nolan, in black jeans and T-shirt under his Kevlar vest, was at the bird's controls. Like the rest of them, Nolan was a civilian now, but the former U.S. Army Airborne Ranger was focused, steady, and strong as he worked the collective, cyclic, and rudder pedals, skillfully piloting the bird below the low-hanging cloud cover of an ink black night, zeroing in on the drop zone.

Thank God for Nolan and a filthy rich father-in-law with a G-5 Gulfstream. Even now, the jet was en route from Manila, where they'd deplaned, to the Zamboanga International Airport, where, if all went as planned, they'd fly out of here in a few days. Without the generous use of Darin Kincaid's luxury jet and the willingness of his pilots—all three former U.S. Air Force and totally up for a break from flying CEOs to board meetings—they'd still be switching commercial flights and waiting out layovers.

Allocation of the Huey, however . . .

"You never did say how you got ahold of the bird." Ethan spoke into his headset mike and watched as a grin broke over Nolan's face.

Dallas, Ethan's middle brother, glanced at Ethan. "*I* could tell you—"

"But then I'd have to kill *him,*" Nolan warned with a

notch of his chin toward Dallas, his grin taking the bite out of his threat. "Let's just leave it at some questions are best left unanswered."

Fine. The fact was Ethan really didn't care what methods Nolan had used to procure the Huey. All he cared about was the end result—although he did have a few ideas on how his brother had come by the bird. Given that the U.S. military had donated a flock of UH-1H Hueys to the Philippine military a few years back, it would be just like Nolan to figure that "borrowing" one back for a little while was a "tit-for-tat" issue. And given the rough situation on the islands these days and that Philippine military aviation assets were pressed into service for VIP transport at a moment's notice, it wouldn't be a stretch that Nolan could have simply *found* the rotary bird perched near some high-profile government building in Manila.

Nolan was resourceful that way. Ethan couldn't even guess how, in addition to getting his hands on the Huey, he'd also come up with the two full Aux fuel bags. Without the extra four hundred gallons of fuel, they'd never have made it the six hundred miles from Manila to Jolo, since the Huey's fuel tank range was less than half of what they needed.

Ethan had no doubts that even though Nolan could have pulled in a few markers from some of his Special Ops buddies who were stationed on the islands and wangled a Blackhawk with a longer range, he would have tapped them only as a last resort.

Farther back, sitting on the floor, Dallas was dressed in his salad suit and wearing face paint like Ethan and Manny. Ethan watched as Dallas, carrying a full combat load of ammo and a bandolier with extra magazines, was busy double-checking his gear. Although it had been a couple of years since Dallas had separated from the Marines, his thoroughness and precision told of his experience in Force Recon.

Marines. Christ. All these years later, Ethan still couldn't believe that Dallas had broken family Army tradition and joined the Marines. Hell, as a rule, a set of legs wouldn't so much as unzip his fly if a Marine was on fire and he could piss on him to put him out— and vice versa. But there was that blood thing.

And that pride thing, Ethan thought, feeling it well up in his chest as he watched Dallas attach an M-203 grenade launcher to his M-4, adding, in Dallas's words, "some boom to his bang-bang."

The middle son of Wes and Susan Garrett was a stickler for details. Dallas had calculated down to the last flare, fragmentation grenade, claymore, and round of ordnance what each man would need for the mission. And then he'd somehow *acquired* it along with the M-4s and Manny's Barrett sniper rifle. Like Nolan, Dallas was resourceful. Ethan wouldn't even bother to ask about Dallas's methods.

Ethan shifted his gaze to Manny Ortega just as his friend kissed the St. Christopher's medal he wore around his neck, then tucked it safely inside his shirt. Manny was Nicaraguan born, but he was a U.S. citizen now, recruited by Uncle while he'd been fighting the Sandinistas during the Contra wars. Manny had been Ethan's friend since they'd made Special Forces back in '89. They'd both been eighteen and as green as their berets, fueled by adrenaline and testosterone and seduced by the allure of being cultural chameleons in foreign lands. Since then, they'd saved each other's asses more times than Ethan could count.

From the far side of the Huey, Manny—also known

as Little Rambo to those who had dared needle him about his movie star good looks and gung ho attitude—flashed his perfect white teeth in a smile that said he was geared to go. Ethan hadn't even had time to brief him. All he'd had to do was call Manny in Boston, where he'd recently made detective on the Boston PD, and say he needed him.

The only question Manny had asked was, "Where and when?" and he'd put in for two weeks' vacation. Because Manny had to catch a commercial flight straight from Boston, they'd connected at the Ninoy Aquino International Airport in Manila only five hours ago, pulled their gear and weaponry together, and Manny still hadn't asked what was up.

"We're going black, boys," Nolan said, giving them all a chance to fix their night-vision goggles before he killed the interior lights.

Ethan folded up his map after double-checking the coordinates for the agreed-upon drop zone at the lee-ward side of the heavily forested island.

Less than five minutes later, it was time.

"I believe this is where you bail, heroes." Nolan's voice sounded distant and tinny through the headset.

Dallas kicked the coil of rope out of the open cock-pit door; then all four men made a quick SAT phone and GPS check. Satisfied, Dallas grabbed the three-inch-thick nylon rope in his gloved hands, backed out the door, and disappeared into space.

"Long way down," Manny said offhandedly as he peered over the side of the bird where it hovered above the beach at about thirty feet.

His statement finally made Ethan grin. He'd seen Manny single-handedly take out a six-man assault team in Afghanistan, outmuscle and outthink a kingpin's handpicked team of bodyguards during a drug sting on the Peru–Colombia border, and win the hearts of the most ruthless women north or south of the equator. Yet the man was scared shitless of heights.

"Look at it this way," Ethan yelled so Manny, who'd already ditched his headset, could hear him above the chopper's roar. "If the height doesn't scare you to death, the fall could still kill you."

Even though he could only read Manny's lips, Ethan grinned, recognizing the words Manny muttered in Spanish as a close cousin to "Fuck you."

After crossing himself, Manny grabbed the rope and set his feet. Then he sucked in a bracing breath and roped down to join Dallas, who should already have boots on the ground on the tiny beach.

"Kick ass," Nolan said just before Ethan removed his headset.

With a clipped nod and brief eye contact, Ethan mouthed, *Later,* and grabbed the rope.

"You bet your ass I'll see you later," Nolan shouted over his shoulder, and Ethan rolled out.

Nolan, Ethan understood, was still a little pissed that he wasn't in on the land assault. Couldn't be helped. His little brother had a baby on the way back home, and Ethan had promised Jillian that he wouldn't let anything happen to her hubby. Besides, they needed Nolan to haul their sorry asses off the island later— provided there was enough left of their sorry asses worth hauling.

They'd counted on the cover of darkness and a strong tropical wind to carry away the sound of the chopper. They'd gotten it. The wind and rotor wash whipped palm fronds into a frenzy and set even the sturdiest trees in the coconut groves along the outer fringe of the rain forest swaying. And as Ethan fast-roped down, undetected by the bad guys—no shots fired equaled no discovery—it was so far, so good. That, he knew, could all change in a heartbeat.

He hit the tide-and-rain-soaked sand only seconds after bailing out, then gave Nolan an all-clear signal with a brief flash from his light. Wasting no time, Ethan adjusted his NVGs, tugged his boonie cap out of his pocket, and settled the floppy-brimmed camo cap on his head. Then he headed through the coconut palms rimming the beach and into the jungle on point.

Crouched down, Camelbak full of water beneath the improvised ALICE packs and hopefully all of them carrying enough firepower to take out any tangos they came up against, Dallas and Manny followed right behind him. Within seconds, the three men disappeared into the undergrowth, indistinguishable from their surroundings as the Huey rose above the clouds and headed back to Zamboanga.

They were on their own now. And to a man, they knew time was running out for Darcy. If it hadn't run out already. It was pushing thirty-seven hours since Ethan had received her message.

I think I might be in some trouble here.... Maybe some bad trouble.

As Ethan climbed a ridge, then skidded down the other side with the help of a trailing vine, Darcy's words caromed around in his head like a pinball, a constant reminder that she was counting on him. When he'd returned her call, his heart had been pumping like rounds from an automatic weapon. But he hadn't reached her at the number she'd left him. So he'd called Sandy Jankowski in London. Sandy and Darcy had started their embassy service together. They kept close tabs on each other. And sometimes, when it was just too hard not to, Ethan kept tabs on Darcy through Sandy, whom he counted on not to give him away.

"I'm scared, Ethan. Really scared," Sandy had said when he'd told her about Darcy's message. "Darcy and I e-mail each other once, sometimes twice a day. It's a pact we made years ago. A fail-safe so we'd know if we should be worried. Her last e-mail was Monday afternoon. That was two days ago. She'd been about to leave for Zamboanga."

"Did she say anything else?"

"God . . . yeah, let me think. Something about a secretary at the embassy passing her some information that she'd found by accident. Darcy was kind of blowing it off, you know. Kind of a cyber head-shake because she didn't have the time to mess with it."

"This secretary? Was her name Amanda Stover by any chance?"

Silence. "How did you know that?"

Ethan knew because as soon as he'd gotten Darcy's message and couldn't reach her, he'd gone online and searched the news sites for the Philippines, specifically Manila. "Amanda Stover is dead, Sandy."

"Oh my God. Ethan—"

"News media is calling it a hit-and-run accident."

Silence rang on both ends of the line. "But you don't believe that, do you?" Sandy asked finally.

Ethan hadn't bothered to answer. "Same media source also states that an unnamed embassy employee has gone missing while on business in Zamboanga. No details available."

Sandy's sob had been audible. They both knew who that employee was.

"Do you know why Darcy was in Zamboanga?"

"Not specifically," she'd said, her voice breaking. "She just said she'd been sent down there on some embassy business. She makes regular trips, so it didn't seem unusual at the time."

Well, it was unusual now. Now that Ethan knew, with certainty, that Darcy had been abducted. It had only taken a couple of phone calls—one to the hotel where he had spoken to a concerned desk clerk who had talked to Darcy just before she'd left the hotel around midnight. The clerk had become alarmed when she hadn't returned two hours later. The other call had been to one of Ethan's contacts in a Special Ops team stationed at Camp Navarro, AFP Southern Command Headquarters at Zamboanga. According to his source there'd been a lot of tango chatter on the airwaves and in cyberspace all of a sudden. Talk of an abduction planned.

And, evidently, pulled off.

There was only one direction to point a finger these days when someone was abducted in the islands. An extremist Islamic terrorist network under the command of Chieftain Kaddafy Janjilani. This particular splinter group, known as Abu Sayyaf, specialized in kidnapping. Ransom was their main source of revenue. And Abu Sayyaf made camp in the jungle on Jolo.

The bastards didn't know it yet, Ethan thought, ignoring the sting of insects and the slap of wet leaves against his face as he humped over another ridge that was green tinged and daylight bright through his NVGs, but they'd just kidnapped the wrong woman.

He moved steadily forward. He hadn't seen Darcy since the divorce. He didn't talk about it. Didn't talk about her. Had never admitted to anyone except himself that he'd never gotten her out of his system.

Damn the woman. She'd always been more trouble than anything else in his life. More trouble and more excitement.

Five years after the divorce, he'd at least thought he'd figured out how to exorcise her from his system: he focused on the job, did what he had to do to get by, and left the past where it belonged. The job was running E.D.E.N. Securities, Inc., the West Palm Beach security firm his father had founded and Ethan now owned with his brothers and sister. Getting by was a matter of taking it one day at a time.

And the past—specifically the part involving Darcy—was history. At least he'd told himself it was until he'd gotten her call.

Then just like that—just hearing her voice again—and he'd known he would never be free of her. Had never *been* free of her. Like a fever or a virus immune to drugs, Darcy Prescott had infiltrated his blood and burrowed deep the first time he'd set eyes on her. . . .

3

THE NIGHT SKY PROVIDED A GLITTERING backdrop beyond the expansive stone terrace flanking the main salon at the U.S. ambassador to Peru's official residence. All that glittered, however, was not limited to the city lights and the candle glow glinting off the delicate crystal dressing an elegantly set table at the by-invitation-only U.S. Embassy party. A king's ransom in jewels sparkled around the necks and wrists and on the fingers of the dignitaries and their ladies in attendance.

Ethan had arrived at the mucky-muck dinner party not more than ten minutes ago. Later than was kosher. Sooner than he'd like it to have been. Unfortunately, he'd had his orders. For him, it was one of those *must attend* functions peopled by U.S. and Peruvian dignitaries, local civic and government leaders, and a smattering of foreign service officers and embassy staff. He and Manny Ortega were the token warriors. The symbols of the best of the best the U.S. Army had to offer.

Not lost in translation was an in-your-face reminder to the local populace of the U.S. presence in Peru combating the ongoing drug trade along the northeastern border with Ecuador that, among *other* things, was commonly known but never discussed or openly acknowledged. Ethan and Manny had both been "requested," in fact, to not only put in an appearance but also show up in full dress uniform, medals shining, boots spit polished.

This was the part of the job Ethan could do without. He understood that diplomacy was as integral to the working relations between the U.S. and South American countries as his A-team's operations in the area were. He understood that he would be called upon to factor into that diplomacy. But the longer he was out in the field, the more comfortable he felt there and the less comfortable he felt with people.

Interesting. He spent weeks on end slinking around the jungle. Didn't have human contact for days sometimes, and even then it was most likely the kind of contact that wielded an assault rifle with the business end aimed directly at him.

Maybe it *was* time he poked his head back among the civilized if that prospect was more appealing than a run-of-the-mill dinner party.

"Smile, *mi amigo*." Manny flashed a grin that generally had a *lay me down and do things to me* effect on women, as a caramel-skinned beauty walked by him. "This beats sucking dirt and crawling on our bellies any day. I know I don't miss the bugs and snakes, at least for a little while. And I have high hopes for the main course. Anything will be better than the monkey meat we've both grown to appreciate and love, don't you think?"

This was true. Ethan would *never* grow to appreciate or love monkey meat, no matter that there were times, in the jungle, where monkey meat and leaves were all they'd had to eat.

"What I think is that I'd like a beer," he said just as a

waiter appeared with a tray of full champagne flutes.

Manny snagged a glass for each of them. When he shoved one at Ethan, he took it with a glare.

Manny laughed. "You have no class, my friend. It's a good thing you have that tall, dark, and handsome thing going for you or the ladies wouldn't give you a second look, you know? Those baby blues are only good for so much play."

Used to Manny's good-natured slurs on his blue-collar preferences, Ethan tipped the champagne to his lips—and saw her.

He simply and literally froze, the glass hovering near his mouth.

She was, in a word, stunning. This slim, creamy-skinned redhead with Nicole Kidman beauty and grace and the most animated and wicked green eyes he'd ever seen.

He couldn't help it. He stared, mesmerized, as she talked to a barrel-bellied Lima suit who leaned toward her and whispered something in her ear all the while trying to get a glimpse down her dress.

It was some dress. A tight little black number. Sleeveless, a little low cut, and short enough to show sleek, slim legs and a whole lot of pale, silky skin.

My God. Lust rolled through him like a fireball dragging a ten-foot tail. How long had it been since he'd touched a woman's skin? Heard a woman's sigh? Felt a woman's heat as he pressed deep inside her?

How long since he'd seen a woman like her?

Never.

She'd taken the WOW factor to new heights.

Her husky laughter as she shook back that amazing mane of long fiery hair and let her admirer down gently had Ethan calculating the blocks back to his hotel and the bed where he wanted to see her stretched out naked and gasping beneath him. Preferably tonight.

"Who is she?" he asked when he caught his breath and his heart had dropped back into his chest.

Standing beside him, Manny followed Ethan's gaze. "The redhead? I don't know. I've never seen her before, let alone met her. Now, however, would be a good time to change that, don't you think?"

Manny took a step forward.

Ethan's hard grip on Manny's arm stopped him. "No. Now would *not* be a good time. At least not for you. Go find your action somewhere else, compadre. That one's mine."

Manny turned. Looked Ethan up and down. And must have recognized the warning in Ethan's eyes for what it was. Friend or no, this was a nonnegotiable issue.

"So, another heart's going to break tonight, eh?"

Ignoring the laughter in Manny's eyes, Ethan drained the glass, shoved it in the general direction of Manny's chest, and cut through the crowd toward her. "Don't wait up for me."

He was waylaid before he got ten feet.

"Lieutenant." Al Hayden—Ambassador Albert Hayden to those who hadn't grown up calling him Uncle Al—smiled with genuine warmth as he stopped Ethan. "It's wonderful to see you."

"And you, Ambassador." Despite their closeness and in deference to his friend's position, Ethan addressed him by his title as Hayden shook his hand. Respect and genuine affection for the ambassador compelled Ethan to cool his jets where the redhead was concerned. At least for now.

There were two types of U.S. ambassadorial appointments. Those bought by men via presidential ap-

pointments when they called in markers and sought the
position for prestige's sake and those earned by the
good guys, the ones who had worked their way up
through the ranks and actually knew what the fuck they
were doing. Albert Hayden was one of the good guys.

"It's been a long time, sir," Ethan said, and noted the
passing of years on the older man's face.

Hayden was a tidy five ten. Ethan had about four
inches on the diplomat. And like Ethan's father, Wes
Garrett, a little gray had started to show at the temples
of Albert's dark brown hair. His eyes were a clear,
vivid gray. And they missed exactly nothing.

"It *has* been a long time. Too long." The ambassador's shrewd gaze studied Ethan through a smile of
affection. "You look well," Hayden decided finally. "I
expected to be calling you captain by now."

Ethan was well aware that in his position Hayden
knew exactly where Ethan had been and what he'd
been doing in the jungles at the base of the Andes
along Rio Napo where it intersected with Rio Marañón
before both flowed into the mother Amazon. Just like
Hayden knew the physical toll the work took on
Ethan's body. And psyche.

"I *am* well," Ethan assured him. "And the new title
starts in a couple months."

Hayden considered him a moment longer, then nodded. "Glad to hear it. And how are your parents and
your brothers and sister? Have you had contact with
them of late?"

"Actually, I spent an hour on the phone with Mom
and Dad earlier today."

Out of the jungle for the first time in three months,
he'd taken advantage of the opportunity to call home

and reassure his always concerned mom that he was fine. That was *after* he'd showered until the hot water had been long gone and the stench of too many weeks without it had been washed away.

"You know Dad retired."

"From the West Palm PD?"

Ethan nodded.

Hayden's snort relayed his surprise. "Can't imagine Wes Garrett content with retirement."

"You know him well." Wes and Al had been in Ranger Bat together at Fort Benning. Served in 'Nam together. When their service was over, Al had turned to politics while Wes had gone back home and joined the West Palm Beach Police Department. A line of duty injury had finally forced him into early retirement last year.

"It lasted all of three months," Ethan told him. "Dad's since started his own business. Corporate and plant security, self-defense training. A little bodyguard work."

"And knowing your father, he sees it as a legacy to pass on to you boys."

"Don't forget Eve," Ethan warned. Nolan's twin sister could hold her own with the three of them. And they all—Dallas, Nolan, and Ethan—had the scars to prove it.

Hayden chuckled. "How can something so pretty and little be such a spitfire? She still planning on Secret Service as a career?"

"She is, yes. Speaking of pretty," Ethan said, taking advantage of the opening to get to his most pressing issue, "do you know her?" He nodded toward the redhead, who was very charmingly mingling with the savvy of one who was well suited to these stuffy events.

The ambassador followed his gaze. "Darcy? She's with the vice consul's office."

"Introduce me."

Hayden cocked a brow and Ethan felt a twinge of regret for a reputation he'd earned along the way as being a bit of a player.

"I'll warn you right now, Lieutenant, Darcy Prescott won't be anyone's flavor of the month."

"How about you introduce me anyway? Sir," he added with a smile, and walked with Hayden across the room.

The fact was, Ethan didn't have a month in mind. While it shocked the hell out of him, one look and he'd been thinking forever.

And after one night with Darcy Prescott in his bed, he wasn't sure forever would be enough.

JOLO ISLAND
PRESENT

There was luck. Then there was dumb luck.

Without a boatload of both, Darcy knew she was a dead woman. It was just a matter of time. Today, tomorrow. Soon.

She made herself as small and as quiet as possible. And she prayed that the twenty or so men gathered in small clusters around a nighttime campfire would forget that less than an hour ago they had lined up to rape her.

Rape. And probably worse.

Sweat, over and above that caused by the cloying jungle heat, rolled down her back. Nausea curled in her belly and rose like bile as she thought back to the ugly scene.

Thank God for Ben. Or maybe she should think of him by his Islamic name now: Rahimulla. Until tonight, though, he'd always been Ben to her. Ben Max

Reyes Ayala. A gangly young man of barely nineteen. A young man who loved his mother and Snickers candy bars. A young and troubled man, apparently, who had gone over to the dark side of Islam: jihad extremism.

And yet he felt loyalty to Darcy.

Thank God that he'd stepped in and stopped them from what would have been a gang rape.

Thank her God. She even thanked their God, who wasn't even a distant relative of a benevolent Allah. Their God was the God of murderers and assassins.

Abu Sayyaf. She'd heard the men murmur the two words like a mantra.

Abu Sayyaf. It meant Sword of the Father to those who believed.

It meant death to those the sword struck down—unless there was value to the cause. She represented value.

On a shuddering breath, Darcy shifted her weight off her bruised hip. She lay on her side where she'd been shoved on the jungle floor beneath a makeshift shelter comprised of a single sheet of torn and filthy canvas. She'd never been a Girl Scout. Didn't like bugs. Even the thought of a snake made her rigid with fear. But worse, even worse than snakes, was the dark. So she was grateful that they'd removed the blindfold early yesterday. Grateful but not foolish enough to believe the action had been prompted by kindness.

She'd slowed them down as they'd shouted, *"Bilis! Bilis!"* (*Be quick! Be quick!*), shoving and dragging her through what she'd known from the scents and the sounds was dense jungle even before they'd untied the length of black muslin from her eyes so she could see where she was going.

And she understood full well that there were only two things keeping her alive—her value as ransom bait and her captors' desperate need for money.

Desperate. Now there was a word she could relate to. For the past two days as they'd marched her up and down hollows and across streams pressing at a torturous pace through a tropical rain forest teeming with wildlife, including brilliantly colored birds and a riot of gorgeous orchids, she'd felt the desperation on all fronts.

How could anything this beautiful and lush be so treacherous?

And how could a body be so tired?

Her hands were tied in front of her now. Her head still throbbed from banging the wall of the van and from what she suspected was chloroform, which they'd used to knock her out. She was covered with bruises and cuts. She needed food. She needed water.

She needed rest. But as another night deepened to the incessant sting of insects, the growl of her empty belly, and the change of the guard watching over her, she didn't dare sleep.

Was too afraid to.

Through weary eyes, she studied her new guard. He was just a boy. Her heart broke for him even though he'd been in line to take his turn at her. Beneath the hatred etched on his horribly young face, he was a beautiful child, no more than fourteen years old. He should be carrying schoolbooks or a skateboard. Instead, he carried an assault rifle and a rage bred by poverty and despair.

But terrorists—twenty or so by her count in this particular band of guerrillas—recruited killers of all ages.

Abu Sayyaf may have been founded as a freedom fighters' organization by a Philippine veteran of the Afghan–Soviet war, but it had devolved into nothing more than a clutch of armed bandits who specialized in kidnapping. Just another offshoot Al Qaeda cell with links to both the Jordanians and the Palestinians. Above all, they were thugs for hire to anyone who could pay the price.

Which explained why they'd taken her. Someone had paid their price. Since two accidental deaths of embassy employees would arouse suspicions, she'd had to be dealt with in another way.

She'd understood that from the beginning. Someone wanted her shut up. Someone wanted her gone—and what better way to have her disappear than to bury her deep in the jungle on some remote island where she would never be found? And the bonus: Abu Sayyaf took all the heat.

She watched the few remaining men who were still awake and passing around a cigarette. Their dark faces were shadowed and weary in the fire glow. Their determination, however, was absolute.

Something slithered through the undergrowth behind her. Every muscle in her body clenched involuntarily.

Oh God.

A baboy-damo?—*wild pig*—she guessed hopefully. She'd seen several of them the past two days as she and her captors had trekked through the forest. But she knew she was fooling herself. Little grass piggies slept after dark.

Snakes didn't.

She bit her lower lip to keep from screaming. Held her breath until she thought she'd pass out. Then swallowed back the unreasonable urge to laugh hysterically at the depth of her danger.

Abductions and terrorists and snakes. Oh my. Life is full of fun adventures.

Get a grip, she mouthed soundlessly, and made herself breathe deeply until her heart rate settled. Until she could think straight again.

She suspected that she was on Jolo. She had sketchy memories of the kidnapping, sketchier still of the time between the abduction and when she woke up at daylight the next morning—at least she assumed it was the next morning. She did remember water. Crossing water. In a boat, maybe. With a loud motor. An outboard? She didn't know. But the reports filtering through the embassy lately all indicated that Abu Sayyaf activity had been heavy on Jolo, and the only way to get there was by air or water.

Even if it was only a guess, it helped to assume she knew where she was. It helped because she knew that if she could figure it out, so could Ethan. And then he would find her.

He had to find her.

She pushed aside the staggering odds of that actually happening and gauged the mood of the camp. All was quiet now. No arguing among the men. No eerie screams from the howler monkeys and baboons. No calls from the hornbills or odd whirring sound of the flying lemurs as they shuttled through the Narra trees.

Again, she thanked God as the memory of the ugly scene earlier made her glance toward Ben. No. *Not* Ben. *Rahimulla.* Rahimulla Sabur. He lay on a thin blanket directly in front of her "tent."

Amazing. It appeared that he was some sort of spiritual leader of the cell of angry, weary, and malnourished guerrillas. Fortunately for Darcy, Ben's mother was a Philippine citizen who worked on the cleaning staff at the embassy. A few months ago, she'd become ill and been in need of medical attention. It wasn't Darcy's job, but she had pulled a few strings, seriously bent a few regs, and made sure Ben's mother had gotten it. The young man had held undying respect for Darcy ever since.

Only his intervention at nightfall had saved her from a gang rape. And only his respect among the guerrillas continued to hold them at bay.

But for how long? That was the question of the day.

"I so apologize, miss." His English had been a little garbled with nerves, but his voice had been filled with regret and shame after the others had backed away, grumbling.

"What will happen to me?" she'd whispered.

He'd only shaken his head, his face grim, and reverted to the Tagalog spoken in the southern islands. *"Tumahimik ka kung ayaw mong masaktan."* Be quiet *if you don't want to get hurt.*

She'd nodded, figuring it was good advice. *"Salamat." Thank you.* And she'd been quiet ever since.

And praying for a plan to come to her. And for that luck she would need to get out of this alive.

But she understood that luck, like time, could run out with the twitch of a hair trigger or a shift back to gang mentality. The key was for her to remain supplicant. The goal was to stay alive. Darcy could handle it. She had to handle it.

First things first. She didn't dare sleep, but she needed to rest.

Rest, however, was as elusive as rescue. Hours passed as she lay awake, her mind reminding her not only of her peril but also of the choices she'd made in her life.

Of the mistakes she'd made.

Of the man she had loved and walked away from.

4

MANY OF THE STAFFERS HATED EMBASSY parties. Darcy loved them. She loved the flash and the dazzle, the intrigue and the politics. She loved the scent of exotic perfumes and cherry pipe smoke. She also loved the opportunity to dress up when too often her days were spent in business suits and her evenings in T-shirts and jeans.

Tonight she'd chosen a short sleeveless v-neck black sheath and spiky heels. It made her feel feminine and sexy. Judging from some of the looks she'd been getting, it made her *look* feminine and sexy. She liked that, too.

The honest truth was that she loved everything about her post in Lima. Sure, she'd put in for Paris on her dream sheet—but it had been just that. A dream. No one drew Paris as a foreign post until they had at least ten years under their belt, and even when a lot came into play, the chances were slim. In her case, Lima was only her second foreign post, so she'd never really expected Paris. And as it turned out, she was glad she'd ended up in Lima. She was absurdly in love with Peru even though she hadn't seen much of it yet.

She was not, however, in love with the Lima city

councilman who had just made it clear that he'd be
open to entertaining her and the idea of a discreet affair if she was up for it.

"Señor," she said, flashing him her sweetest smile,
"you flatter me. But I think you also tease me. Your
wife is so lovely and she obviously cares for you a
great deal."

Folding her hands companionably around his arm,
Darcy walked the councilman toward the wife in question to ensure that his overture got cut off before the
high notes. "Look how she looks at you."

In fact, wifey was glaring rapier-sharp daggers at
Darcy, but she didn't let it stop her.

"You are a lucky woman," Darcy said, handing the
gentleman over to his lady, "to have a man so enchanted with his wife."

"Enchanted?" the elderly woman said with a curious but nonetheless pleased look.

"Of course." Darcy smiled between them. "He was
just telling me how dear you are to him. How much he
adores you."

The would-be Don Juan nodded a smile to Darcy—
an acceptance and even affectionate admiration for her
expert maneuvering—and drew his wife to his side.
"You would doubt that, *mi amor*?"

They were cooing like lovebirds when Darcy
walked away, fully aware of another pair of masculine
eyes watching her.

She'd noticed the handsome lieutenant the moment
he'd walked into the reception room a little while ago.
How could she not have noticed him and his compan-
ion, for that matter? Anyone would be hard-pressed not
to. They were quite the striking pair.

She was used to seeing an American military presence in Lima. Marines guarded the embassy and historically the official commanding the joint military offices within the embassy was the highest-ranking officer of the branch with the heaviest military presence. Currently it was the captain of the naval contingent.

So, yes. She was used to seeing military men. She was not, however, used to seeing men like this one. Or reacting to them the way she was reacting to this Army lieutenant.

And react to him she did.

The American was not the more handsome of the two, she noted, taking in the flashing black eyes, flirtatious smile, and poster boy perfection of his military brother. But with his dark brown hair, deep-set blue eyes, and singular and edgy presence quietly proclaiming he was in command, capable, and, if need be, a ruthless warrior, he was definitely the more compelling.

He was wearing his formal dress greens. The uniform did little to conceal the breadth of his shoulders and the lean, toned musculature of his body. The black stripe running down the outside seam of trousers that bloused at the top of his black boots identified him as an officer. The green beret he held in his hand identified him as Special Forces. As did the insignia of crossed arrows on his lapel.

His rank—1st Lieutenant, which he wore on his epaulette—indicated that he was driven. The numerous ribbons and awards lined up in neat rows above the left breast pocket of his jacket indicated that he was also an overachiever.

For some reason, that made her smile, then smile

again when she realized he was watching her size him up.

And well, well. Look who was walking her way with the ambassador in tow?

"Darcy. You look lovely." Ambassador Hayden folded her into a fatherly embrace, then dropped a light kiss on her forehead.

An amazing man, was Albert Hayden. Sincere, honest, and, in contrast to the perception of most diplomats as being driven by politics and ego, Ambassador Hayden was one of the most caring men she knew. On all levels.

He cared about his country. He cared about his ambassadorial function. But on a more basic level, he cared about people and family. And he viewed all embassy employees as part of his extended family. Most specifically, he watched out for those new to the post— and in many cases on their first extended stay away from home and away from the United States—as if they were his children.

This was not Darcy's first post. Neither was she a child. She wasn't a fool, either. She recognized the fatherly warning in the ambassador's *watch your step with this one* look as he introduced her to Lt. Ethan Garrett.

Interesting, she thought as Ambassador Hayden gave her a discreet nod, then walked off to join another group at the far side of the room.

"Lieutenant," Darcy said, and accepted the hand he extended. "It's a pleasure to meet you."

"Miss Prescott," he murmured in a voice that was deep and smooth and had a totally unsettling effect on her. Then in a gesture that she should have found pretentious and affected but instead found oddly gallant, even charming, he brought her hand to his mouth and kissed it. "I assure you, the pleasure is mine."

Well, now.

His hand was rough, strong. His fingers tensile and lean. But his lips, where they lingered over the back of her hand, were incredibly soft. As soft as the breath that whispered across her skin and sent a shiver of arousal eddying through her system.

And not by accident.

The lieutenant knew exactly what he was about.

He was seducing her—launching a full frontal assault. And the look in his eyes when he straightened and met her gaze told her he wanted there to be no mistake about his intentions.

The eyes that held and captured her attention were a stunning, vivid blue. Intense and probing, alive and knowing. She'd never experienced such pure male appreciation as his gaze held hers much longer than was comfortable.

And yet she didn't look away. Truth was, she couldn't. She'd never reacted to a simple look with such instant awareness, such electric arousal. Even worse, he knew the effect he had on her. At least he had a pretty good idea if the smile tilting his lips was any indication.

Nice lips. Supple. Full. And he smelled . . . umm . . . he smelled of sandalwood and lush exotic spices.

Whoa.

She just might be in a little bit of trouble here. Not a position where she generally found herself with men. She understood men, could hold her own among them. But this man . . . this man was different.

He had a lean and hungry look about him—like a big jungle cat on the prowl. Sleek and dark and dangerous. And the way he was watching her made her think he might pounce at any moment.

She didn't know whether to be annoyed or excited by that notion. One thing she could not be was impassive.

She covered her hyperawareness of the testosterone aura surrounding him with a flirty tilt of her head. It was either that or jump out of her skin under his onslaught. "Been out in the jungle a little too long, Lieutenant?"

He smiled. Not at all offended. In fact, he clearly found her speculation amusing. Not that he addressed it.

"Sit with me at dinner," he said instead, his voice as dark as the night, as tempting as the original sin.

He didn't beat around the bush, did he?

She could think of a hundred reasons to say no. Starting with a self-confidence that made no bones about his plans for her and ending with the peal of her internal alarm system warning that he was a big juicy bite of something that might taste great but would be a whole lot more than she could chew.

My God, the man was potent. And arrogant. And tempting.

No wonder the ambassador had felt the need to warn her.

And no, she thought again, Ethan Garrett was not the most stunningly handsome man she'd ever met, but she'd been right about the compelling part, because she was actually thinking about what an affair with him might be like.

To *compelling* she added *dangerous.*

"I believe the place cards have already been set out," she said at long last, not knowing whether the little skip of her heart was prompted by relief or disappointment that she'd come up with an excuse.

"Place cards," he repeated with a frown.

She nodded. "Afraid so. I imagine it's a little too late to adjust the seating now."

"Ah, well." He smiled—another one of those devastatingly intoxicating smiles that did unreasonable things to her body temperature and respiration.

With a nod and a respectful, "Ma'am," he left her in the middle of the room.

Feeling like she'd been hit by a tank.

When Darcy entered the dining room with Sandy Jankowski—a coworker in the vice consul's office—an hour later, it came as no surprise that the lieutenant was already seated at the table.

"Who's the hunky SF lieutenant with the gorgeous baby blues?" Sandy asked with a grin. "And why does he look like he wants to eat you alive?"

Sandy was a petite brunette with big brown eyes and an irreverent smile. She and Darcy had become fast friends in the year since they'd started their PCSs in Lima.

"Ethan Garrett," Darcy said, and felt her pulse spike under his blatant scrutiny. "And to answer your second question, I have no idea."

Sandy laughed at the bewilderment in Darcy's tone. "Were I you, I think I'd be finding out."

"I don't know," Darcy said. "He might be a little too much for me to handle."

"Sweetie. Those are the best kind. Now go forth and flirt before the poor guy busts a vein."

Sandy gave her a gentle nudge in the lieutenant's direction and took off across the room.

Inertia more than a conscious decision propelled her in his direction. He rose when she walked toward him, watched her with those hungry eyes. She felt an instant and alarming shock of an answering need.

Oh yeah. This guy is colossal trouble.

"Miss me?"

She smiled, because for God's sake, what else could she do? "You're very confident of yourself, aren't you?"

"Confident that I know what I want when I see it."

She tilted her head. "I think I was right. You *have* been in the jungle too long."

He chuckled. Like his voice, the sound was deep and throaty and embracing. She managed to stay on her feet, but it felt like her bones had just liquefied.

"Well, would you look at this." He pulled out the chair beside his, feigning surprise. "What a nice coincidence. We seem to be seated next to each other after all."

She glanced from him to the place cards that sat side by side amid fine china and polished sterling and paper-thin crystal and did, for a fact, have their names printed in gold script. She had no doubt that he was responsible for shuffling the seating arrangement with a nifty bit of sleight of hand.

"Tell me, Lieutenant Garrett," she said as she took a seat. "Are you always this resourceful?"

He bent down as he pushed her chair in for her. His warm breath whispered across her ear. "When compelled, yes."

She stalled a shiver and smelled— "Cherry? Do I smell cherry?"

He sat down beside her and reached into his breast pocket. She actually salivated when he produced an open roll of cherry Life Savers.

"Oh my God. I haven't had one of these since I left home."

He held the roll out to her. She popped a Life Saver into her mouth with an appreciative, "Umm. Wherever did you find them?"

He didn't answer her for the longest time. He just watched her before finally saying, "If the look on your face is any indication of how you respond to pleasurable stimulation, I'm thinking I'll have to keep that my little secret. That way when you want something sweet, you'll have to come to me to get it."

He truly should have been assigned to a tank division. "Has anyone ever suggested that subtlety's not your strong suit?"

He pocketed the candy, all the while holding her gaze with an intensity that made her heart skip. Again. "I generally find subtlety a waste of time."

When she could speak beyond the lump that had suddenly lodged in her throat, she reached deep for composure. "Speaking of time . . . you don't believe in wasting any, do you?"

"No, ma'am, I don't. Life's too short."

Yes, she thought. This man would know about how short life could be. A warrior's wariness lay beneath all the heat in his eyes. He was a soldier. Not just any soldier. He was Special Forces. Elite of the elite. He knew about life and death. He experienced both every day.

Oh yeah. The self-confident lieutenant was as close to danger as she had ever come. There was a certain excitement in knowing that. Knowing that someone like him would be this interested in the youngest daughter of Delmar and Mary Prescott from Cincinnati, Ohio, whose most exciting moment to date had been boarding the plane to Peru.

Somewhere in the haze of all this excitement and riveting sensual awareness was the truth. She had reason to beware of this engaging alpha warrior whose intentions were as clear as the blue of his eyes. He could burn her. He could burn her quite badly if she wasn't careful.

But as the night wore on and her defenses wore thin, the fear of stepping into the flames with Ethan Garrett gave way to the bigger fear of what she'd be missing if she stood outside the circle of his fire.

Somewhere between the entrée and desert, and despite Ambassador Hayden's warning look and what she suspected would be a monumental error in judgment, Darcy decided to take a huge leap of faith and a giant step closer to the brink of what just might be her ruination.

"Just how much time do you plan on spending in Lima, Lieutenant Garrett?"

She could see it in his eyes. His beautiful, expressive blue eyes. He knew he had her, he *had* to know, yet the only indication he gave was a subtle shifting of his body closer to hers. "How much time do I need?"

5

"ROGER THAT." ETHAN SPOKE QUIETLY INTO his SAT phone as daylight of the second day broke down through the jungle like a strobe blaring through the overhead canopy of green on green. "Later, Bro."

He disconnected, then let his head drop back against the white bark of a gnarled dapdap tree with a muttered, "Fuck."

Dallas sat to Ethan's left at the base of the tree that dripped with brilliant red flowers. On his other side, Manny ripped open a power bar and said nothing. He knew from experience that when Ethan had something to say, he would say it.

After several long moments, though, Dallas grew impatient. He broke a silence so tense it hummed like a trip wire strung between them. "So I take it Nolan didn't have all good news."

Ethan inhaled deeply, let air out on a heavy breath. "No. Not all good news."

They'd been on the move all night. It had been slow, treacherous tracking. An hour ago, they'd had a breakthrough. Manny had found a trail. It was several hours old, but it was the lead they'd needed. Provided it led them to the terrorists who had taken Darcy. Until they closed in and got a visual, that was still up for grabs.

But Ethan knew. On a level that he couldn't begin to explain, he knew this was it. They were getting close.

But they'd needed rest. And he'd needed commo with Nolan.

When Ethan made contact with little brother, he found out Nolan had been busy. Nolan had called up some markers, oiled a few gears. It was because of his contacts at Camp Navarro that they'd had a bead on the tango's entry point into the island in the first place. The Air Force pilots flying out of the base at Zamboanga loved a chance to play outlaw, show off their toys, and indulge in a little unsanctioned extracurricular surveillance.

Their latest gimme—and all hell would break loose if the base commander got wind of it—was last night's midnight flyover in a plane equipped with forward-looking infrared aerial surveillance. Cruising thousands of feet above the island, the monitoring equipment had spotted not only the three of them but also a larger group about six hours ahead of them. Which meant they were on target to close in tomorrow.

That was the good news. The bad news was, in addition to them and the terrorist cell, the infrared technology had also picked up a mass of activity moving in from the base of Bud Tumangtangis.

Ethan dragged a hand over his face before breaking the news to Manny and Dallas. "Tourists and missionaries are abducted on a routine basis and the Philippine government makes noises but no tracks to find them. Seems that when an American embassy employee falls into the mix, however, the military decides to get its ass in gear and hunt them down." He paused, shook his head. "They're heading inland. A full company."

Dallas muttered Ethan's earlier assessment of the situation. Manny stood in silence.

They were so fucked. So was Darcy.

"So if the terrorists don't kill her, she's now in danger of getting caught in the crossfire from the Philippine military who are on a seek-and-destroy operation against Abu Sayyaf."

With a grim nod at Dallas, who now clearly regretted stating the obvious, Ethan stood, to the complaint of his knees. "Let's move."

Ethan kept in shape. He ran. Lifted weights. But it had been years since he'd slogged through a jungle, up and down crevasses and hills, carrying approximately seventy-five to one hundred pounds of combat gear.

"You know, this group might not be our bad guys," Dallas pointed out carefully as they set off, following the trail.

"It's them," Ethan said, and kept on walking. He knew they were on the right track, just like he'd known Darcy was the one the night he met her.

It had always been that way with Darcy. The first time he'd set eyes on her, he'd felt an unexplained connection. It was like a live wire, taut and tingling, had drawn them together.

He felt the same unsettling electric connection now. Felt it on a visceral level. Felt it living in his bones.

"Spread out . . . three to five meters," he said just loud enough for Manny and Dallas to hear. "And watch your six."

Ethan figured they still had four, maybe five hours before they made visual contact. But there could be trailers in the group and he wanted to make damn sure the three of them spotted any tangos before the tangos spotted them.

He had full confidence in Manny doing just that. Manny was an expert sniper, could pick off a target with the Barrett 82A1 .50-caliber semiautomatic rifle he was carrying at a thousand yards, no problem. How Dallas had come by that premium piece of firepower Ethan could only guess. It was a state-of-the-art weapon with a range of almost two thousand yards—and it was military issue.

Like every other piece of equipment and ordnance "commandeered" for this mission, Ethan didn't really want to know where Dallas had gotten the sniper rifle. The fact was, Ethan already knew everything he needed to know—about himself, about Dallas, and about Manny.

They weren't James Bond. They weren't MacGyver. They couldn't make an explosive device out of an MRE, a flashlight battery, and a little duct tape—although Dallas could make damn near anything with his roll of silver tape.

They were, however, among the best-trained fighters in the world. It may have been a few years since their last sanctioned op, but to a man, they'd never forgotten the regimen of combat training they'd received. Training that was designed for close encounters and geared for annihilation.

And as he pressed forward through the tropical heat, Ethan had no doubt it would come to that.

Just like he had no doubt he would find Darcy.

A cold sweat layered over the thick film of perspiration already soaking his body.

Sweet Jesus God, let her be alive.

She had to be alive. The thought of her dead was agonizing.

Darcy Prescott was the most vital human being he'd

ever known. Just standing next to her or lying beside her or buried deep inside the sweet silky heat of her, he'd felt more alive than he'd ever felt in his life.

He might not have been a part of her world for the past five years, but he'd always known she was alive; he'd always known where she was. It hadn't been enough, but it had been bearable. Losing her now would not be.

LIMA, PERU
EIGHT YEARS EARLIER

Ethan was barely aware of the murmur of the other members of the dinner party seated around the ambassador's dining room table. Hardly heard the laughter, the inane chatter. All the glittering jewels and designer gowns of the women in attendance were lost on him.

He heard only Darcy. Sweet Christ, she had him tied in a pretzel knot. He saw only her, in her simple black dress and wearing a simple silver chain around her neck. Saw the gentle ebb and flow of her pulse where that thin silver necklace lay against her skin. Saw the fiery sheen of her thick silky hair, the mobile fullness of her lips when she laughed or sipped delicately from her wineglass.

Every move was sexy. Every sound she made was a turn-on. And her scent. Floral but not too sweet. Fresh but not quite innocent. He'd never been so far gone on a woman so fast, never felt such immediate, gut-clenching need.

And he couldn't believe his good luck when after about an hour of carefully guarded small talk she asked, "Just how much time do you plan on spending in Lima, Lieutenant Garrett?"

His heart damn near stopped.

He had her.

Talk about a gift from the blue. He wasn't sure why, but this bright and beautiful woman was not only up to speed on his plans for her; she was also up for what he had in mind. It wasn't just the invitation in her question that told him; it was the invitation in her eyes.

Thank you, God.

He smiled into her beautiful all-American face. "How much time do I need?"

She sliced him a coy glance and lifted a water goblet to her lips.

And he almost went down in flames.

He didn't remember much of the rest of the dinner. He must have been a party to the general conversation, though, because the pompous ass on his right—an attorney on vacation from Baltimore who had wangled a dinner invitation because he was a distant relative of the naval base commander—kept peppering him with questions about the Green Berets the entire time.

Hell, it was his first decent meal in months—seven damn long courses—and he couldn't swear to eating beef or grubs.

But he did swear. Several times under his breath during the interminable two-hour meal when Darcy would smile at him a certain way and those green eyes would make promises of heaven. When his thigh "accidentally" brushed hers beneath the table his groin tightened like a fist. When their hands met, oh so briefly, the silk of her skin shot a goddamn 10,000-volt burst of electricity from his fingertips straight to his dick.

Jesus.

He'd turned into an animal in the jungle. It took every ounce of his control to keep the beast from howling at the moon and throwing the sexy redhead in the tight black dress down on the closest horizontal surface.

And wouldn't it just do wonders for U.S.–Peruvian diplomacy if he flipped up her skirt and put it to her between the butter knife and the sugar cubes?

Finally, *finally*, the dinner was over.

After making what he hoped were the right noises to anyone who seemed to care, he excused himself and Darcy from the throng. Gripping her hand tightly in his, he led her out the door and into the back of a cab.

Where he sat.

Eyes dead ahead.

Fists clenched on his thighs.

Ordering himself not to act like the rabid dog he'd turned into sometime around the third course.

"Problem, Lieutenant?" That silk and honey voice sounded so amused in the seat beside him, he considered telling her exactly what the problem was.

She wouldn't look so smug if she knew what he wanted to do with her. *To* her.

"I'm at the Hotel Bolivar," he said, doing what he thought was a remarkable impression of a man in control. "Will that work for you?"

When she said nothing, he gathered all of his restraint and looked at her. And oh God, he wanted this woman.

Her smile faded. Her breath actually caught.

He knew what she saw on his face. Need, squared. Greed, cubed.

For a moment, he thought he might have scared her to death—or at least into making a fast exit out of the cab.

He must have been holding his breath, because he felt it sough out of his chest on a slow, heavy sigh when she very clearly said, "My apartment's closer."

Sweet mother of God.

She scooted forward and gave the driver her address.

And Ethan lost it. She was so slight. So slim. Her hips so sweetly curved. Her ass so round and tight.

He reached for her, drew her onto his lap, and kissed her. Hard. Hungry. From the gut.

She made a low, humming sound deep in her throat and opened her mouth for his tongue. And damn, he thought he'd come right there in his dress greens and embarrass the hell out of both of them.

"Okay," he said, his breath hitching, his hands shaking like hell as he pried her arms from around his neck and set her away.

Deep breath. Another. "Okay. Just . . . um. Okay. Christ. *Christ,* Darcy, I want you so bad I'm afraid I'm going to hurt you."

He breathed in deep through his nose, let it out through his mouth, fighting dizziness in the wake of all the blood that had rushed from his big head to his little one.

"Lieutenant?"

Just the sound of her voice did things to him. Good things. Bad things.

When he thought it was safe, he chanced a look her way.

Aw God. Her cheeks were flushed pink. Her lips were swollen from that one heavy-handed kiss. Scared. She should be good and scared.

But her eyes said she was far from it. Her eyes looked all sleepy and heavy-lidded as she lifted her hand to his mouth, slid her index finger along the seam of his lips, and in a voice that grabbed him by the balls and twisted whispered, "You're not going to hurt me."

On a strangled groan, he covered her hand with both

of his, sucked her finger into his mouth, then forced himself to drag her hand away again. He cupped it in both of his and pressed it against his chest where his heart beat like crazy. "Darcy—"

"You won't hurt me." She turned her palm into his and laced their fingers together. "But if I were in *your* shoes, Lieutenant? *I* might be a little afraid of getting hurt."

It made him laugh. A weary *oh my God, I can't believe I'm so far gone* kind of laugh. It was the reaction she'd wanted. And it was the relief he'd needed.

He lifted her hand back to his mouth. Kissed her knuckles. "How much farther?"

"So, Rocketman . . . is there more where that came from?"

Ethan groaned, pushed out a chuckle, and if he'd had the strength and the breath, he would have dragged her on top of him and hugged the hell out of her. But he didn't have the strength. And he could still barely breathe.

Then there was the mortification factor. Christ, it had been all over in two deep thrusts.

He turned his head on the pillow, smiled an apology into her sleepy, amused eyes, and thought, *I am the luckiest sonofabitch on earth.*

Two seconds ago, he'd been as embarrassed as hell. He hadn't lost control like that since he'd been sixteen and one huge randy hormone.

And here she was, smiling. Making it a joke. Making everything okay.

He'd make it up to her for going off like a rocket the moment he pressed into her incredible wet heat. Swear to God, he was going to take her places she'd never been before for being so generous and for telling him with her sweet, forgiving smile and really fine sense of humor that it was okay. She wasn't judging him by his less than stellar nanosecond performance.

"That's *Lieutenant* Rocketman, if you don't mind."

Her soft laugh sounded lush and sexy against the pillow. "I stand corrected."

"Did I tell you I was a sprinter in high school?"

Still smiling, she sat up. "Never would have guessed it."

He grabbed her wrist and pulled her back down beneath him.

Levered above her on his elbows, he stroked a strand of her incredible hair back from her eyes. Soft. Her eyes were as soft as summer grass.

"God, you're beautiful. Why aren't you ticked off?"

"Let's just say I'm an optimist."

Yeah. So was he. And she was giving him more than enough reason to be optimistic about a lot of things.

The animal lust was quenched. A new tenderness replaced it. He ran a finger down her bare arm, amazed all over again by the silken feel of her skin. "Got to love an optimist. Don't love this so much, though. You've got too many clothes on."

His fault. They'd barely made it inside her apartment and he'd attacked her. Dragged her to her bedroom and dealt with the minimum amount of zippers and cloth and managed to roll on a condom to make what had just happened happen.

It had been that or die. He'd been sure of it. He was going to implode from the inside out.

Lord did he have a lot to make up for. Starting now.

He reached behind her and slowly slid down the zipper on her dress. "I hope I didn't ruin this."

Another sultry look on that gorgeous face had every muscle in his body knotting with need. "What you need to worry about," she said, lifting her arms so he could slide the dress up and over her head, "is ruining *me* . . . and I don't feel even a little bit damaged."

He had to be dreaming. He *had* to be. He touched her again, just to make sure.

"Not that you have any reason to believe me," he shrugged out of his shirt and kicked off his pants, "but I have every intention of well and truly wrecking you before this night is over."

She reached behind her back and unhooked her black lacy bra. An adorable dimple dented her left cheek. "And you plan on starting this devastation . . . when?"

6

DARCY SEMIDOZED WHERE SHE'D BEEN shoved down against the red bark of a Narra tree. Was it forty-eight? Seventy-two hours ago that this nightmare had started? More?

She didn't know. She knew only one thing, and of that one thing she was certain.

She was past the fear stage.

The body and the psyche could only handle so much stark, raw terror before one or the other shut down. She'd reached the point of no return several hours ago. And she'd made a choice.

She chose to be pissed off. And she chose to live.

Provided she got lucky. It all came back to that.

She lifted her head and shoved the damp hair from her face with her bound wrists. Another morning had passed. Her captors had slogged through the heat and humidity, dragging her through the thickening undergrowth, and pressed deeper into the jungle. Slower, though. They moved much slower than they'd traveled yesterday. Part of it was due to the terrain.

Moss and vines covered hidden rocks and made them slippery. Heavy undergrowth and gangly roots snagged her feet and slowed everyone down.

Earlier, morning rain had pelted down in buckets, welcoming and cool for the thirty to forty minutes it had lasted. In its aftermath, the sun boiled down through the tree cover; now steam rose from the forest floor like thick, damp heat from a dryer vent. Wet ferns and leaves clung like her soaked clothes, slicing her bare arms and legs and drawing insects to the scent of the blood oozing from the thin cuts; moss and grass clawed at her sodden sandals, bogging her down in the muck on the more level stretches.

Thank God they stopped much sooner in the day to make camp. Watching but unable to hear their conversations, Darcy got the impression that this was a predetermined spot. Like they'd planned on stopping here for a reason.

And something about that conclusion added an additional element of unease. Were they meeting someone here? Or was this where they planned to kill her and bury the body?

She shook off the thought and concentrated on the good news.

She was bug bitten, bruised, cut, and hungry—but she was alive. Her captors suffered the same fate. While they were more acclimated to the jungle heat and better dressed in long-sleeve shirts and pants to combat the sting of the jungle, they had to be as exhausted as she was. From what she could tell, they had little food, less water. The only thing that was abundant was the tension. And it was mud thick.

While she couldn't hear what they were saying at the moment, she'd kept an ear open through the laborious march. Verbal spats had broken out with too frequent intervals among the terrorists. Apparently "thick as thieves" didn't hold any weight with these guys. The only thing that tied them together was their extremist doctrine of hate. Right now that hate was focused on her—the cause of their infighting.

While they were fluent in English—if necessary, they growled orders to her in English—most of the men conversed in Tagalog. At times they reverted to the local dialect—Chavacano, a bastardization of Spanish and English—apparently thinking that she couldn't understand them.

They were wrong. Darcy had held her current post in Manila for close to two years. As she had with her other posts in Lima and Tel Aviv, she'd familiarized herself with the local languages. In the case of the Philippines there were many, but she'd concentrated on the two most widely used in the area—Tagalog and Chavacano.

Her efforts were serving her well now as they made camp amid renewed arguments and vicious glares in her direction.

As she'd done from the onset, she continued with a low profile. She sat in silence. She didn't make eye contact. She didn't complain. She did what she was told and prayed that Ben—Rahimulla—could keep the younger warriors at bay.

But as she drew her knees to her chest and gauged the mood, she feared that some of the younger, angrier members of the group would eventually hold the most sway. They still wanted to rape her. And then they wanted her dead.

Can't have it both ways, boys, she thought, for once in her life understanding the true meaning of gallows humor.

The terrorists constantly challenged the wisdom of capturing a hostage associated with the U.S. Embassy. They feared American reprisal if it was proven they were responsible for her abduction and argued that they had nothing to lose by killing her, withdrawing to Basilan Island, and joining a greater force of their Abu Sayyaf brothers.

A small faction, led by Rahimulla, held out for holding her for more ransom—no doubt his attempt at keeping her alive. It also confirmed her original conclusion that they'd already been paid by someone to abduct her. And thinking about who had most likely paid them, she realized that was the biggest betrayal of all.

She couldn't think about that now. Instead, she prayed that they would keep listening to Rahimulla, go for more money than they'd already received. At least then she had a chance of being released. Provided, of course, someone would cough up the ransom demand. It wouldn't be the U.S. government. She understood that. They didn't negotiate with terrorists. But her parents would. Or Ethan.

She let out a deep breath. Who was she kidding? Her folks didn't have any money. And Ethan. Ethan didn't negotiate. Ethan acted.

Please, God, let him be acting now.

In the meantime, she had Rahimulla. Bless him. Whenever the chance arose, she thanked him with a look for his efforts.

But Rahimulla was losing momentum. His arguments were holding less and less water. He was losing support by the hour. Which meant she was losing, too.

And knowing that, for the first time since this started, she thought about the possibility of dying here.

What happened next had her wondering if maybe dying was such a horrible fate after all.

The men arrived with much fanfare—albeit quiet fanfare.

If Darcy hadn't seen a flurry of movement on the far side of the camp—which was only about fifteen yards in diameter—she wouldn't have noticed the arrival of another terrorist band.

Her heart sank as she counted at least a dozen new men and boys.

"It just had to get worse, didn't it?" she whispered skyward.

No one seemed particularly surprised to have met up with the other men. No one but her—and the woman who suddenly appeared, bound and battered, as they dragged her behind them.

Oh God.

Oh . . . my . . . God.

Darcy's stomach twisted in sympathy and horror as she got a good look at the hostage.

She was a mass of bruises and cuts, her skin sunburned and peeling. Her long hair was a matted straggly blond that hadn't seen a brush or shampoo in— Darcy's heart clenched—how long had the woman been captive?

Long, Darcy decided with a sinking sensation in her chest.

Very, very long.

The woman stood there, weaving on her bare and battered feet. Her hands were bound in front of her and tied to a rope like she was a head of livestock. Her head was bowed, her shoulders hunched beneath a filthy and ragged camo T-shirt. Baggy green shorts hung on her thin hips. Bruises in varying colors and cuts in different degrees of healing or infection covered her emaciated frame.

She looked beyond exhausted. She looked beyond defeat. Beyond, perhaps, sanity.

Absent. Her body was here—but Darcy wondered if her mind had gone somewhere else.

Darcy wanted to go to her, prop her up. Hold her close. Shelter and protect her from what must have been barbaric sins committed against her.

Darcy hadn't even known she'd risen and leaned toward the hostage when Rahimulla's hand on her arm stopped her. A quick shake of his head begged her to stay put.

For the longest moment, she held his gaze, fighting with the urge to disobey him. But Rahimulla was the only thing standing between her and possibly the same fate as this poor woman. And Darcy wouldn't be any good to either one of them if she ended up dead for her efforts.

So she stayed where she was. Mouth shut. Fingers clenched so deep into her palms, she felt the sting from her ragged nails.

And she watched with an aching heart.

The woman could have been anywhere from twenty to sixty. Darcy couldn't see her face beneath the fall of snarled hair. Couldn't see her eyes. But Darcy was aware suddenly that she could hear her.

She'd thought she'd imagined it at first. But the sound became increasingly clear.

Soft continuous moans.

Keening little cries.

So low and so tortured, Darcy knew the woman wasn't even aware she was emitting them.

Darcy's heart clenched tighter—so tight it physically hurt.

In the midst of all that agony, the hair went up on the back of her neck and suddenly Darcy realized she wasn't the only one doing the watching. She tore her gaze away from the woman and directly into the face of what appeared to be the leader of this new contingent of rejects from the human race.

From the beginning, he'd seemed to command an inordinate amount of respect from all of the terrorists. Heads bowed all around when he spoke. Boys and men alike hopped to when he issued a quiet order.

And when she met his eyes—cave black, deep-set, and filled with disdain and judgment—she knew that her fate had just shifted to another set of hands.

He stalked toward her in his jungle fatigues, dragging the woman by the rope. He was tall and rail thin, his posture erect. His beard was ragged and unkempt, shot through with bits of gray. When Rahimulla filled him in on who Darcy was and why she was still alive, the slow, disgusted sneer curling his thin lips revealed broken, yellowed teeth.

There was no mistaking his opinion of Rahimulla's decision. Just like there was no mistaking that not only had the leader board changed, but her life expectancy had changed as well.

"Shut her up." His voice was whisper soft yet as deadly as the AK-47 he held in his scarred hand. "Or you both die today."

With a hard tug, he pulled the woman toward Darcy.

The woman stumbled, went down hard on all fours. Before Darcy could get to her she rolled to her side and curled into a fetal position, protecting her head with her arms.

Protecting herself. As she must have tried to protect herself from being beaten and kicked many times in the past.

"Sick son of a bitch," Darcy muttered under her breath, and walked on her knees to get to the fallen woman.

The butt of an assault rifle punched Darcy hard between her breasts and brought her up short.

The impact made her gasp and lose her balance. Steadying herself, she looked up and into the eyes of pure evil.

"You dare speak?"

She held his gaze defiantly.

"You do not speak, American infidel." He gave the rifle a hard shove that sent Darcy sprawling on her back, her sternum exploding with knifelike pain. "Shut her up," he repeated.

Darcy was still sprawled on her back, trying to catch her breath, when he walked away.

Gritting through the pain, she worked herself slowly to a sitting position. Rahimulla had turned his back to her.

Darcy understood. He was completely submissive to this new leader. She couldn't think about what that meant. She could only deal with the moment.

Back on her knees, she moved to the woman's side.

"Shhh," Darcy murmured gently, approaching her like she would a wounded animal. "Let me help you.

"Can you hear me?" she asked softly, leaning over the woman, who was little more than skin and bones. "I'm Darcy. I'm not going to hurt you. You're not alone anymore."

Darcy reached out, touched her hand to a frail shoulder. The woman flinched so violently that Darcy drew back, startled. And the keening grew louder.

"It's okay," Darcy said after a nervous glance toward the leader showed he was quickly losing patience. "I'm not going to hurt you," she repeated. "I'm not one of them. I'm an American. From Ohio," she added, thinking the more details she could provide, the better chance she had of reaching her. "What about you? American? German?" Darcy speculated, seeing up close that the woman's hair was a golden blond beneath the snarls and dirt.

And still she made those horrible sounds of despair.

Darcy looked across the camp where the terrorist leader now sat cross-legged in front of a group that had gathered around him. They had scared up some food and water for him. He drank and ate and talked, all the while sending threatening looks her way.

It was do-or-die, Darcy decided, looking back to the woman. She had to quiet her down or it was all over for both of them.

Gathering her breath and her courage, Darcy looped her bound wrists over the woman's head, then clamped her arms tightly around her slim figure.

The woman immediately flinched and fought to pull away. Darcy held on tight. In the end, the woman didn't have much fight in her. Less strength. Making soothing sounds, Darcy eased her painfully fragile body to a sitting position and held her close; held the woman's face against her breasts as she would a child, absorbing her almost inhuman sounds of pain.

And when the fighting finally stopped and the trembling began, Darcy just held on tighter.

"It's okay. It's okay," she whispered over and over

again. "You're going to be okay. You have a friend now. You have me. Hold on. Just hold on to me. We're going to get through this. We're going to get through this together."

She lied. She knew she lied. She didn't know any such thing. But a lie was much less painful than the truth this woman had lived.

So Darcy lied for her. To ease her mind. To quiet her. To convince her of something Darcy was no longer sure she believed herself.

And she lied for herself because the alternative was too horrible to contemplate, let alone believe.

Finally, *finally,* the poor soul fell silent. Fell asleep—or passed out—in Darcy's arms.

Thank you, God.

Darcy let out a relieved breath. And continued to hold her. No matter that her arms ached and her hands were going to sleep. She held on.

And that's how they stayed. Darcy was not going to let her go. Because the truth was, Darcy needed this woman almost as much as she was needed by her. After too many hours of uncertainty, Darcy needed something to think about other than herself.

Exhausted, she let her cheek rest on the woman's dirty hair. Darcy closed her eyes . . . and tried to think about anything but where they were, what would happen to them, and the sad truth that the only plan she had was staying alive until Ethan found her.

If Ethan found her.

If he found *them.*

She'd been so certain that he would. But the longer this went on and the more feral the arguments among her captors, the less certain she was that Ethan could even locate her, let alone rescue her.

To combat those thoughts, she mentally pictured Ethan slinking through the jungle at this very moment, searching for her. But mostly, she simply thought of him. Of the husband she'd never stopped loving long after love had ceased to be enough to keep them together.

7

DARCY WASN'T A TOTAL INNOCENT. BUT NEI-
ther was she a player. She'd had relationships. And
they'd been important to her. She never engaged in sex
with a man just for sex's sake. Had never slept with a
man without knowing him, liking him, and respecting
him, either.

At least she hadn't until she met Ethan Garrett.

Yet here she was. Half-dressed and horizontal with
a man she had met less than three hours ago at a formal
embassy dinner party. A man who had wanted her with
an urgency that had thrilled and excited her and left her
breathless.

Above the thrill, though, beyond the rush, a curious
and warming tenderness was far and above the reaction
that took hold in the aftermath of the stealth in which
he'd just taken her.

My God, had the man taken her. In truth, he'd lost
control. His need had been huge. For her. It was hum-
bling and empowering. Yeah. She had the power at the
moment, and considering the will of the warrior lying
beside her, that was the biggest surprise of all.

The only thing she clearly understood was his em-
barrassment.

Well, we just couldn't have that.

"So, Rocketman . . . is there more where that came from?"

And just like that things were okay. The look in his eyes shifted from mortified to "all was right with his world."

He undressed her slowly then. And made her tremble. He had such a soft touch for a man with such big scarred and calloused hands. And he had such a fine smile.

Between silly, sexy banter and deep, drugging kisses, he laid her back down. And taught her things about sensual pleasure she'd never known she was capable of feeling.

"Here?" he whispered, his mouth making love to her breast while his fingers delved deep inside of her, stroking, finessing, finding the most exquisitely sensitive places.

"Um," she sighed, and moved against his hand, loving the feel of his wet mouth playing with her nipple, the slight stubble of his cheek abrading the soft tissue of her breast, the skill of his hand where he caressed her.

He rose above her, his eyes dark and dangerous as he knelt between her legs. With his hands on her knees, he eased her thighs apart. "I want to look at you. I need to look at you."

She'd never felt so exposed. Or so vulnerable. Or so totally, wholly sexual.

"You're so pretty. So pink. And so slick and wet," he whispered, watching where he touched her, then watching her face as he told her what he wanted to do to her.

Her inner muscles clenched involuntarily around his

fingers as she imagined his mouth there where he said he wanted to make love to her.

She'd never known. Never experienced the true meaning of craving—for one man's hands, one man's mouth, one man's body—until Ethan taught her the extreme measure of the word.

And the pleasure . . . *My* . . . *God.* So much pleasure as he slid off the end of the bed and dragged her by her hips to the edge. His face was intense and dark, intent on complete possession as he knelt on the floor and draped her legs over his shoulders.

"I'm going to take you so high," he promised, his warm breath feathering over her clitoris before he made a first, lingering sweep with his tongue. "So high."

He was selfless. He was relentless as he made good on his promise. And he was single-mindedly, ruthlessly thorough.

She gripped the sheets at her hips and simply drowned in the exquisitely carnal indulgence of his mouth making love to her. Gentle, then aggressive. Giving, then greedy.

She came with a cry and a burst of raw, electric sensation. And when he slowly brought her down with gentle nuzzling, settling kisses against that part of her that he'd made the center of her universe, she didn't even try to stall a groan.

"My . . . God," she managed on a trembling breath.

His dark eyes were soft with laughter and lust and a smug male expression that told her he was pleased with his results as he gazed up the length of her body. Whispering soft kisses against her pubis, he nuzzled between her legs as if he couldn't get enough of the taste and the scent of her wasted on sex and decimated by his devotion to ruining her.

With a final kiss to her belly, he stood, then, burying a knee into the mattress, lifted and shifted her until he slid her back up the bed with her head on the pillows.

Lord, he was beautiful. She'd been right. Beneath his dress uniform, he was all lean muscle and carved sinew. And the proud erection that jutted toward her was irrefutable proof that he was far from finished with her.

He stretched out on top of her, suited up again, slipped inside of her, and with long, deep strokes and lush, lazy glides took her on another incredible ride.

No ten-second wonder, this time. He made sure he drew out the process, extended the pleasure that she'd thought he'd already wrung out to the very last drop. She'd thought wrong.

Huge and thick and hard, he plunged into her again and again. She clung to him as he burrowed his big hands beneath her hips and tipped her up and against him for better contact. And she felt herself shooting for the top again.

Her heartbeat rioted out of control; her blood pooled and throbbed at the miraculous spot where they joined until, with a final, deep thrust, he pushed her over the brink and into oblivion.

Good. It . . . was . . . so . . . good.

"So, how you doing?" he asked several long moments later as he lay beside her, his head propped on one hand, gently caressing her breast with the other.

"I'm . . . um . . . can I think about that for an hour? Maybe two?"

She felt as much as heard the rich rumble of his

chuckle against her side. "I take it you're well on the road to ruin?"

Ah yes. There had been talk about ruination, hadn't there? And she'd more or less told him to bring it on.

"Here's another question. I'm not going to hear any talk about Rocketman from you again, am I?"

Eyes closed, she smiled and arched into the wonderful feel of his rough hand playing so gently with her breast. "Depends," she said, turning her head on the pillow to look at him.

She lifted her hand and caressed his jaw.

He turned his face into her palm and lightly bit her. "On?"

"On what kind of punishment you plan on meting out if I do."

The smile he gave her was playful and sexy and just a little dangerous. "I was thinking more along the lines of a reward."

He reached across the bed for her nightstand and his roll of Life Savers. "Want some candy, little girl?"

JOLO ISLAND, PHILIPPINES
PRESENT

Adrenaline pumped through Ethan's blood like he'd been straight-lining caffeine. His heart beat so hard he could hear it in his ears, feel it in the tips of his fingers. His hands shook with the rush of it; he had to steady his binoculars on the log directly in front of him so he could focus.

Hunkered down on his belly behind the cover of forest grass and a rotting tree trunk approximately three feet in diameter, he peered through his binocs at the terrorist encampment twenty meters away. He ignored the mosquitoes buzzing around his face, was only peripherally aware of the screech of a hornbill echoing through the treetops high above.

He only had eyes for one thing. Darcy.

They'd found her. And she was alive.

She's alive.

Thank you, sweet Jesus God, she's alive.

Now they just had to figure out how to keep her that way. Her and the unexpected other hostage.

Hell. Just what they needed. A twofer.

They'd caught up with the slow-moving Abu Sayyaf band a little over two hours ago. Had shadowed them from a distance, looking for an opening or a weakness that would help them plan for Darcy's extraction.

It had been just half an hour or so since the tangos had stopped and made camp. For the first time since this started, Ethan was not only getting a good look at Darcy; he was also getting his first long look at what they were up against.

The tangos were a ragtag band of older men, young militant bulls, and a few hungry-looking boys. Christ. Some were no more than kids but every one of them had an abundance of one thing to feed on. Hate. Hate that was spoon-fed along with their deadly jihadist doctrines.

Yeah. Some were boys—and they'd grease him in a heartbeat if he gave them the chance. He didn't plan to.

He scoured every area of the tight perimeters of the camp. The most vigilant were the younger ones—no doubt motivated by a do-or-die edict and yet another kind of hunger: to convince the men that they had earned their place among the ranks.

Their weaponry was pretty much what he'd thought it would be. He spotted several AK-47s. Funny how the Russian-made Kalashnikovs always managed to find their way into terrorist hands. So had enough knives to stock a butcher shop, as well as an ancient but no doubt effective shoulder-mounted RPG launcher.

Big surprise. They were outgunned and outnumbered—by his best count, by around thirty to three. And besides being familiar with their surroundings, the tangos had another advantage. They had nothing to lose.

Ethan did. He had everything to lose.

On either side of him, almost invisible in their salad suits and face paint, Dallas and Manny were also well into recon mode, counting heads, assessing weaponry, already plotting the best method of extraction.

Ethan was on board with them—until he zeroed the glasses back in on Darcy and his heart started slamming around in his chest again like machine-gun fire.

God, look at her.

She was exhausted.

She looked bruised. And so damn beautiful he could barely breathe.

Her white T-shirt was filthy and torn. Her khaki shorts were caked with mud. And there was blood. On her bare arms, on her legs. On her poor feet that had taken a beating on her forced march through the jungle in little more than soles held on with thin straps of leather.

Yet no matter how bad she looked, the other woman—*Jesus.* He didn't even want to think about the hell the other captive must have gone through.

She lay dead still on the ground, her head on Darcy's lap. Not moving, barely breathing.

Darcy appeared to be keeping guard over her. That

was Darcy, he thought grimly. She'd look out for someone else long before she'd take care of herself.

Like the other captive, Darcy's hands were tied in
front of her. Her eyes were closed. She was so still he
knew she was dozing—until an AK-47–wielding thug
walked over to her and kicked her feet.

Her head snapped up and she almost toppled over.
The woman jumped with a scream and Darcy quickly
leaned in close to her, murmured something fast, over
and over until she finally quieted and inched closer still
to Darcy.

Ethan clenched his jaw, felt his muscles tighten
with the need to spring into action and hurl himself at
the sonofabitch who dropped a canteen at Darcy's
feet.

A hard hand on Ethan's shoulder held him steady.
He didn't have to look to know it was Dallas. He *did*
have to take a deep breath to get it back under control.

The slightest move could have revealed their
position—and he'd almost blown it.

If he'd gone with his gut, he'd be with her now.
Yeah, he might have taken out a few of the bastards before they'd killed him. And then they'd have killed
Darcy. Probably Dallas and Manny and the other
hostage, too.

No. Now was not the time. This was not the moment.

He cut a glance at his brother. Nodded that he was
okay. That he was in control again. And then he set his
mind to the task.

He had to make this impersonal. Make it a job. Extraction. That was the goal. Darcy was the target. And
he wouldn't think about the bruise on her cheek. Or the
way she gently helped the other hostage drink before

chugging down her own share of water like she hadn't had any in a month.

And he wouldn't think about the blood—*God damn the blood!*—on Darcy's pale skin.

Deep breath
Clear head.

He was a machine. He was on a mission.

And he would not fail.

Like he'd failed Darcy and their marriage.

Ignoring the way his stomach dropped at the reminder, he gave Manny and Dallas a hand signal to withdraw.

As silently as they'd arrived, they crawled on their bellies, backing away.

It was 1900 hours. A couple of hours yet until dusk. They would wait. They'd firm up their plans, then take turns snagging quick combat naps. Then they'd set the field in preparation to go in at dawn and catch the terrorists off guard. Given the one-to-ten odds, the best thing they had going for them was the element of surprise.

The worst thing going against them was the other hostage. They couldn't leave her, but damn—one of the reasons Special Ops worked in small teams was mobility. Fewer boots on the ground made for fast, unobserved movement.

He'd known Darcy might slow them down. But this other woman—who knew if she could even walk? Guess they'd soon find out.

Five meters to his left, Manny made his way through the jungle like a panther stalking prey. He moved with the stealth and efficiency he'd learned alongside Ethan in the rain forests in northern Peru.

That was back in the Contra days when the covert

budget was mostly funneled into Central America.
Ethan and Manny and others like them had been pulled
out of Honduras and deployed under the few-and-far-
between doctrine in South America.

Yeah. They'd been few and far between then just as
they were today. It hadn't stopped him from doing his
job then. It wouldn't stop him now.

Only when they'd retreated a full two clicks away
from the terrorist encampment did they regroup to plan
their extraction strategy.

"So—life's just full of complications, eh?" This
from Manny.

Yeah, Ethan thought, knowing Manny was thinking
about the other hostage.

"Wouldn't have wanted this to be too easy," Dallas
said with a grim smile as he shrugged out of his ALICE
pack.

"Here's how I see it going down," Ethan said, and
laid out his plan.

Fifteen minutes later, each man knew his role and
his assignment. Pared down to the most basic elements, Ethan would snag Darcy, Dallas would grab the
other woman, and Manny would do what Manny did
best. He'd cover their six when the hell that was sure to
break loose did.

"I'll take first watch," Manny said. "Go ahead and
catch some z's."

Ethan shook his head. "There's something I have to
do first."

Dallas's look stopped him as he checked his Beretta,
then reholstered it.

"I'm okay," Ethan assured his brother and Manny,
who were both watching him carefully. "I've just got to
let her know we're here.

"In the meantime, see if you can raise Nolan. Let him know we've found her. Tell him we had to extend an additional party invitation for the extraction."

Dallas was already digging out his SAT phone.

"Make sure the GPS is working and establish some approximate time frames and coordinates on where he should pick us up. See if there's a more direct route out of here than the way we came in. Oh yeah—and make sure Nolan knows we'll probably be hauling ass under fire." He turned to leave. "I'll be back in a few."

"I'll go with you." Manny stood at the ready.

Ethan shook his head. "Not necessary."

Two dark scowls told him how uncertain both men still were of his control.

"I'm fine," he restated, and Dallas finally nodded. He understood. Ethan had to let Darcy know that he was here.

As he stole silently back toward the enemy camp, he told himself he was doing it for her. Told himself he couldn't let her think she was alone a moment longer.

The truth was, he was doing this for himself. He couldn't bear the weight of Darcy's anguish.

The look on her face when she'd been startled awake by the guard—aw God. It haunted him. She hadn't let the thug see her fear, though. But she hadn't been able to mask her despair. Not from him. And he couldn't leave her lost in it for one more moment than was necessary.

It was near dark by the time Ethan reached the terrorist camp again. Bellied down beneath a piece of deadfall, he tugged his boonie cap low over his forehead and watched for the better part of an hour, assessing the risk, developing a plan of action.

The tangos were sloppy. They didn't appear to be guarding against an assault. In fact, the only things they were guarding were the women, and they'd put a boy to the task. That would all work in their favor when the three of them returned to get the women out of there.

Finally satisfied with a course of action, he crept slowly closer. Moved with a stealth born in another jungle. A jungle where he had been the hunter and the men and the drugs they traded had been the hunted. A jungle where he had learned to become invisible and as silent as the earth. A jungle where he'd learned to kill and live with it.

He still lived with it.

It took him an hour to move into position where he was close enough to give Darcy a signal. And while he waited for the right time, blending into a night that was as close as the guard who ran roughshod over her, he remembered another time, another place, where running had never been a part of her plan.

8

"I'VE GOT TWO WEEKS' VACATION COMING.
Spend it with me."

It was five in the morning. Predawn light, as soft as
the breeze sifting in through the bedroom window, lay
in a gentle arc across the bed and the woman by
Ethan's side.

He'd just spent the most amazing night of his life.
They'd made love all night long. Now she was lying in
his arms, lean and spent and the softest damn woman
he'd ever held.

And he was far too cognizant of the fact that Darcy
Prescott was the first thing in a very long time that had
compelled him to want to make anything but war.

Occupational hazard. Christ. He *had* been out in the
jungle too long.

She yawned and gave a sleepy allover stretch, then
nuzzled her face into his neck on a deep, drowsy sigh.
"Hmm?"

"Spend some time with me," he repeated.

"Okay."

He tucked his chin, looked down at her. And chuckled. *"That* was easy."

Her eyes opened slowly—gorgeous green eyes that

he loved to watch dancing with laughter, turning smoky with need when he came inside of her, or drifting, slumberous and misty, when she was gloriously and truly spent.

He didn't see any of those reactions now. Right now, her eyes were filled with a somber uncertainty.

"I'm not, you know. Easy," she clarified with a hesitance that told him how uncomfortable it made her for him to think that she was. "You're a first for me. I don't make a habit of falling into bed with men I hardly know. And I've never fallen into bed with a man I've just met."

He stroked a hand over the top of her head, loving the feel of her silken hair beneath his rough palm. He met her serious, serious eyes. "I know that. How could you possibly think I didn't know that?"

And he had known. For all her confidence and flirting, there had been an innocence to her responses, a wonder to her reactions, that had touched him deep, deep inside.

She brushed her fingers lightly along his chest, her touch tentative. He covered her hand with his.

"What's happening here, do you think?" she asked in a small voice.

He understood exactly what she was asking. It had happened so fast. The attraction. The emotion. The need. They'd both felt it. It was confusing as hell. Anyway, it had been at first. Not anymore. At least *he* wasn't confused.

He drew her tighter against him. If he had a velvet ribbon he'd tie her to him and never undo the knots.

Amazing. His life, his work, required solitude, fostered the need for it. For so long, he'd been alone. With his thoughts. With his actions. With a conscience that spoke out with far too little conviction as the years rolled by and the silent, secret battles faded to jobs well done. Hell, he didn't even have nightmares anymore.

And now this. After just one night he couldn't imagine what his life would be like without the amazing grace she'd brought into it. With her, he didn't have to be a soldier, a hunter, a killer. With her, he didn't have to be afraid for a life that could be over with the slightest drop of his guard.

To rot in an unmarked grave and decompose into rain forest loam.

With her, he could just be a man.

"Ethan?"

She'd asked him what was happening between them. He pressed a kiss to the top of her head. "That's what we're going to find out in the next fourteen days, okay?"

The statement was for her. He understood that she needed some time to get used to "them." He didn't. He knew exactly what was happening, and he didn't need another week, another month, another year, to get things in perspective.

He loved her. It was that plain. That simple.

For the first time in his life, he was in love. Knocked on his ass, ready to slay dragons, filled to the bursting point, in love.

Crazy. It was the craziest damn thing he'd ever heard of. A man didn't just fall in love with a woman over dinner and marathon sex. And yet he had.

He understood, though, that a woman—especially one as special as Darcy Prescott—didn't fall in love with a man given the same set of circumstances. She needed a little time to come up to speed.

Still, by the time he'd lifted her up and settled her over him and she'd taken him deep into her lush, welcome heat, he'd developed some hellish high hopes that maybe this woman would.

"We'll start out with the *conchitas à la parmesana* for an appetizer." Ethan handed his menu back to Madam Jacques.

"And for your main course, monsieur?"

"The whitefish."

"The *corvina à la milanesa*?" The middle-aged Frenchwoman waited tables and tended bar in the restaurant she ran with her husband.

"Yes. Please."

Darcy had taken him to the French restaurant their second night together in Lima. One could not live on lovemaking and cherry Life Savers alone, it seemed. God knew they'd tried.

The next evening, they'd gone back again. And now it had become a habit.

"And for you, mademoiselle?"

"Ceviche, please," Darcy said, smiling.

"Bon. Très bon." Their hostess gathered the menus and walked away.

"What?" Darcy asked with a laugh when Ethan shuddered.

"Ceviche? Raw fish?"

When she smiled and tilted her head like that it lit up her face and did weird things to his heartbeat. "I'm sure you've eaten worse out in the jungle."

"Not by choice." He lifted his Pisco sour. He'd developed a taste for the powerful brandy topped with foam and bitters when Darcy had introduced him to the drink the first night they'd come here together. They'd been back several times since then. And he'd enjoyed several more of what he had since learned was the national cocktail of Peru.

"*Salut.*"

She touched her glass to his over the table. "*Salut,*" she murmured, and tipped her glass to her lips.

And like he'd been doing hourly, he fell a little deeper in love. With her face. With her spirit. With an unflappable optimism that sometimes left him slack-jawed with awe. Most of all, he fell in love with the way she made him feel about himself.

With her, he could forget some of the things he'd done, some of the places he'd been.

And he couldn't get enough of her. In or out of bed.

Which worked out great because she couldn't seem to get enough of him, either.

"So what's a nice girl from Ohio doing so far from home?" he'd asked one night as they lay on her bed, naked and cooling down under the slow, lazy paddles of an overhead fan.

"Following a dream," she'd said simply, and turned on her side, facing him.

"You have big dreams, do you?"

"My parents did. For me. For my older sister."

With her slim fingers tracing a line back and forth along his naked hip she quietly told him about her dad. "He's a big, barrel-chested teddy bear of a guy. Worked—still works—in a Cincinnati tool and die factory. Loves to laugh."

"Is that where you got your green eyes? And this amazing hair?" He lifted a thick strand, wrapped it around his fist.

"Both are my mom's doing."

"She must be very beautiful."

"She is. And she's smart. Yet she's waited tables for minimum wage and tips for years."

"Maybe she likes it," he suggested.

She shook her head. "Maybe. But she works like a dog—Daddy, too. They wanted us to go to college."

"Us?"

"Me and my sister, Della. You talk about beautiful."

"I *see* beautiful." He leaned in and kissed her. "And what does Della do?"

"She's a social worker. By the time I graduated, she was already burned out, and she'd only been at it two years."

She shook her head and propped a pillow beneath her cheek. He turned on his side so he could touch her. Couldn't get enough of touching her.

"Made me think twice about what I wanted to do, you know? I still knew it had to be important, something to make the folks proud. Anyway, now I still get to help people but not with the kind of horrendous problems that Della saw."

Now she helped Americans abroad in her position at the vice consul's office in Peru.

The scrape of her chair on the tile flooring brought Ethan back to the moment. She'd scooted up closer to him so she could take a sip from his drink.

"I hear you do your job well," Ethan said after giving her a hard time about drinking her own drink.

"What exactly is your relationship to Hayden?" she asked, understanding that anything Ethan heard he had to have heard from Hayden.

"I hear," he said, ignoring her question and digging a little deeper to get an answer to his, "that sometimes you stick your neck out a little too far."

She lifted a shoulder. "I do what needs to be done."

And then some. Hayden had related an incident when a U.S. college student on holiday had gotten drunk and rowdy at a bar and ended up in jail charged with theft of property.

"And that includes going into a very rough part of the city by yourself trying to find someone who would stand as witness for a spoiled rich American college kid who shot off his mouth to the wrong person?"

"He was innocent. At least of the theft charges. He could have rotted in that jail cell."

"And you could have been raped, or killed, or both poking your nose into that end of the city."

According to Hayden, if a local *policia* hadn't come along by accident and scared a street thug away, it was hard telling what might have happened to her.

Ethan tensed all over just thinking about it. Per Hayden, Darcy sometimes took too many chances.

"Don't ever forget that you're in a foreign country, Darcy. The rules change drastically outside U.S. borders. Hell, it wasn't that long ago that the Shining Path planted a bomb outside the U.S. Embassy."

The Shining Path was a Maoist revolutionary group with hard-dying plans to overthrow the Peruvian government with their doctrine of killings and torture.

"Since Toledo was elected president, that's not happening so much anymore," she assured him.

"It doesn't mean it won't happen again."

The Shining Path, along with other extremist groups, might have lost a lot of momentum, but there were holdouts. And the holdouts were the most extreme members of the groups.

And God knew Ethan saw the dregs of humanity in his work.

There were so many bad guys out there. They'd

never scared him, until now. And now he was scared for Darcy.

"All I'm saying is be careful, okay?"

"Okay," she said to mollify him. "Enough about me. What about you?" she asked, and lifted her hand to fuss with the hair at his temple in an attempt to distract him.

It worked. He let it work. He didn't want to get angry. He didn't want to get all dictatorial on her and start issuing ultimatums about not sticking her neck out, so she'd stay safe.

And he didn't want to wreck the mood.

He shrugged and drifted on the soothing feel of her fingers. "Basic stuff. Three brothers and a sister. Mom's a teacher. I think she plans to retire next year."

"What about your dad?"

"Quiet man. Smiles a lot. You'd like him. And he'd love you. He was Army, too, before he went into law enforcement. Special Ops. Rangers. A 'Nam vet."

"Ah. So you're carrying on the family tradition. Saving the world."

He grunted and sobered, uncomfortable talking about something he hadn't thought about in a very long time. And yet it did make him think and remember why he'd enlisted.

"Yeah, well, that's what I thought when I signed up. I was going to make a difference." He'd actually been that naive.

She sat back in her chair, frowned at him. "You say that as if you don't think you do."

Okay. This was a mistake. He'd opened a door to a topic he didn't want to talk about. Not with her.

He didn't want her touched by some of the things he'd done as an agent of the U.S. of A. Things she wouldn't want to hear about. Things that would drain the blood from her face and erase that adoring look from her eye.

"How about we talk about something else?" he suggested.

It hurt her a little that he'd shut that door. He could see that. And he was sorry. But it wasn't negotiable.

She let the subject drop with a soft smile. "What would you like to talk about, then?"

"How about we discuss that incredibly sensitive spot right . . . um . . . here," he suggested, distracting her with a wandering hand on the inside of her thigh.

He loved how she shuddered and went all sultry for him. No games. No false modesty. Just open, hungry desire.

Madam brought their appetizers and he drew his hand away from certain trouble. Although he started to wonder if Darcy might be willing to meet him again for a quick, hot session in the tiny unisex bathroom at the back of the restaurant.

He got hard just thinking about that spicy little quickie they'd shared there last night.

"I don't suppose," he said, his voice sounding so rough that he alerted her to his intentions before he even voiced them, "that you'd like to meet me in the back hallway?"

She grinned. "Once was a little risky, don't you think? Twice would definitely be pushing it."

She glanced over her shoulder as Madam headed back toward the kitchen. "Madam likes us now, but she might take a different view if she knew what we'd been up to last night."

Last night when he'd taken her up against the bathroom door in a heated frenzy of love and lust and urgency.

"Then again, Madam is French," he pointed out hopefully.

"You are a bad, bad man," Darcy said with a laugh as she helped herself to the platter of appetizers.

"And you're just now figuring that out?"

He got the blush he wanted and was certain she was thinking about the same thing he was—a naughty little game he'd talked her into playing earlier this afternoon.

He filled his own plate and indulged in something almost as good as sex. "I don't know what all is in this and I don't care. It's unbelievable."

"It's some kind of shellfish," she said as she sucked one off the half shell with open delight. "Flash baked, not raw," she added when he looked a little wary of the delicacies swimming in butter, lemon wine, and Parmesan cheese.

He followed suit until all that was left was the sauce, which they sopped up with delicious homemade bread and devoured with unabashed hedonism.

That was another thing he loved about her. She enjoyed. Everything. Whether it was a lavender-gray sky at sunset, a song that she would stop and listen to as if it were a prayer, the glide of skin on skin. Or now, as she touched her fingers to the worn blue-and-white-checkered tablecloth, absorbing the much-washed feel of it between her fingertips. A very tactile person, was Miss Prescott. And touching him, being touched by him, was one of her favorite sensory experiences.

From the corner of his eye he saw Madam Jacques walk past, a smile on her face. She had grown used to seeing them together. Apparently, he was a good tipper, because she always gave them the best table in the house.

Even though the evening was warm, a small fire burned in the fireplace by the window that overlooked the garden. From the kitchen he could hear Jean, where he cooked in battered copper pots, barking orders to the little cholo Indian boy who bused tables and helped Madam serve their customers.

When their entrées arrived, Darcy dug into her fish, then ate every bite of the cold baked sweet potato and chunk of corn on the cob that accompanied it. And then when they were both as full as ticks, they still indulged in some lucuma ice cream that made him think of peaches and that exotic and tender flesh between her thighs.

After lingering over their drinks, they finally decided to walk back to her apartment.

"They call it *garúa,*" she told him when he commented on the mist that settled over the city. "It makes everything seem sort of dreamlike. I love this time of year here."

It did feel like a dream. The warm Lima night and the contact of their joined hands felt too good to be real as they walked back to her apartment. He'd given up his hotel room after their second night together, earning little more than a raised eyebrow and a curious grin from Manny, who had connected with an old lover himself.

Later they made love. Slow and sultry. Long and lazy. Ethan drifted off to sleep with Darcy in his arms and his mind a blank slate.

It was a gift. A gift of peace that she gave him.

In her arms, he forgot about the hellish places he'd been. Forgot about the reality of the silent, secret wars he fought, about the men he'd killed before they could kill him.

With her, he didn't have to be a warrior.

With her, he only needed to be a man.

He'd known her less than a week. And she'd changed his life completely.

Changed him to the point where he'd never be the same again.

To the point where he knew he didn't ever want to be.

9

"IT'S GOING TO BE DARK SOON," DARCY SAID softly even though the entire camp was asleep— including the woman who was lying with her head on Darcy's lap.

She didn't care. She just needed to talk. Needed to hear the sound of her own voice. Something real in a surreal nightmare.

"It's something, isn't it? How nightfall just sort of drops like a log in the jungle? It's daylight. Then it isn't.

"I'm not much of a fan of the dark," she confessed, looking forward to the transition with all the enthusiasm of going under the knife without anesthetic.

She looked down. The woman had surrendered to a combination of exhaustion and fever. Or possibly she'd just shut down mentally as well as physically. Sleep was one way to escape the mental anguish of her ordeal.

Despite the oppressive heat, icy chills ran down Darcy's spine when she remembered the horrible, otherworldly sounds the woman had made before finally quieting.

"Wish I knew who you were," Darcy said, resting a comforting hand on the woman's shoulder.

"Amy."

It took a moment for Darcy to react. And then her heart picked up a beat. "Did . . . did you say something?

The silence that followed was so long and so absolute that Darcy decided she must have been hearing things. So long that when, at last, she heard another almost indiscernible whisper, it startled her.

"Amy."

A surge of adrenaline shot through Darcy's system.

"Amy?" she whispered back so the guard wouldn't hear. "Is that your name?"

Without lifting her head, she nodded.

Darcy's surprise was so huge it made her light-headed. "Oh, Amy. I'm so glad to meet you. I'm Darcy. And I have a friend back in the states named Amy," she said, working to soothe, relieved beyond belief that Amy had finally initiated conversation. "Are you from the states?"

"New York."

"You're from New York?" Darcy asked, more to keep her talking than for confirmation.

"Buffalo. And I'm . . . I'm not crazy. Sometimes . . . sometimes I just want them to think I am. They . . . they leave me alone that way."

Darcy glanced up at their guard again. He stood a couple of yards away, his back to them, deep in conversation with another one of the terrorists. Another teenager. She looked across the camp. No one was paying the least bit of attention to them.

By the time she zeroed back in on Amy, a lightbulb had burst on in her head.

"Amy . . . would you be Amy Walker?"

Another slow, hesitant nod.

My God. Everyone at the embassy had assumed

Amy Walker was dead. It had been months—maybe six months—since the office had received an inquiry about the American teacher who had disappeared. Darcy hadn't worked the case herself, so she didn't know who'd made the contact, but if she remembered right, they'd expressed concern over not hearing from Amy. The last anyone had known, she was in Manila.

"How do you know that?" Amy whispered.

Darcy lowered her head closer to Amy's. "I work for the vice consul's office in the U.S. Embassy in Manila. I remember seeing a missing-American report on you. My God, Amy, you've been missing for months."

"Close as I can determine, five months, one week, and two days."

"I'm so sorry." It seemed like such an inane, useless thing to say.

"Yeah. I'm sorry, too."

Finally, Amy sat up—and gave Darcy her first good look at her face in the fading light.

As ravaged as she was with fatigue and starvation and God only knew what unspeakable things had been done to her, Darcy could now see what the missing-persons report had described as a twenty-five-year-old white female. Blond. Blue. Five six. One hundred and fifteen pounds. Only there wasn't much more than ninety pounds left to her, if even that.

"So, what did you do to land in Camp Wish-I-Were-Dead?" Amy asked with a tentative smile—as if it had been a very long time since she'd had reason to use one.

Amazing. After all that had happened to this young woman, she still had the backbone to crack a joke. She was half-starved, bruised and battered, and probably ill, yet she'd found a way to stay alive and stay sane.

"Seems I know a little too much about something I

shouldn't know anything about," Darcy said, figuring no good would come of exposing Amy to her suspicions. "What about you?"

"Just the opposite. I was trying to find out something I know nothing about. I must have asked the wrong questions of the wrong people." She gave Darcy another hesitant smile. "So . . . I suppose it's a stretch to hope you've got a fail-safe escape plan in the works."

"Sorry." Darcy didn't tell her about Ethan or her hope that he would come for her. This woman couldn't take any more letdowns. "But if we could figure out how to fire that relic of a grenade launcher we could wreak some serious havoc."

"Guess we're pretty much screwed then, aren't we?"

Yeah, Darcy thought, but didn't say as much. They were pretty much screwed.

"How badly are you hurt?" Darcy asked.

"I don't know. My ribs are awfully sore. I think . . . I think I might be sick. I . . . I get the chills sometimes."

Darcy touched the back of a bound hand to Amy's forehead. As she'd suspected all along, it was warm. "You have a fever."

"Yeah. I figured as much."

They fell silent for a time before Amy broke it. "What I said . . . about not being crazy? It's . . . it's true . . . most of the time."

The single tear leaking down her dirt-streaked cheek told the rest of the story. Most of the time, she wasn't crazy—but some of the time, it was very, very hard not to fall into that pit.

Darcy reached for her and, looping her bound wrists around her, drew her close again.

And then Darcy held on while Amy cried.

• • •

All sorts of night sounds reverberated through the rain forest as Darcy lay on her side drifting in and out of a restless sleep.

Beside her, Amy shivered. *The fever,* Darcy thought. It was getting worse.

They hadn't had much more opportunity to talk after Amy had cried herself dry, because their guard had returned to his post. Fortunately, though, since Amy had quieted down they'd been pretty much ignored.

For how long was anybody's guess.

Darcy didn't know how Amy had survived this long. Darcy had never been so tired. So deep in her bones, weary in her mind exhausted. And yet she couldn't truly sleep. Some of the problem was psychological; she recognized that she was afraid they might shoot her or Amy while she slept.

Other reasons were physical. Pain for one. Hunger for another. But a pressing need to empty her bladder was the most compelling.

When she'd finally been given water, she'd drowned herself in the warm, stagnant wetness of it, not knowing when she would be offered more. Their daily food ration consisted of some kind of cold mush that might have been a mixture of corn, rice, and wallpaper paste. With little more than a cup of the gruel to sustain her since morning, there wasn't much to hold up the urine flow.

On a deep sigh, she conceded that she had no choice. Careful not to wake Amy, she pushed herself stiffly to a sitting position. God. She felt like she was a hundred years old. Every joint ached. Her head throbbed. Insect bites burned and itched. And her feet felt like bloody stubs. If she didn't have an infection from a deep cut on her left heel, she would have soon. Infection in the jungle was a death sentence—at this rate, it could do her in before her captors made up their minds to kill her.

She inhaled deeply. If she was going to die, she'd just as soon do it with an empty bladder. For her mother's sake, she wished for clean underwear. And thinking of her mother, who never let her leave the house wearing anything but clean undies—*what if you're in an accident and end up in the emergency room? What would the doctors think?*—brought tears to her eyes even as she smiled.

Her mom must be so worried. And Daddy.

Oh God. Daddy.

She bit her lower lip to keep from crying. Then she dug deep and squared her shoulders.

She wouldn't give the bastards the satisfaction of knowing she'd had a bad moment. And she told herself the moment was over. And then she made it *be* over.

She studied the guard who paced slowly back and forth in front of them. Not far away, huddled around a low-burning fire, the other cell members were knotted in a tight little clew, like the worms they were. Whether they stuck tight for defensive reasons or because each simply didn't trust the others out of his sight she didn't know.

Rahimulla no longer stood watch over her. The new kid on the block must have ordered him away. In fact, Rahimulla hadn't spoken to her all day. Worse, he would no longer look her in the eye. Not good signs.

But she didn't want to think about that now. She wanted to pee.

Careful not to disturb Amy, Darcy got the guard's attention.

"Sir," she said softly, as she had been ordered to address her guards, even though this one was another boy. *Lito,* she thought. *Or maybe not.* She didn't want to know their names.

Since the only time Darcy spoke was when she had to relieve herself, there was no need for further communication. They all knew the drill by now.

The boy glared but finally nodded, which was her signal for permission to stand. Not making eye contact with him, she stood, submissive, and waited, giving him the sense of power he seemed to need. At long last, he made a gesture with the nose of his assault weapon indicating that she could walk to the edge of the clearing.

He followed as she limped to the fringe of the encampment, then stood within three feet of her. Beyond modesty at this point, she reached for the snap on her shorts. It took some fumbling with her bound wrists, which were raw and weeping from the hemp rope, but she eventually managed the zipper. It was only because her guard was young and apparently embarrassed that he turned his back and left her to her business.

She hadn't any more than squatted down in the midst of some leafy ferns when all the hairs on her arms stood at attention. She froze, still as a tree, while her heart bounced around inside her chest like a pinball.

All of her muscles tightened. She felt instantly overwhelmed by awareness. Of what, she didn't know. But something—something was about to happen. She was certain of it.

She made quick work of her business and dropped to her knees so she could pull up her shorts.

She glanced back at her guard. His young profile was limned in night shadows cast through the foliage from the small fire burning in the middle of the encampment. He seemed relaxed. As if the world hadn't just rocked beneath his feet as it had beneath hers.

Hyperaware of the very air that she breathed, she snapped her head back front. And just as she did, something fell past her field of vision and dropped to the ground a few inches in front of her. She heard it more than saw it.

A minute whir of sound.

A minuscule flash of color that startled her.

She caught a cry of surprise before she gave anything away. Her fingers trembling from excitement as much as from fatigue, she felt around on the ground in front of her, silently pushing aside grass and forest rot—until she finally felt something.

Something small and round and . . .

Her pulse spiked like a fever.

A Life Saver. It was a Life Saver!

Oh God, oh God, oh God.

Ethan. Ethan is here.

She almost wept with relief before getting ahold of herself.

With a trembling hand she snatched it up, afraid that even in the dark her guard would see it. Or accidentally run across it. She knew it was cherry even before she popped it into her mouth.

She bit her lower lip to hold back a joyous cry or a frustrated snarl—she truly didn't know which. It took every ounce of her dwindling control not to look up or around and try to spot him.

He was here. Somewhere. Close. *So close.*

She wanted to run to him, to fall into his arms and weep with relief and joy, and . . . and she couldn't.

She couldn't go to him. Not yet. She couldn't give

him away. If he'd meant for this to be the time, he'd have simply come and gotten her. Instead, he'd sent her a signal.

A Life Saver.

A cherry Life Saver!

So that she'd know he'd come to save her life.

She lowered her head, her heart pounding so hard she was afraid the guard would hear it. Tears stung her eyes.

Oh, God, thank you.

And for some reason, she was suddenly more frightened than the night she'd been abducted. Knowing that Ethan was so near and not being able to reach out to him was torture. Like standing ankle-deep in the snow in bare feet and freezing to death while watching a fire burn through a locked window. Like dying of thirst while staring at a lake full of water that was out of reach.

And she was afraid the fire would burn out . . . or the water would evaporate before either could help her.

But this was Ethan. Not a mirage. Not a dream. He was real. He was here. And he *would* get her out of here.

Her faith in him had to sustain her. And it would.

It did.

She carefully stood and refastened her shorts. With the guard's permission, she walked past him on shaking legs and resumed her position on the ground. Where she sat, then lay on her side, her eyes watchful, searching, her spirits buoyed.

She couldn't see Ethan. He didn't want her to see him. But she knew that he was out there in the dark waiting for the moment to strike.

For now, it was enough. She had to make it be enough.

Despite her hunger, despite her pain, she found a strength of will, of purpose, deep inside. She'd need every ounce of both when the time came.

Silent tears of relief leaked down her cheeks. Ethan hadn't let her down. He'd promised her once he would never let her down.

And she wouldn't let him down, either. She'd be ready when he came.

10

DARCY HAD SOME TIME OF HER OWN COMING when the handsome lieutenant asked her to spend his vacation with him; she didn't hesitate to cash it in.

"I've been in Peru almost a year and I haven't taken the time to venture outside of the Lima city limits more than a couple of times," she confessed.

"Well, we're going to rectify that during the next few days."

He hadn't been lying. The first day, they drove south of Lima to Pisco and braved the sand dunes on a wild dune buggy ride. He'd laughed and she'd screamed and later they'd fallen into bed, in each other's arms, blissfully happy and thoroughly exhausted.

He had a sense of adventure, this lieutenant of hers—and she had begun to think of him as hers, wisely or not. Peru suited him well. The country was, she was finding out, a place pulsing with adventure.

To the west of Lima and fringed by stark desert was the sparkling Pacific. They drove there in a day, then stood wrapped in each other's arms laughing at the antics of thousands of playful sea lions as they dived in and out of the icy ocean.

It took Darcy and Ethan two days to travel back to

the little coastal city of Trujillo. Here the surf was incredible. Of course, Ethan had to ride it and then drag
her out on a small canoe made of reeds and lashed together with string. The locals called the small boats *pe-
queños caballos,* "little horses," and with Ethan
manning the paddle, she got the ride of her life.

She felt like she was living in a dream, beautiful
lover, beautiful country, when a few days later she
stood with Ethan at one of the most stunningly beautiful places she'd ever seen—the base of the Andes and
El Misti volcano just outside the city of Arequipa.

Smoke rose from the crater in magical drifting
wisps; all around them the brilliance of hot pink
bougainvillea blooms filled her senses with color.

The man at her side filled her with wonder and awe.

The days since that first night with Lt. Ethan Garrett
in her bed had been wild and intense and incredible.

Sometimes she had to stop and catch her breath. Remind herself that she'd just met him. And they never
spent much time talking. At least not about him.

But it was so good between them.

So good, it sometimes frightened her.

Daily—while she watched him lather his gorgeous
face and shave in front of a bathroom mirror wearing
nothing but a towel low on his hips and the scars on his
body that he wore like armor—she'd cautioned herself
that she'd just met the man.

A man the likes of whom she'd never before encountered. Never dreamed existed.

And she was a fool to not enjoy every moment he
wanted to spend with her.

Their last day in Arequipa, they played tourist.
" 'Arequipa is known as the city with the prettiest

girls,' "she announced, reading from a pamphlet she'd picked up at a welcome center.

He plucked a bougainvillea blossom from a nearby vine and tucked it behind her ear. "Not possible."

Then he leaned in and kissed her with a gentleness that never failed to make her knees go weak. "I'm looking at the prettiest girl in the world."

Because she was so filled with emotion, she made a joke of it. "You're so cute when you're corny."

He pulled her to him, held her loosely with his fingers laced at the small of her back. "How about when I'm horny? Am I cute then, too?"

His erection pressed against her belly and made her laugh and shiver at the same time. "Since I've never seen you any other way, I guess the answer would be yes."

"Got to love that word." He kissed her so sweetly then, it brought tears to her eyes. "Got it in you to say it again?"

And then he did the unthinkable. He went down on one knee. Slipped a ring out of his pocket.

Her world went red, white, and fuzzy.

"I know this is fast," he said while around them villagers and tourists grinned at the romance of it all. "And I know it's a little crazy. But I know something else, Darcy."

His beautiful blue eyes searched hers with the first, the very first hint of uncertainty she'd ever seen him show. "I love you and I never dreamed I could love anyone as much as I love you. Marry me and I promise, I'll never make you sorry."

She must have started crying, because she couldn't see for the mist that clouded her eyes. Couldn't see the beautiful old buildings made from volcanic ash. Couldn't see the lushly flowering bougainvillea that climbed and twined around stone walls and ironwork fences.

She could only see him. Nothing but him.

"Marry me," he repeated, holding her gaze.

She'd had a total of two serious relationships in her life. They'd been sweet and uneventful and in the end they'd simply fizzled. In both cases, she and the man had parted as friends. And it was as friends that she thought of them still.

What she had with Ethan Garrett was too exotic to call friendship. Too intense to call casual. He made her laugh, made her yearn, made her feel, in turns, safe and cherished, then afraid and out of control. Above all, though, he made her feel alive.

Darcy knew his body intimately. Knew every nuance of those intense blue eyes, knew exactly how to make them widen with shock or go smoky with pleasure.

She knew everything about him. Everything but the one thing she wanted to know the most and that he protected with evasive kisses or clever subject changes. She did not know *him*. The man. What made him feel the deepest. What made him want. What made him cry.

And yet . . . as he looked up at her, hope laced with the secrets in his eyes, she was desperately, hopelessly, in love.

Eight days. She'd known him eight days.

And she said yes without hesitation.

Darcy liked to think it was because of her connections at the embassy that they managed to get the paperwork rushed through the channels. Ethan never said, but she suspected that his relationship with Ambassador Hayden might have actually been the master key that turned all the bureaucratic locks.

It didn't matter. All that mattered was they had their marriage license. And that her family and Ethan's were happy for both of them.

"I know it's sudden, but I love him, Mom," she'd laughed on the phone the next day. "I just wish . . . well. I'd always thought Daddy would walk me down the aisle and give me away.

"I'm sorry," she said, happy but tearful, "but Ethan's leave is almost over. We may not see each other again for months. If we don't do this now . . . well, we so want to be married. Can you forgive me?"

Of course, her mother had. And Darcy's daddy had leveled a good-natured threat to Ethan about not hurting his baby girl, before welcoming him to the family.

"We'll plan a reception at home the first chance we get," Darcy promised them because she knew, deep in her heart, that this did hurt her parents—and Della. Darcy and her sister had always promised they'd be in each other's weddings.

"I love your family," Darcy told Ethan later the same day.

He had called his mother and father. She'd spoken with them both as well as with his sister, Eve, who had just happened to be home visiting at the time.

"They loved you, too." Ethan wrapped her hand in his where it rested on his thigh. "I'm going to make you happy, Darcy. I'm never going to make you sorry."

There was such passion in his eyes that she cried.

Just like she cried the next day at City Hall. With Manny Ortega standing as Ethan's best man and Sandy Jankowski as Darcy's maid of honor, they swore to love and to cherish until death parted them.

• • •

Thanks again to Al Hayden pulling some strings they honeymooned in Brazil . . . long stretches of sandy beaches, long nights of hot, steamy sex. Lazy days of getting to know and love each other even better.

"No . . . no!" Darcy repeated on a laugh and, twisting, somehow managed to pull away from Ethan's hold on her waist before he dragged her deeper into the surf.

Splashing through the thigh-deep Atlantic, she ran and laughed and sprinted for the beach.

"You can run," he taunted from behind her in his best villain's voice, "but you will never escape me."

Darcy had foolishly thought she'd made a great escape when he grabbed her from behind. Ignoring her laughing shrieks, he scooped her up in his arms and trudged back into the surf.

"Pervert," she sputtered through a grin when he carried her back into the water until they were submerged to their waists and he slipped his palm under her bikini bottom to cup bare skin.

"You love it."

"On a public beach? Not so much," she assured him, scooping wet hair out of her eyes.

"Then you shouldn't wear that suit you're almost wearing."

"It's Brazil. It's hot."

"And so, dear wife, are you."

He let go of her legs and they floated down into the water. Before her feet hit the sandy bottom, she wrapped her legs around his hips and hooked her ankles at his waist.

"You are killing me, here," he growled, and banding his arms tight around her ribs lowered his head for a deep, carnal kiss. "And as you pointed out this is, after all, Brazil," he reminded her while his hands wandered south again.

"Public beach," she cautioned him, and with a well-timed move that caught him off guard dunked him, then made another break for the beach.

"There are words for women like you," he called out when he surfaced.

She turned around, pleased with herself for getting the drop on him. *"Tease?"* she suggested, liking the sound of it and the idea that she could drive him crazy.

Something in his expression held her where she stood. With the surf licking around her ankles she watched him wade toward her. The sun glinted off his sleek, tan skin. Salt water streamed down his body and matted his hair.

When he reached her, he touched a hand to her face. Smiled. *"Important.* That's one word. *Everything.* That's another. *Loved,"* he said, adding the most important word of all. "God, Darcy, you are so loved."

He would never stop surprising her, this man who was now her husband. And he had the damnedest ability to make her cry.

She leaned into him, wrapped her arms around his neck. "You are the darnedest man."

He touched his forehead to hers and pulled her close as the surf eddied around their ankles, eroding the shifting sand beneath their feet. "That's a good thing, right?"

"Yeah," she said, cupping his precious face between her hands. "That's a very, very good thing."

He was so strong and vital and so in need of her. And she was so very, very much in love with him.

Later that day, levered on his elbows above her, in a twilight brilliant with the first evening stars and a moon that cast a pale yellow glow over the bed in their honeymoon suite, he told her just how much.

"Darcy . . ." He whispered her name as he entered and withdrew in deep, slow strokes. "You'll never know . . . never . . . know."

Breathless with love and sensation and weepy with the weight of knowing this was their last night together, she clung to him.

"Never know," he repeated, cradling her head in his hands, "how much I love you."

And much later, after he'd emptied himself inside her and they lay in the dark, their bodies limp and damp with perspiration, he spoke into the night. Whispered as if in prayer. "I existed until I met you. Now I'm alive."

"I don't want you to go," she blurted out, and finally let the tears fall.

He wrapped her tightly against him. Murmured words of comfort, words of love, and she sensed that this strong, brave warrior came very close to doing a little crying of his own.

11

ETHAN EXPELLED A SILENT BREATH OF RE-
lief when Darcy didn't give him away. He'd seen her
snatch up the Life Saver like it was a lifeline. Seen her
pop it into her mouth. Good. It was all good. She was
alert enough to destroy the evidence, in control enough
not to let on that she knew he was here.

That's my girl.

She was smart. *Darcy has always been so smart,* he
thought with a swell of pride that did amazing things to
calm his heartbeat and level out his breathing.

Even battered and exhausted and starving, she had
her wits about her.

Hugging the main trunk of a clump of dapdap trees
and balancing his weight with a foot on an adjacent
trunk, Ethan waited and watched as she stood, then remained statue still until her guard motioned permission with the muzzle of his AK-47 for her to return to
camp.

Not once did she look up or look around. Not once
did she let anyone see her excitement. But Ethan saw.
He saw the little things that only a husband would
recognize.

Ex-husband, he reminded himself as he waited for

another fifteen minutes, then shimmied slowly and silently down the tree.

Thirty minutes later, he rejoined Dallas and Manny back at camp.

If they were relieved to see him back in one piece, they didn't show it. Dallas went back to sleep.

Manny sat up, scrubbed his face with his hands. "I'll take second watch."

"No. Go back to sleep," Ethan said. "I'm good here."

The fact was, he was too wired to sleep. Manny must have recognized it, because he lay back down, tugged his boonie cap over his face, and was out within seconds.

Ethan opened up an MRE, forced himself to eat and drink so he'd be shored up physically for the confrontation to come.

So close. He'd been so close to her. And all he could do was wait. Hope he'd eased her mind.

He went over and over their plan in his mind, playing devil's advocate, looking for flaws, poking at weak spots. But he couldn't punch any holes in it. Only fate coupled with the Philippine military could do that.

He'd consciously blocked the fact that at this very moment a full company was marching in from the north and sandwiching Darcy in the middle. The potential of their making a showing was the wild card that could truly muck things up.

To a man, Ethan, Dallas, and Manny knew their only hope was beating the military to the terrorist camp.

We've got to get them out of there before the company of soldiers arrives. End of story, Dallas had said earlier.

Even knowing they might be cutting it close, Dallas

agreed that the hour before dawn was the best time to strike. They had the advantage of NVGs, but the women didn't. They couldn't run through the jungle in pitch-dark. At least not very far very fast.

So, they waited. And didn't kid themselves that they weren't on a damn near impossible mission.

One thing Ethan had learned about war in the trenches: battle plans were painstakingly made, but they usually got chucked the moment the first round was fired.

Then everything got real, and hypothetical and logical flew out the window.

In the meantime, fighting was what they hoped to avoid. A quick in and out and it would be all over but the shouting before anyone even knew Darcy was gone. Darcy and the other woman. God.

Anyway, that was the plan. And they would follow it to the letter until they had alphabet soup. Then instinct would take over.

Ethan's instincts had always been good.

He swallowed the last of his meal and stared in the general direction of the tango camp. Yeah. His instincts had always been good.

Except when it came to his marriage.

LIMA, PERU
EIGHT YEARS EARLIER

Ethan didn't want to leave her. Didn't want to leave her in the bed where they'd started their marriage.

He didn't want to head back to the field.

It was a first for him. He'd always been eager to get back on the job. Not this morning. This morning, he just wanted to be a husband. Just a husband.

But he left anyway, to the tune of the tired but true cliché playing over and over in his head.

Duty called.

He left his wife of three days asleep and snuggled deep into the bed he'd had to force himself to crawl out of.

He couldn't say good-bye. Couldn't stand the thought of seeing her cry. But he thought of her. Every hour of the flight as he sat alone in the plane and the cloud cover below obscured the rain forest to which he was about to return he thought of her.

He was still thinking of her when he went from lover to covert killer the next day.

"What?" he asked, his heart rate revving off the charts when he and Manny arrived back at base camp and they saw the look on Weasel's face.

Something was wrong. Something was bad wrong. Ethan felt it without a single exchange of hellos as their team members gathered to meet them.

"What, god damn it? Tell me what's wrong!"

Tears began streaming down Weasel's cheeks. Ethan felt his gut tighten with dread.

Thomas "Weasel" Griffin was six four and 250 pounds of steel. He was quick with a laugh, quicker with his fists, and in the three years they'd been on the same team Ethan had never seen Weasel break down.

It was scary as hell to see it now.

Runner Ward clamped a supportive hand on Weasel's shoulder. And started talking.

Oh God. Oh, Jesus God.

Worse. It was so much worse than anything Ethan could have imagined.

He wanted to scream. He wanted to hit something.

But he stood, stoic as a judge, as he listened to Runner relay the grisly news.

Brody "Gumdrop" Addison was twenty-three. But he'd been made by the cartel—and now he would never be twenty-four.

He'd wanted to be a teacher when he got out of the SF. He was so patriotic he bled red, white, and blue. And he had a kid sister back home who'd gotten hooked on crack cocaine and it had messed her up good.

So Brody had wanted to fight the bastards. He wanted to take down the drug lords at the mouth of the river where the flow was the most fierce, not at some small-time tributary where small-time criminals pled out to lesser charges before some namby-pamby bleeding-heart judge. Brody wanted to stop the traffic before it ever hit the streets. So he'd ended up in this hellhole, playing both ends against the middle and doing a damn fine job of it.

Until he'd gotten made.

"They strung him up like a damn animal," Weasel said, his face crumpling again with anger and pain. "And then the fuckers skinned him alive."

Ethan could hear Brody's screams in his head as Runner told him and Manny how they'd found the body yesterday.

Ethan couldn't speak. Could barely breathe. Was dizzy with grief and rage and hatred.

Brody was dead. There was no denying that fact. And as far as Ethan was concerned, there was no denying what had to be done.

He stumbled to the edge of camp and puked his guts out. Tears ran down his cheeks. For the loss of a brother. For the loss of a soldier whose family would never know he died a hero's death because what went on this far south of the border would never be publicly acknowledged.

... *Unfortunate accident during a routine practice drill* ... would be specified on the death certificate. And Brody's mom and dad wouldn't even have a body to cry over.

Very quietly Ethan wiped his cheeks, then gathered his personal arsenal. The concerned looks didn't last long as one by one, led by Manny, the rest of the team armed themselves.

Without exchanging a word, they headed into the jungle.

Two days later, they dealt swift and merciless revenge. They didn't follow anyone's orders. They followed their guts. And they executed at least a dozen of the bastards who had tortured and murdered one of their own.

Ethan couldn't get out of the Peruvian jungle soon enough. Couldn't get to his wife—to her sweet, giving warmth, her innocence and love—soon enough.

Still, it was six months before he could slip away for a weekend in Lima.

Turned out, it was still too soon.

He hadn't decompressed from the Brody incident. He couldn't talk to her. Couldn't smile for her. All he could do was make love to her. Sometimes with a violence that left him ashamed. And then with a gentleness bred by guilt that would never atone for the way he'd used her.

She didn't complain. She never complained. She

just stroked his hair and held him in the night and asked nothing from him but to give up his demons to her.

"Tell me. Tell me what hurts you so," she begged one night in the aftermath of a stormy lovemaking session that left him raw and edgy and her destroyed and clinging.

It was all she wanted. For him to tell her. And he couldn't do it. Couldn't dirty her with his sins.

So he lectured instead: "Are you being careful like I asked?"

He couldn't see her face in the dark. He didn't have to, to know he'd frightened her.

"Ethan?"

"Answer me, damn it!"

Filled with an unreasonable anger, he shot out of the bed and stalked to the window. The midnight breeze cooled his naked skin, but not his rage, as he propped his hands on his hips and fought a gnawing anger toward a world few people knew about and even fewer would believe.

A world where men were heartless and soulless and life had no more value than a dime bag. It was a world he knew too well and was as much a part of as the predators he hunted.

"Yes," she said finally. "I'm being careful." Her voice sounded small with hurt and uncertainty.

He was being a sonofabitch. Letting out a deep breath, he turned to her, ashamed.

She'd flicked on the light by her bed. She sat on her hip, her feet tucked under her. Naked and pure—with something very much like fear in her eyes.

He swore and went to her. Knelt in front of her. Pressed his face into the softness of her breasts.

"I'm sorry. I'm . . . I'm sorry, baby. But I worry. Christ, I worry about you, Darcy. I worry so much."

She touched a hand to his cheek. "I'm okay. I'm okay."

She didn't get it. She would never get it.

"How much longer do you have on your PCS here in Lima?"

She lifted a shoulder. "Six months, seven months."

"Perfect." He pulled back and gripped her by her shoulders, feeling his first flicker of hope. "You can go back to the states then. Find us a place to live until I get out. You'll love Florida. Or we can live in Cincinnati if you want to be close to your family. I don't care. I don't care where we live, just so—"

She pressed her fingers to his lips, silencing him. "Ethan." A deep furrow creased her brow. "I'm not going back to the states. I've already received my new PCS. I'm going to Israel."

He hadn't heard her right. He was sure he hadn't heard her right. For the past six months he'd been working it all out in his head.

As he sweated out the rain forest days and skulked through the heat of the nights on the hunt, he'd worked it out. She would go back home. Where she would be safe. Counting on that was what had kept him sane. What had kept him going. Knowing he could at least stash her someplace even if he couldn't be with her.

"Sweetie, no." He palmed her cheeks. Ran a hand through her hair. "Change it. Get a stateside assignment if you want to stay in the service, but don't go to Israel. For God's sake, that's worse than here."

She looked at him through those beautiful green eyes as if she didn't know him. And it shook him to the core.

"Ethan. This is my career. This is what I've planned for. What I'd dreamed of. I'm not going back to the states. Not for a long while yet."

"Darcy—"

"No. Listen. You think I don't worry about you? You think that every single moment of every single day I don't stop and wonder where you are? What you're doing? If you're safe? You think I don't know how dangerous your work is?"

"Baby." He drew her tightly against him. Whispered into her hair. "We're not talking about me. We're talking about you."

"No." She pulled out of his arms so she could look at him. "We're talking about *us*. Not me. Not you. *Us*. Don't ask me to give up what you wouldn't ask of yourself. What we do is part of who we are. It's part of you and me together, Ethan. I never dreamed you didn't understand that."

Stunned, he rose from the bed again, raked a hand through his hair. And said exactly nothing.

He didn't know what to say. He just wanted her out of harm's way. He wanted her someplace where she couldn't be touched by even the fringe of the muck he lived.

She walked up behind him where he stood in her open bedroom window. "It'll be okay. We'll be okay."

She pressed herself against him from behind. Warm, soft, breakable. Wrapping her arms around him, she rested her forehead against his naked back. "Just . . . just trust me to take care of myself. You have to trust me, like I trust you. If I didn't trust you to stay safe, it would make me crazy, Ethan. So I do. I trust you. I *have* to trust you. And you have to trust me."

He turned in her arms, pressed his face into the top

of her head, and breathed in her fresh floral scent. Breathed it like he'd never breathe it again. And he hung on.

He knew she was right. If he didn't trust her to stay safe, he'd go insane.

And he didn't trust her.

JOLO ISLAND
PRESENT

Darcy awoke with a start; her heart beat like a bass drum in a parade march.

It was pitch-black. Something was wrong. She wasn't in her bed. She was—she blinked, looked around as things came into fuzzy focus.

Disappointment quickly replaced the confusion. She definitely wasn't in Kansas anymore. It didn't take long to figure that out and to remember exactly where she was.

She was in a terrorist camp. She was being held hostage.

But there was hope. Finally.

Ethan.

Last night, Ethan had come.

Or was it still tonight? She couldn't believe she'd actually fallen asleep. And for how long? A few minutes? A few hours? She had no way of knowing.

But she did know that he'd come. She *knew* that.

Didn't she?

A sudden and frightening uncertainty had her heart kicking up again. It couldn't have been just a dream.

Ethan had come. *He'd come.*

A latent and too familiar panic piggybacked with uncertainty and worked hard at convincing her otherwise.

She settled herself with several deep breaths and the

vivid memory of how sweet that cherry Life Saver had tasted on her tongue.

Yes. *Yes! The Life Saver.* It had been so sweet. Dirt and all—amazing how quickly standards nose-dived when survival was on the line. But the sweetest thing of all was settling the question. He *had* come for her. She could still taste the faint flavor of cherry on her tongue.

Lying very still on her side, with her bound hands beneath her cheek for a pillow, she glanced over at Amy. She was sleeping soundlessly, curled into herself like an orphaned kitten.

In the middle of the camp, the fire had burned down to nothing but a wisp of smoke and ash. It had to have taken a while for it to burn down that low—which meant that Darcy *had* slept. And for more than a few minutes. Not that it mattered, but she wondered what time it was. Wondered if Ethan was, at this moment, hunkered down at the edge of the camp, waiting for the absolute right moment to get her out of here.

Quiet. It was so, so quiet that she marshaled her breath so it wouldn't disrupt the volume of the silence. She looked down at Amy again. She was sleeping so soundly. It was the reason Darcy hadn't told her about Ethan earlier.

Darcy hadn't wanted to wake her; she knew that Amy would need all the strength she could muster when the time came to run. Now Darcy knew it couldn't wait. This night wasn't going to last forever—even though it felt like it was—and she felt it in her bones that Ethan would come after her before morning.

"Amy," she whispered, bending down close to her ear.

"Nonononono . . . please," Amy whimpered, and if possible curled into a tighter ball, "please . . . please . . . don't . . . don't . . . don't—"

"Amy. Sweetie. It's Darcy. It's okay; it's okay," she assured her when the younger woman stilled abruptly.

Amy lifted her head and focused on Darcy's face. And in that moment Darcy saw the depth of Amy's torment at the hands of these animals.

Somehow, she managed to pull back from it. Breathing hard, she nodded at Darcy to let her know she was back in control.

"So," Amy whispered, still trembling from residual fear. "You weren't a dream."

Darcy shook her head. Smiled. "No, but there's a lot of that going around. How are you feeling?"

"I'm okay," Amy said, but her eyes had a vacant and glassy look. And she'd started shivering again.

"Amy, I have something to tell you. Don't make a sound. Don't react. Just listen, okay?"

And while their young guard dozed, leaning against a tree, Darcy told Amy about Ethan contacting her.

Darcy could see the disbelief in Amy's eyes, the hesitance to hope, the fear that it was all a wild story.

"When will he come?" she whispered in a tiny voice that pushed through her constricted throat.

"I don't know," Darcy confessed. "But it'll be soon now. And you need to be ready. Do you think you can run?"

"I was born to run," Amy whispered with a tremulous smile as the truth of Darcy's words began to sink in.

Darcy gave her a grin.

And together they waited. As seconds ticked to interminable minutes, minutes to an excruciating hour.

12

"IT WAS A SIDE OF HIM I'D NEVER SEEN BE-
fore," Darcy admitted to Sandy during their lunch
hour.

It was a week after Ethan's first return trip to Lima.
And things had been eating at her.

"And this surprises you? That you don't really know
the man you married?" Sandy dug into her ceviche.
Both women had developed a taste for the raw fish during their tour in Lima.

"For God's sake, you knew him all of what? Eight
days before you married him? When I pushed you toward him that night at the ambassador's party, I was
thinking more in terms of a flashy affair. I never
dreamed you'd end up marrying the guy."

Darcy felt like she was betraying Ethan even men-
tioning his behavior to Sandy, but ever since he'd left
last week to return to his team she'd been having trouble dealing with things between them.

"Don't misunderstand," she said carefully. "It's not
like I'm having second thoughts. I'm not. I love him.
He loves me. It's just . . ."

When she trailed off, Sandy concluded gently, "It's
just that it took this long to sink in that you have no

idea what he's endured, what he's done, what he has to live with."

Yeah, Darcy thought with a deep sigh. It was just that. Soldiers bore two kinds of scars. The physical ones. And the ones no one would ever see.

"I guess I thought he would share things with me. Unload, you know? Instead, he seems to be transferring the real danger that he's in to an imagined danger for me. He wants me to quit the State Department—or at the very least opt for a stateside station."

Sandy tipped up her wineglass, drank, then said frankly, "Sweetie, it's true what they say, you know. These SF guys, they're wired a little different than the rest of us. They have to be to handle what they do. He wants you safe. Figures he's the one to ensure that. And he can't. Because he can't be with you all the time.

"But, having said that," Sandy continued, "I've seen the way he looks at you. He loves you. So give it some time, okay? Give him some time. This is all new to him, too."

Darcy hoped Sandy was right. Hoped time could fix things that Darcy'd never thought might be broken between her and Ethan. In the meantime, Ethan was under enough pressure; he didn't need her to add more.

In the following months, whenever he managed a return trip to Lima she concentrated on making him happy. She cooked. She teased; she shared photos from her childhood and absorbed every word when he told stories about his. They even managed to squeeze out a five-day trip back to the states where both families had gotten together in West Palm to get acquainted. She'd loved the entire Garrett clan—and they'd loved her. Same for Ethan and her family.

Everything started to seem normal—as normal as it

could be considering they saw each other only once every other month or so and each time he came out of the jungle he seemed a little wilder, a little more distant, than the last.

Each time, it took more days to get that smile out of him and to get past the "be careful lecture" and a disturbing pattern of accusing her of lying to him—not about other men but about taking unnecessary risks in her job.

She'd settle and soothe and eventually, he'd finally let it go—though he never gave up on suggesting she return to the states for good.

Sometimes it turned into an argument—she didn't have that red hair for nothing. And then they'd make up and make love with a desperation that left her decimated and confused.

The hardest part came when she left for Tel Aviv. They had no idea when they would see each other next. And when he walked away to go back to the jungle and she boarded her plane she felt like he was taking a huge part of her soul with him.

JOLO ISLAND
PRESENT

"Jesus. Are those what I think they are?" Ethan whispered, adjusting his NVGs to get a clearer look as Dallas dug two mines out of his ALICE pack.

"Call 'em an early birthday present," Dallas said, and went about his deadly work.

"And me without a cake."

Dallas grunted. "I'll be damn happy that I won't be lugging 'em around anymore. Suckers weigh a ton."

It was 0330 hours. They'd geared up an hour ago. Then they'd headed back toward the enemy camp to lay a line of "attitude adjusters" for any tango who might think he wanted to follow them once he realized they were minus two hostages.

"I didn't even know these bad boys—or should I say bad girls—were still in production."

The M-16A1 antipersonnel mine—affectionately referred to as "Bouncing Betty"—was a mean piece of work. It was also effective—provided the bad guys were obliging enough to set off the trip wire. Once that happened, somewhere between the primary and secondary explosion anyone in close proximity would find their head and their ass in different zip codes—no sleight of hand involved.

"Just because the U.S. military doesn't carry 'em in its arsenal anymore doesn't mean they don't flood the black market." Concentrating on his work, Dallas placed a mine, set the trip wire, secured it with some duct tape, then carefully camouflaged it with ground cover.

Ethan made a mental note to avoid this route on the way back through the forest, while Dallas set the other mine.

Twenty or so meters behind them, Manny was systematically laying down a line of claymores. Unlike the trip mines, the claymores fired via a remote detonation device. Loaded with a couple of pounds of C-4 and enough projectiles in the form of pellets or nuts or bolts to scatter in a fifty-meter kill zone, the claymores gave a helluva bang for the buck.

Ethan crept back to check on him. "How's it going?"

"Got to love it," Manny said with a grin, and read out loud the instructions stamped on the claymore. " 'Front toward enemy.' Christ. Only in the U.S. military.

"Here." Manny handed one to Ethan. While making light of the overobvious instructions, Manny was dead serious about what he was doing. "Place it over there."

Ethan took the claymore and positioned it where Manny told him. In addition to being an expert sniper, Manny was also a pro with explosives. Before joining Ethan's A-team in Peru, Manny had worked for Uncle Sam training Contras to fight the Sandinistas in Nicaragua. He'd blown a lot of bridges the few years he'd been deployed in Central America. Ironically, some of them were bridges Manny's own father had engineered.

Dallas joined them. "All set?"

"Locked and loaded," Manny said with a grim nod.

They'd already decided. Manny would guard their flank, pick off tangos with the Barrett, and detonate the claymores if the need arose. Hopefully, it wouldn't. Hopefully, they'd get in, get out, and get gone before anyone was the wiser and they'd never have to fire a shot.

Armies, however, didn't win wars on hope alone. Neither did a three-man extraction team facing thirty-to-three odds.

Ethan looked from Dallas to Manny. "Okay. Let's do this . . . and so help me God," he clenched his jaw, pinned them with a hard look, "if either one of you gets yourself shot, I'll whip your ass from here to West Palm, you got it?"

To a man, they knew the odds of getting out of this in one piece were slim and none. And to a man, they were up for it.

"You worry about your own ass, brother mine."

Manny grinned. "And I'll cover both of your asses, so let's skip all this touchy-feely shit and get it done, eh?"

• • •

At 0400 hours, Dallas was in position at Ethan's side. Condition 1: magazines locked, chambers loaded and ready to fire. They were bellied down behind a long line of protruding rock covered with creeping purple vines, reconning the tango camp.

"Quiet as a cemetery," Dallas whispered after a long, thorough look through his binocs.

Ethan grunted. "Not the metaphor I would have chosen."

To the right, on their rear guard, Manny and his sniper rifle were positioned about four meters up in a rubber tree.

Ethan gave Manny a hand signal. *We're moving in.*

The butt of the Barrett hit Manny's shoulder as he sighted down the scope he'd mounted on the rail of the barrel.

Ethan nodded to Dallas and without another word they readied their garrotes.

"Wait," Dallas said, adjusting his binocs. "Fuck. We've got trouble."

Ethan lifted his glasses. And felt his blood run cold.

Darcy had nodded off again. Sitting up. Her back against a boulder, Amy curled up by her side.

But now she was awake. Wide awake. Startled awake.

It was an occurrence she was getting used to.

But something was different this time. Something other than Amy had awakened her. Something other than the hunger gnawing at her belly.

She gave her pupils time to adjust, squinted into the dark and the quiet searching for what had taken her from unconscious to hyperalert.

And then it occurred to her. Her guard. He was

standing at attention directly beside her. Which was odd. He'd never come this close before.

A prickly unease sent shivers along her bare arms when he snapped to attention. She followed his gaze across the dark expanse of the camp—and by the light of the campfire stared directly into the eyes of evil.

The new leader—she'd heard some of her captors refer to him as Omar—was walking toward her. And there was no mistaking the look in his eyes. This time of night, with the rest of the camp asleep, he could only have one thing in mind.

Darcy swallowed hard when he stopped in front of her.

"Get up."

Except for her heart—it was beating so hard it was about to pop out of her chest—she didn't move.

Beside her, Amy stirred. "What? Is it time to—"

"It's okay," Darcy interrupted quickly. The last thing they needed was for Amy to inadvertently give away that they were waiting for Ethan.

Omar glared at Amy with heightened interest. "Time to what?"

Amy shot to a sitting position when she realized the terrorist leader was here and addressing her.

"T . . . time to get up," she improvised, reading the look on Darcy's face. And then Amy looked, really looked, at the way Omar was watching Darcy.

"Oh God," Amy whispered as Omar grabbed Darcy's upper arm and hauled her roughly to her feet.

"No . . . no, take me," Amy cried. She struggled to stand. "Leave her alone. Please, sir. Take me. I'll do anything you want."

With an iron grip on Darcy's arm, Omar dragged her against him.

"Leave her alone!" Amy screamed. "Leave her—"

He moved so fast neither of them saw it coming. Omar backhanded Amy across the face so viciously that she stumbled backward and fell, hard, to the ground.

"Amy!" Darcy fought to get away as Omar started dragging her across the campsite.

He jerked her back against him so hard it felt like he'd wrenched her arm out of her shoulder socket. "Fight me and you will die. Submit and I may let you live."

"You didn't have to hit her!" Reeling with pain, horrified at how still Amy lay, Darcy pried at his fingers.

"You would prefer I hit you?"

"I'd prefer that you let go of me." She met his eyes with a defiance bred of rage.

He grabbed a handful of her hair, jerked her flush against him. The knife appeared out of nowhere.

Darcy gasped when he wrenched her head back and set the blade to her throat.

"You are no longer dealing with old men and boys who have not yet learned the proper way to deal with infidels."

Darcy swallowed, closed her eyes. This was it. It was over. She was going to die. With Ethan so close. So close.

She braced herself. Felt the sharp point of the knife prick her skin . . . and thought of her mother.

Somewhere in the haze of terror and acceptance that she'd never see home again, a muffled pop of sound registered. She felt something warm and wet spurt across her face. And then the knife and Omar's grip on her hair fell away.

She opened her eyes, heard another pop just as Omar folded in a lifeless lump at her feet. Before he fell, she saw his face. Blood ran out of a hole the size of a pencil eraser, right in the center of his forehead.

It had no more registered that she was still alive and Omar was dead than a hard hand clamped around her mouth. Instinct had her gasping and fighting to get away as she was drawn back against an even harder chest.

"Shhh. Shhh. It's me, babe," a harsh voice whispered in her ear. "You're okay. I've got you now."

Ethan.

She went weak with relief. He was here. He was really here. And because of him, she was alive and Omar was dead. The adrenaline that had been fueling her for days suddenly let down. Her knees buckled and she had to hold on tight to Ethan's arm to stay upright.

"Keep it quiet," he whispered so softly she could barely hear him. "Can you stand?"

She wasn't sure, but she nodded.

Very slowly, he removed his hand.

"Ethan," she whispered, and sagged into him. "Oh God, Ethan. Thank you."

"Thank Manny," he said into her hair. "He's the shooter."

She pulled back and looked up at him. "Manny? Manny's here?"

"Dallas came along for the ride, too. But let's save the chitchat for later, okay? We've got to get out of here before the entire camp wakes up."

Her chest was thick with emotions she couldn't sort or identify. Relief. Joy. Guilt.

Ethan. She was looking at him and still couldn't believe he was real. He looked so good. Even covered in face paint and shadowed by the night, his eyes hidden behind some high-tech-looking goggles, he looked good. Felt good. Strong and solid and steady.

And because of her, he was in horrible danger.

She couldn't think about that now. They were a long way from safe.

She started moving, then startled at the flurry of action at her feet. She looked down. And saw Dallas. Even through the camo paint and goggles, she recognized him.

He grabbed Omar by the feet and dragged him into the jungle brush rimming the perimeter of the camp. The body of her guard—the second pop, she would realize later—lay lifeless on the ground by the canvas tent. She was still digesting the idea that not only Ethan but also Dallas and Manny had come after her when Dallas was back, dragging the dead guard away to hide the body with Omar's.

A rage—for the senseless violence, for the loss of life, for little boys who carried big guns and died in the name of hate—immobilized her.

"Hey." Ethan lifted her chin with a finger, commanding her attention. "Don't think about it."

Darcy saw him though a haze. Saw him nod in reassurance as he unsheathed a knife and with one exacting swipe sliced the rope binding her wrists.

She muffled a sob. Pain shot through her fingers like tiny needles as full circulation returned.

"Can you walk?"

She nodded.

He glanced toward Amy. "Can she?"

Amy was hunched into herself on the ground. But she was conscious now. Her eyes were wide with terror.

On shaking legs, Darcy went to her. "It's okay," she whispered.

Amy stared at Darcy in terrified silence while Ethan squatted down and cut the ropes binding Amy's wrists.

"It's your face," he whispered. "It's covered in blood." Darcy looked up over her shoulder. "His," Ethan added with a hitch of his chin toward the spot where Omar's body was hidden.

Darcy lifted the hem of her shirt and hurriedly wiped away what she could of the blood.

"We've gotta move. Now," Ethan reminded her gruffly.

Dallas materialized again and held a hand out to Amy. She shrank away with a whimper.

Gone, Darcy realized. Amy had withdrawn where none of this could reach her.

"It's okay," Darcy promised her. "He's going to help us. Amy," she whispered, trying to make the young woman tune in to her. "You can trust him. He won't hurt you. I promise you," she added as Amy started that horrible keening sound again.

"Oh, sweetie, no. Shhh. Don't." Darcy cupped Amy's face in her hands. Pressed her thumbs over Amy's lips and whispered urgently, "We have to be quiet. Come on. You have to get ahold of yourself. We have to go. We have to go now, before anyone wakes up."

But now was already too late.

A shout rose from across the camp.

Ethan looked over his shoulder just as a burst from an AK-47 exploded into the silence.

13

ETHAN PUSHED DARCY BEHIND HIM, SHOV-
ing her toward the cover of the jungle. "Go. Go!" he
shouted, laying down a line of ground cover with his
M-4.

Dallas hauled the other captive into a fireman's
carry and sprinted out of the line of fire.

Walking backward, Ethan sprayed rounds toward
the terrorists, who, with few exceptions, were running
around like chickens with their heads cut off. Some
had grabbed their AK-47s and were firing from the hip,
shooting wildly into the dark hoping to get lucky.

When Ethan reached a stand of trees, he pulled the
pin on a frag grenade, counted to three, then hurled it
into the center of the camp.

Beside him, Dallas, with the M-203 grenade launcher
attached to his M-4, fired into the thick of things. Amy
rocked and hummed in a shell-shocked stupor a yard
away. Darcy had wrapped herself around the other
woman and was doing what she could to reassure her.

Men screamed when the grenades hit their mark.
Shrapnel rained down like volcanic ash, and the scene
went as Hollywood as a blood-and-guts war movie.

Only this wasn't fiction. This was too goddamn real.

"Go!" Ethan shouted to Dallas when it was obvious that while they'd taken out several tangos and sidelined a few more, they were still way down on the odds chart.

Manny was still in sniper position in the tree. He was picking off tangos before they ever knew what hit them.

Grabbing Darcy's arm, Ethan hauled her to her feet and headed at a run for the path they had painstakingly marked to avoid the claymores and Bettys.

He didn't ask if she could make it. There wasn't time. When she stumbled and went down, he hauled her to her feet and kept on going.

Ethan lost complete track of Dallas and Manny. He knew only that his brother and the woman were ahead of them, and Manny would stay back to provide cover.

An earth-jarring explosion shook the ground behind Ethan. Another went off directly on its heels.

Way to go, Betty!

The first and secondary explosion of the trip mine was quickly followed by an earsplitting series of blasts and piercing screams. Manny had set off the claymores and sent more jihadists to their warped version of Allah.

That was the good news.

The bad news was, there were still plenty of bad guys left to chase them.

The really bad news—one of the bastards had gotten lucky.

Ethan had taken a round in his leg.

And he was losing blood like a high roller lost chips at a rigged craps table.

Dallas stowed his NVGs on the move as dawn broke over the rain forest within a half an hour of the fireworks at the tango camp. They'd planned it that way. While he and Ethan and Manny could have made good time in the dark, the women didn't have the benefit of the NVGs. They'd had to make accommodations.

Although, Dallas thought, *this woman who'd been a hostage could have found her way through a series of caves without so much as a candle.*

Man, could she move.

Fear was a helluva motivator—and it hadn't taken long for him to realize that she was as afraid of him as she was of the terrorists.

As soon as the fireworks let up, he'd taken a chance and stopped. Set her on her feet.

She'd shivered out a serrated breath, looked at him like he'd been belched up from the bowels of hell—and taken off at a dead run.

"For the love of Mike," he'd muttered, and sprinted after her.

That had been over an hour ago. She hadn't slowed down yet. At least she was going in the right direction.

Batty. She was as batty as a haunted house. *Not her fault,* Dallas conceded with equal measures of sympathy for her and hatred for the animals who had made her this way.

"Damn," he swore aloud. The woman could move. He had to hump like hell to keep up with her. Of course, he was carrying at least seventy pounds of rifle and gear.

For as frail and fragile as she looked she set a helluva pace. Only when they were a good two or three Ks from the terrorist camp did she start to slow down. And he could tell that it wasn't by choice.

She was about to collapse from exhaustion.

And just as he was thinking it, she did.

Great. Just what he needed. Another hundred or so pounds to carry.

Sucking air, he dropped to his knees beside her.

She'd landed, facedown, on a bed of vines and ferns at the base of a coconut palm.

He touched a hand to her hair, intending to push it away from her face so he could see if she was passed out or just down-and-out.

She moved so fast, he almost didn't catch her.

"Stop it! Stop it," he said more gently when he'd wrestled her to her back on the ground.

He pinned the lower half of her body with his hips and thigh, secured her arms above her head in one hand, and propped himself up with the other.

Then he caught his breath. And got his first good look at her.

God, she was a mess. She wasn't any bigger than a minute. But she was a scrapper. He felt the brunt of her moxie in what was going to be a helluva bruise on his ribs where a sharp, bony elbow had connected. With a vengeance.

"Christ, woman. Chill, all right? I'm not going to hurt you. Jesus. If you're going to fight or run every time I look at you sideways, we're going to have a long couple of days."

He glared down at her, as much in disgust as in concern over the swelling on her face where the king creep had clipped her. But now wasn't the time to go soft. Now was the time to reach her.

"You think I'd put my neck on the block to get you out of there alive just so I could kill you?"

She stared up at him through distrustful blue eyes set in a bruised and battered face. "Who are you?"

Ah. She speaks. "I would be your ticket out of this tropical paradise."

"A hired mercenary?"

Dallas rolled his eyes. "Don't I wish. But I'm just a

dumb dweeb, okay? I volunteered for the job—wasn't smart enough to ask for money, although, I've got to tell you, I'd have thought twice if I'd known I'd have to put up with the crap you're dishing out."

For some reason, that got an itty-bitty smile out of her.

Which could mean she found him amusing or it was just loony-toons time. He decided to go with amused. He smiled, too. "Fine. Laugh at my expense."

She didn't say she was sorry, but he decided she looked the part. And that worked for him.

Finally. A thread of sanity.

Maybe her screws weren't as loose as he'd thought they were when she'd launched into that high-pitched hissy fit back at the tango camp and woken up half of the third world.

"Are you . . . Army?"

He grunted. "Bite your tongue, woman. I'm a Marine. Ex-Marine," he corrected. "My brother was Army, but I don't hold it against him and neither should you. He's the one who coordinated this little snatch and grab."

"Your brother? Ethan?"

He nodded. "Yeah. Ethan. Darcy tell you about him?"

"Just that he was coming."

"Yeah, well, Manny and I tagged along for grins and giggles."

"Manny?"

"You'll meet him later. Now can I let you up without worrying about you running again? And before you answer that, think about the probability that I might just let you go this time and you can figure your own damn way off this godforsaken island."

She actually seemed to think about it. "No," she said finally. "I won't run."

He didn't figure it was much of a concession on her part. She probably couldn't have run another yard if she wanted to.

And he suddenly realized he needed to get off of her for reasons that were totally inappropriate. It shocked the shit out of him that he'd even let his mind wander in that direction.

"Here," he said, rolling away and pulling out the tube to his Camelbak. "Drink.

"Whoa. I said *drink,* not *drown.* Easy now," he cautioned when she sat up, then sucked water down like she'd drain an ocean if he gave her a big enough straw. "Easy. You'll make yourself sick."

But she was already sick, he realized, studying her glassy, feverish eyes. They were sort of a winter sky blue. Cool, bordering on gray. And were probably very pretty when they weren't glazed with fever and fear.

"How long have you had the fever?" he asked, shrugging out of his ALICE pack, then digging around for the medical supplies he'd stocked anticipating that Darcy might need them.

"Don't know. Days. Maybe weeks."

He jerked his head back around to look at her. "*Weeks?* How long have you been out here?"

When she told him, he felt an icy rage expand to roughly the size of a glacier. He wondered what her story was. Wondered what all had happened to her during those months of captivity—figured he already had a pretty good idea judging by the way she recoiled every time he laid a hand on her.

Yeah. He wondered what had happened to her. And

by the same token, he didn't want to know. Didn't need to know to do his job. So he just clenched his jaw and fished around in the pack until he found the antibiotics.

"You allergic to anything?" he asked, filling a syringe.

She shook her head, regarding him warily. "What is that?"

"Just your garden-variety antibiotic. We need to get something into your system to fight whatever bug bit you until you can get proper medical attention.

"Arm or hip?" he asked, peeling the paper off a sterile gauze pad soaked in alcohol.

"Are you a doctor?"

"Not so my bank account would notice. But I've had some basic training and field experience. It's okay," he said with an encouraging nod. "I know what I'm doing here."

She still didn't want to trust him. She still wanted to be afraid. To her credit, she fought both impulses. She held out her arm. Must be she'd finally figured out that he was the best thing she had going.

"God," he said, feeling sick with sympathy for how emaciated she was. "Nothing but skin and bone. It's gonna hurt like hell."

She actually laughed. "I don't think so."

Meaning she knew what hell hurt like and this didn't even come close.

"Just the same," he said more gently, "let's go for the hip, okay? At least there's a little meat there to absorb the sting."

Very little, he realized after she warily turned her back and lowered her shorts—barely far enough to reveal a pale, skinny hip.

She tensed, but that was all the indication she gave that he'd hurt her.

"Sorry," he said, and capped the syringe. "How long since you've eaten?"

She whipped around so fast he had to grab her arm to steady her. "You have food?"

It was the most animation he'd seen on her face since this nightmare started. He couldn't help himself. He stared, caught off guard. Despite the sunburn and bruises and grime coating her cheeks, the snarled and matted hair hanging in her eyes, he could see the promise of a quiet, credible beauty.

And that was something he didn't want to think about, either.

"Yeah," he said, and dug back into his pack. "I have food. You'll have to settle for meat loaf and mashed potatoes. It's the best I can do."

Her eyes widened like a kid's on Christmas morning. He opened up the MRE and handed it to her before she attacked him—and who could blame her if she did.

"Slow now," he cautioned, handing her a plastic fork. "I'm thinking your system's going to have a little trouble handling starch and protein for a while."

If she heard him, she didn't acknowledge. She dug in like a stray dog that hadn't had a meal in weeks.

And she probably *hadn't* eaten in weeks.

He watched her in silence. If he knew his terrorists—and unfortunately he did—starvation wasn't the worst of what they'd done to her. It made him physically ill to imagine how the bastards must have used her.

Leave her alone. . . . Take me. I'll do anything you want.

He'd heard her loud and clear from his position on

the perimeter of the camp. She'd been ready to sacrifice herself for Darcy's sake. Which told him several things about her character. She was loyal. She was brave. And she knew from experience that she could survive whatever that sick son of a bitch had in store for her.

That particular bastard would never abuse a woman again.

"What you were willing to do back there . . . for Darcy. It took some guts."

She looked up from her almost empty meal, met his eyes for a brief moment, then looked away. Far away. So far away, he wondered if she was with him anymore.

He dug a pack of disinfectant alcohol wipes out of the first-aid kit. "Here," he said, handing her some.

She looked at the wipes. Tears filled her eyes. "Thank you," she said so quietly he could barely hear her.

Then she used the wipes on her face and hands like they were an indulgence the equivalent of a bubble bath.

A tear finally spilled down her cheek and she just sort of wound down; her hands, holding the filthy wipes, dropped to her lap.

It was a matter of pride, he realized after a moment. She must feel a yawning absence of pride. She'd been reduced to existing like an animal. Had been treated like an animal. The chance to wash her face—a small reminder of normalcy—only magnified the horror of her captivity and everything that had been taken away from her.

"It's all over," he said, surprised by the gruffness of his voice. "You don't have to think about it anymore."

She spoke to her lap. "It will never be over."

No, for her it wouldn't, Dallas realized. And she would think about what had been done to her in this jungle forever.

Not your problem, Garrett, he told himself as he gathered up anything that could tell the bad guys they'd been here.

He dug back into his pack, came up with a pair of extra socks and a roll of duct tape.

"We need to do something for your feet," he said when she frowned at him. "Sorry I can't do better."

This time he waited for her to make the first move. It took several deep breaths before she got up the courage to extend one bare, battered foot.

Christ. She was tougher than leather to have made it this far on those poor cut and infected feet. The infection was probably the source of her fever.

He opened the first-aid kit again, propped her foot on his thigh, and dabbed each cut with alcohol. She gritted her teeth and barely flinched. He knew it had to sting like hell. Then he dressed the cuts with antibiotic ointment. He didn't bother with Band-Aids. They'd just come off.

She watched him like a hawk the entire time, but she didn't say a word. Didn't utter a complaint. She didn't relax, either, until he rolled a sock onto her left foot, then loosely bound it with duct tape.

"It's not much, but it'll give you a little protection," he said when he'd finished treating and wrapping the other foot.

He handed her a couple of ibuprofens.

"Thank you." Her voice wobbled.

He told himself not to. But he looked up and into her eyes.

Oh, hell. She was near tears. She wouldn't cry over

the pain, but she'd tear up with gratitude. With those blue eyes and that blond hair, he couldn't help but think of his kid sister. Eve was a blue-eyed blonde, too. Maybe a few years older than this woman. If anyone had done this to Eve . . . if anyone had abused her this way . . . he'd make the bastards pay.

He swallowed hard, realized he wouldn't mind doling out a little more frontier justice on the barbarians who had done this to her.

"What's your name?" she asked, startling him back to the reality that they were two strangers who knew nothing about each other.

"Garrett. Dallas Garrett."

"I'm Amy," she said, then added as if it was an afterthought, "Amy Walker."

It was a soft, simple name for what he'd decided was a tough, complex woman.

And they didn't have time for social hour—just like he didn't have the inclination to get acquainted. She was a job—an unexpected and unwanted one at that—and he didn't need to know her to get her safely out of here.

He stood, shrugged back into his pack, and picked up his M-4. "We've got to keep moving."

It had to hurt like hell, but she pushed to her feet. Not so much as a whimper.

More points for the gutsy little blonde with the pale baby blues. Even more when this time she waited for him to lead the way.

14

THE LOSS OF BLOOD WAS MAKING ETHAN light-headed. He knew he should have stopped before now, but he'd wanted to put as much distance between them and the tangos as possible before they took a break.

He'd shed the NVGs when daylight had broken a half an hour or so ago. Now he paused to try to catch a breath and scan the terrain around them. Through a tangle of stringy vines and fern fronds something caught his eyes: a rock formation half-hidden by a clump of dapdap bleeding red flowers and a small stand of palms.

If he hadn't been bent over, sucking air and leaning on his rifle for support, he never would have seen it. Which meant that anyone else passing this way probably wouldn't see it, either. Could be it was their best shot at laying low for a while without being detected.

He headed for the outcropping. Like she had all morning, Darcy stuck close on his heels. Because she was exhausted, because the terrain was a bitch, Darcy was oblivious to the fact that he was weaving on his feet and leaving a blood trail a myopic bloodhound could have followed.

Beneath the jut of rock Ethan discovered that the earth dropped off into a gully and exposed a tangled tree root system. Behind the roots and a curtain of hanging moss erosion had carved a tidy little bowl into the earth. It looked like the opening to a cave when in fact it was just a five-by-five-foot indentation that would easily hold two people. They could tuck in behind the roots and for the most part be hidden from anyone they didn't want to find them. If they got lucky, no one would.

He gritted his teeth against the pain, slid down the embankment, and ducked in under the network of roots. Supporting his weight on his good leg, he leaned heavily against the wall of dirt. He'd have liked like hell to sit but was afraid that if he did, he'd never get up again.

Darcy eased in beside him. And for a moment, there they stood, catching their breath, hidden from view by the cover of open tree roots, ferns, and vines.

"You don't need to stop for me," she said, closing her eyes and resting her head against the wall of brown earth. "I can go on."

"Yeah. Well, I can't."

Her eyes snapped open. Ethan tried to distract her by handing her the M-4. "Anyone shows up that you don't like the looks of, just point and squeeze."

She looked from the automatic to him. "What's wrong?"

It took all of his strength to shrug off his ALICE pack. His hands were shaking so hard he couldn't open the compartment containing his first-aid kit. "Guess I'm just a pansy ass. Need my midmorning nap," he mumbled, heard the slur in his voice, and knew he was drifting toward some very deep shit. "Look, you're going to have to open this for me."

And that's when she took a good long look at him.

Ethan knew what she saw. The tight set of his mouth against the pain. The sweat that beaded his brow beneath the floppy brim of his boonie cap. Sweat. And yet he felt cold.

"Oh God." Her green eyes widened in horror. What she hadn't been able to see walking behind Ethan in the darkness was glaringly clear in the light of day. "You've been hit."

"Always were a quick study," he said through alternating waves of pain and a cold, blessed numbness.

"Where?"

"Thigh."

She dropped to her knees in front of him. And gasped.

"Ethan. Oh my God, Ethan. There's so much blood."

"Looks worse than it is."

And he'd go to hell for lying.

He'd taken the hit high—close enough to his pride, his joy, and his joystick that he could have been singing soprano if the round had hit him an inch to the right. His pants were soaked with blood all the way into his boots. His thigh burned like blazes. And then it burned like the fires of hell when she ripped his pant leg open.

She swore shakily and tore frantically into his pack for the first-aid kit. He hissed in a breath through clenched teeth. "Gawd damn! Could have warned me, sweetheart," he gritted out when she doused the wound with alcohol.

And that was all she wrote. His legs went out from under him. He landed on his ass in the dirt.

"Ethan. Blood is spurting everywhere."

"My belt," he mumbled. "Need . . . need to stop the flow."

This much blood meant only one thing. The slug must have hit the femoral artery. Not severed it or he'd have bled dry and been dead by now. But the artery had been nicked well and good.

"Take off my belt," he repeated, fighting to stay conscious. Stay with the program. If he went down, so did she, and that just couldn't happen.

While she fumbled frantically with his belt, he applied pressure to the wound with the flat of his hand.

"You used to be a lot faster at that."

She was near tears as she struggled to undo the buckle. "Jokes? You're cracking jokes at a time like this?"

"Ease up, babe. Just slow down. Take a deep breath. You can do it. Atta girl. There you go. Now slip it under my thigh."

"Where do I put it?"

"Up. Higher. Higher. Okay. Good," he said when she had it situated just below his groin. "Now fasten and tighten it."

Her hands shook as she drew the leather through the buckle. "There's just so much blood," she said again in a tremulous voice.

"We're gonna take care of that right now. Good. Okay. Tight. Tighter," he said through gritted teeth, and fought to keep from passing out. The pain was excruciating.

"How we doing?" he asked to keep himself from sinking closer toward unconsciousness.

"I don't know. I don't . . . —Oh God, I need help. Where's Dallas? And Manny?"

"They're taking care of business," he told her, although, like Darcy, he wished like hell one or the other of them would show up. Chances of that were slim and slimmer as the escape plan had been to fan out, then meet up later at pre-established coordinates.

"Darcy." He lifted a hand to her hair. "Don't lose it now. Not now. We've got to get you out of here. And you're going to need me to do it."

"How? You can't go on. You can't possibly walk like this. You'll bleed to death."

"I'm not going to bleed to death, okay?" he said, working to reassure her and damning the tremor in his voice that gave away just how weak he was. "Not here in this shit hole."

She closed her eyes. "I'm so sorry I got you into this."

He forced a smile. "And here I thought you were glad to see me."

The bleakness in her eyes was heartbreaking.

His leg felt cold. "How's the bleeding?"

She swallowed and checked. "Slower. A lot slower."

"There ya go. See? We're cookin' now."

He could tell she didn't buy it. And it was up to him to make sure she did. He needed her solid. He needed her steady. Because if he bought it here, she was going to have to keep it together until Manny or Dallas circled back and found her. If they found her.

He rubbed his thumb across her cheek. Didn't know if it was his blood or the blood of the bastard Manny had greased covering her now. "You're a mess, babe. You know that?"

She turned her face into his hand. Pushed out a

pained laugh. "You're not exactly spit-and-polished yourself."

"But I'm still hot, right?"

Another small, strained laugh. "Yeah. You're still hot. Not to mention you're still full of yourself."

He met her eyes. Green eyes he'd dreamed about every night since he'd lost her. "And you're still the most beautiful woman I've ever seen."

She became very quiet. And they both knew why. This was old ground. No point treading it. Not here. Not now.

"So. How's life been treating you?" he said, trying for snappy, but it came out slurred. "Present situation excluded."

She shook her head.

"Shit," he said when a thought struck him. "You've got to be starved. I've got MREs."

"You expect me to eat? While you're bleeding to death?"

"I told you. I'm not bleeding to death. Come on. You believed that pansy-ass remark?"

"Ethan—"

"Here's the way it's going to work," he said, finding it harder and harder to keep things in focus. "You're going to drink. I'm going to . . . drink. You're going to eat. I'm . . . going to eat. Then we're going to clean . . . this thing up," he pointed to his wound, "slap some antibiotic paste and a dressing on it. With me . . . so far?"

She nodded, not looking at all convinced.

"We're going to rest . . . for a bit while you tell me how you got into this fix; then we're . . . getting the hell out of here."

It was a solid plan. In a little while—when he felt a

little more comfortable risking it—he'd turn on his SAT phone and try to raise Dallas and Manny.

Good plan, he thought again as he fought to keep his eyes from rolling back in his head. Solid plan.

Would have worked, too, if he hadn't picked that moment to pass out cold.

"Anything?" Manny cut straight to the chase.

Dallas tipped his SAT phone back down to his mouth, his expression grim. "Negative."

It was the second time in as many hours that Manny had raised him to see if he had news from Ethan. This had been the longest fucking day of his life. And it looked like it was far from over. "Any luck with the GPS?"

"That's a big no. Either Ethan doesn't have it on or it's inoperable."

Dallas had fixed Manny's location at about half a click north. About a quarter of an hour ago he and Amy had made the designated rendezvous point the team had set ahead of time.

"Roger that," Dallas said. "I made commo with Nolan just before you called. He's going to see if he can get a bead on Ethan from his transmitter. In the meantime, no news is no news."

He glanced at his watch. It was 0930. "Check back at 1030. That'll give No a little time to scare him up."

"Will do. I'm going to go ahead and double back, see if I can pick up a trail."

"Luck, man."

"Watch your six." Manny broke the connection.

Dallas scrubbed a hand over his face and stared into space. He didn't like this. Not one freaking bit. They should have raised Ethan by now. And they should be halfway to the beach if they wanted to stay on their timetable. Nolan had given them a setting that would halve the time of their trek to the beach where he was supposed to pick them up in approximately thirty-six hours.

Overhead, the canopy of leaves was alive with the chatter of birds and the occasional serrated screech from a howler monkey. A small, clear-running stream had carved out a four-foot bank just below them. The water cut a meandering path over a rocky basin. It made a lazy gurgling sound as it poured over and around dead-fall and stones in its path.

Just above the stream, he found a good place to lay low and rest, well hidden in the elbow of a downed tree that had broken off about four feet from the ground. Jungle brush had grown up around the downed trunk that hung from its base at a ninety-degree angle. Huge fern fronds, a patch of monster tongues that he recognized as bromeliads—Eve had a potted one on her patio—and strings of trailing yellow orchids had totally overgrown the site.

It was like sitting in an airy tent in the thick of some little girl's fairyland with flowers and jungle grass soft and springy beneath them and freshwater nearby.

Well, it was no fuckin' fairyland, Dallas reminded himself with a disgusted grunt. It was a terrorist haven, and the woman sitting beside him in their makeshift hideout knew firsthand the extent of these particular terrorists' brutality.

He was bushed suddenly. Running on the backside of an adrenaline rush that had finally given up the ghost. A seventy-two-hour march without much more than a few hours of sleep caught in fragmented combat naps would do that to a man.

And now this thing with Ethan.

"Are they lost, do you think?"

He blinked, then looked at Amy. Since he'd tackled her earlier and they'd had their little meet and greet, they'd marched on for another four hours. And for most of that time Dallas had tried to think of her as the other woman hostage. Nothing more. Nothing less. But when she looked at him that way, with those waif blue eyes and that poor bruised face, he couldn't quite manage to put an impersonal spin on it.

She was Amy. And she was something.

In the hours since dawn, while he'd set a pace that would prompt a Marine in his prime to bellyache and bitch, she'd gutted it out in stoic silence. Half-starved. Sick with fever. Walking on cut and bloodied feet.

"Don't know," he said finally, dragging his gaze away from her face. He rolled his head, then worked his shoulders. "Could be they're in a gully and something's blocking the signal on the SAT phones. Maybe the equipment's on the fritz. Or it could be they're laying low and don't want to risk commo or turning on the GPS transmitter in case the tangos are close by."

Speaking of tangos. Manny's recon said they were still out and about—in decidedly fewer numbers but still on the hunt. Dallas didn't think it was necessary to share that bit of news with her. But he did have a question.

"You say you were in the jungle for months?"

She nodded.

"In the past few days—before you hooked up with the thugs who had Darcy—did you see anything or hear any scuttle about the Philippine army?"

She frowned. "No. I don't remember that I did. I didn't speak Filipino when they brought me here, but I got pretty good at figuring it out after a while. I didn't hear anything about an army. And I never got the sense that they were particularly worried about being pursued."

Well, that was good news. Maybe the army had turned back. Maybe the team didn't have to sweat that a company of uniformed men would still show up, shoot first, and ask questions later.

He glanced over at where Amy sat no more than a foot away with her knees drawn up to her chest. And his curiosity finally got the best of him. "How did it happen? That you got kidnapped?"

She cut him a quick glance, then just as quickly looked away. "Sometimes you just get lucky."

Yeah. If bad luck was luck.

Okay. So she didn't want to talk about it. "Well. Your family's going to be happy to get you home."

She closed her eyes, rested her forehead on her knees. And didn't say a word.

Damn it. He should stop. But he couldn't. "Surely you've got a husband . . . or a boyfriend waiting for you?"

Nothing.

He waited a beat. Was going to drop it, then heard himself ask, "Mother? Father?"

Finally, she lifted her head. "No. No one." And if bleak were a color, it would be the color of her pale, gaunt face beneath her poor sunburned skin.

Because he felt too much sympathy, still too much curiosity, and somewhere in there even a kernel of satisfaction that she wasn't married or hooked up with someone, he backed away. Way the hell away.

"How's the duct tape holding up?" He nodded toward the makeshift boots he'd made her.

"Okay. Good."

She didn't say anything else. She just nibbled on her lower lip and looked worried.

Yeah, well. He was worried, too, but he didn't want her to know that. Ethan was no raw recruit; he knew the drill—and he wouldn't break protocol or contact unless something was bad wrong.

"Look. Ethan's smart," Dallas said aloud to reassure himself as much as her. "He knows how to take care of himself. And he'll take care of Darcy. We'll hear from him. We just have to give him time."

"Maybe we should go look for them."

Amazing. The woman was so sick and exhausted she could hardly hold her head up, yet she was willing to mount a search.

"Manny's on it. We need to stay here in case Ethan shows."

Sometime during their hike, Dallas had told her about Nolan and Manny—mostly so she wouldn't run like a scalded dog when Manny popped up unexpectedly, as Manny was wont to do.

"Why don't you try to get some rest?" Dallas looked up at the sky through the netting of vines, leaves, and yellow orchids that hid them. And heard the sudden whirling sound of bird wings—lots of bird wings.

And then he heard nothing.

The hair on the back of his neck stood at attention.

Something had spooked the birds. He had a pretty good idea what that something was.

They had company.

15

DALLAS TOUCHED AMY'S ARM.

She flinched. Shit. She still flinched every time he touched her.

He pressed his index finger to his lips. Mouthed for her to be quiet and reached for his M-4.

Silence. Absolute and crackling with unknowns.

Amy buried her face between her updrawn knees and her chest. He could see her struggle to keep her breathing regular. And she was losing the fight.

A twig snapped. It came from his right. On the rise above them. No more than ten meters away.

Beside him, Amy started to shake.

Keep it together. Keep it together, kid.

But it was the impossible dream.

He could see she was gearing up for a major panic attack. *Fuck.* If it came on her like the one she'd had back at the tango camp that had roused the vermin from their spider holes, they were up shit creek.

And he couldn't let that happen.

Just as he heard a man's voice—speaking Tagalog—he also heard the beginnings of a hollow, high-pitched little moan.

Double fuck.

Amy was going to go off like a storm siren.

He had to do something to shut her up—and he had to figure out how to do it in a nanosecond.

He set aside the M-4, gripped her by the shoulders, and when her mouth flew open he clamped his hand over it.

Eyes wide, she started to struggle.

Dallas pressed her onto her back and with his hand still covering her mouth tried to corral her thrashing limbs. She kneed him in the groin for his effort.

Smothering a moan of acute, blinding pain, he fought to get control of her—while she fought just as hard to get out from under him.

He knew. He just knew what she must be thinking. How many times had she had to fight and still been brutally violated? And how could she possibly separate what he was trying to do from what had been done to her?

He wished there was another way. But there wasn't. So he held her down. Or tried to. She was as slippery as an eel. Fast as an otter. He needed another hand. And there was only one way to get it and still keep her quiet.

There was no help for it. He lowered his head to hers.

I'm sorry, he mouthed into her terrified eyes, and replaced his hand with his mouth.

He swallowed her squeal of surprise and pinned her arms above her head.

Once he had her wrists manacled in his hand, he lifted his head and quickly clamped his hand over her mouth again.

Her eyes were wild with panic when she stared up at him.

"I'm not going to hurt you," he whispered against

her ear, and used the weight of his legs to still the thrashing of hers. "You've got to trust me here. Trust me, Amy. You have to be quiet. If they hear you, we're as good as dead. But they won't spot us if they don't hear us. You can do this. Come on, Amy . . . trust me to know they'll never find us. But you've got to be quiet."

Beneath his chest, her heart beat like a squadron of Blackhawks revving for a spin up. Rapid and strong and piston-fire hard.

Her breathing was fractured; great heaving sobs soughed out, pressing her breasts against his chest and confirming what he'd already guessed. Beneath that loose, out-of-shape shirt, skinny little Amy Walker was stacked.

And this was no time to think about that.

"Easy, now. Come on, sweetheart. Trust me. Trust me," he whispered over and over again, and finally, *finally* felt the slightest indication that he was getting through to her.

Either that or she'd exhausted herself.

Thank you, Jesus.

The men's voices grew louder as they grew closer.

He lifted his head, met her eyes.

It's okay, he mouthed. *Be still. Be still. I've got you. I won't let them get to you. Trust me. Trust me.*

The closer the voices came, the louder the noise as the men stomped through the brush. And the harder it became to tell if it was her heart or his that was pummeling his chest.

He continued to hold her gaze. Made pleas with his eyes. Made promises.

And finally—*finally*—made the connection that settled her. She went limp and still beneath him.

Releasing his first true breath since she'd gone off

on him, he glanced to the left. Not four feet away he spotted several pairs of combat boots. Heard the sound of a zipper going down. The splat of liquid against soil as a tango tapped a kidney.

Dallas looked back down at Amy. His face was less than an inch from hers. Her eyes were still wide and wild with terror. But she was quiet. It was killing her, but she was quiet. And still he didn't lift his hand from her mouth.

He just nodded. Mouthed, *It's okay. It's okay. You're doing fine.*

Freckles. At this range, he couldn't miss them beneath the sunburn. They feathered across the bridge of her nose, drifted wide over her bruised cheeks. And made her look all of twelve years old.

The breasts poking against his chest put an end to that notion in short order.

And the beginnings of a boner pressing into her stomach damn near sent him into orbit.

What the fuck?

Whoa. That was just wrong.

As slowly and inconspicuously as possible, he lifted his hips, balanced his weight on his knees, and broke the belly-to-belly-contact. The last thing she needed was to get all freaked out because he had a temporary unexplained testosterone surge. Not to mention a lapse in rescuer-to-rescuee protocol.

Protocol, hell. There was no protocol for this. And there was no excuse for him going off half-cocked— literally—and giving her another reason to spook on him.

He chanced a look at her face. Realized he still had his hand pressed over her mouth. He swore under his breath. It was a wonder she could breathe.

He lifted his hand fractionally—a test to see if she was going to keep quiet.

When she just lay there, her eyes still wide and searching his with a wariness shot through with a tentative trust, he let up on the pressure on her mouth.

She licked her lips, blinked, and turned her head to the side. But not before her cheeks flushed hot pink.

Dallas hung his head. Let out a deep breath. *She hasn't had enough humiliation, asshole? You had to add to it?*

Long moments passed as he sort of straddled her in a modified push-up on his knees and elbows. Long moments when he was aware of her breathing, the warmth of her skin from the fever and exertion, and how very, very still she was.

He made himself tune back into the tangos. From the sounds of things they were all zipped and tucked again and heading down the embankment for the stream.

Once there they seemed to be arguing. He didn't speak the language, but he didn't have to to realize that somebody was pissed off.

They were still muttering when the sound of their voices finally faded away.

He let out a pent-up breath.

He should move. He should move off of her now.

But for some reason he didn't. He needed to say something. Explain, somehow, what was freaking unexplainable. At the very least, he should apologize.

Um, yeah, about that, um, flashlight in my pocket.

"I . . . I think they're gone."

He snapped his gaze to her face. And yeah, they were gone. And yeah, he should still move.

"There could be trailers," he said, and stayed exactly where he was.

Amazing.

Only moments ago he'd wanted to put as much distance between them as possible. Now he couldn't come up with a remotely plausible reason that he should move even an eighth of an inch.

Then she licked her lips again—and he thought about how those lips had felt pressed beneath his. Something he hadn't had a chance to digest when he'd been relatively certain they were both going to get their heads blown off if he didn't shut her up.

Her lips were wide and full. Nicely shaped. Angelina Jolie lips. Soft and supple beneath his.

Shit.

He was getting hard again.

He scrambled off of her in a flash.

Sitting on his ass, his elbows on his knees, he hung his head in his hands—and breathing was a helluva lot harder than it had been a second ago.

Silence settled like a bomb.

"I'm sorry," they finally both said at the same time.

He looked at her over his shoulder. "*You're* sorry?"

"For flipping out on you. I almost got us killed."

He shook his head. "Like you don't have reason to flip out? Forget it," he added. "You did fine."

Several more moments passed while he tried to figure out how to apologize. "About what happened," he started, staring straight ahead and away from her.

"Nothing happened," she said quickly but so quietly that he knew it had freaked her out, too.

He drew in a deep breath. Let it out. "Yeah. Something happened." He shook his head. Lifted a hand.

"Things . . . things happen, you know, in the heat of the moment. Under stress. It's not an excuse. I just . . . I just want you to know. I'd never do anything on purpose, you know . . . to make you uncomfortable, okay?"

He'd begun to think she wasn't going to respond when she very softly said, "Okay."

He felt way too much relief. "Okay. Good."

And then he looked over his shoulder. And almost lost his breath.

She was sitting there. Just sitting there framed by a curtain of trailing yellow orchids and pink bromeliads. The sun had broken through the cloud cover. Dappled rays slanted down through the vines and played along the rise of her cheekbones, flickered at a jawline that was purple with bruising.

And for a moment there, despite the bruising, despite the snarled dirty hair, despite her sunburned skin and the suffering in her eyes that she refused to let defeat her, she was one of the prettiest things he'd ever seen.

Finally, Darcy thought. Ethan was coming around. It was almost noon. He'd been out for nearly two hours.

"Ethan. Come on. Stay with me. Please, stay with me this time."

She'd found smelling salts in the first-aid kit and passed them under his nose again.

He jerked and batted her hand away. "Fuck. Uncle . . . uncle, okay?" He blinked several times and finally opened bloodshot eyes.

He stared into space, then slowly shifted his unfocused gaze to hers. "Well, hey. Aren't you just the prettiest damn thing? You *are* real, right?"

Darcy said a silent prayer of thanks. "I'm as real as it gets, cowboy."

He sliced her a bleary grin. "We goin' for a ride?"

She laughed because crying wasn't an option. Even though she wanted to. "Not this very moment, no. How are you feeling?"

He rolled his head on his neck. "Ready to leap tall buildings."

"Yeah, well, let's not put that to the test just yet."

He looked down at his leg, squinted like he was trying to get things in focus. "You've been busy. I slept through all that?"

"I suppose *some* people would call it sleep."

Darcy called it passed out. For a while she'd even considered calling it comatose. It had scared her to death. All the while she'd cleaned the wound, applied the antiseptic ointment she'd found in the first-aid kit, and then packed it with gauze she'd prayed. She'd apply pressure, loosen the tourniquet, swear, tighten it again, and apply pressure again.

An hour, then two had passed.

It had given her a chance to look at him. Really look at him. Even through the camo face paint and beard stubble, Ethan's face was beautiful, familiar. She'd thought when she saw him again that she'd see a stranger's face.

Five years, however, wasn't that long even though it had seemed like a lifetime.

They had loved so much. And screwed things up so badly.

He had a scar over his left brow that hadn't been there the last time she'd seen him. She wondered what other scars he carried—outside and in.

And that was a road that led exactly nowhere, she'd

finally told herself, relieved when the bleeding had stopped.

"How are you *really* feeling?" she asked again.

"Couple of quarts low."

"Think you can drink something?"

He nodded, still looking a little fuzzy around the edges. When he tried to boost himself up so he could sit up a little straighter, he finally gave it up with a disgusted, "Fuck."

"Might want to bump that estimate to three quarts," she said, watching him carefully when she positioned the tube from his Camelbak to his mouth.

"Just need some fluid." He made a valiant effort to take on as much water as possible. "I'll be good as new."

Yeah, and she was the tooth fairy.

He let his head roll back against the dirt wall, exhausted from the effort of drinking. "How long was I out?"

"Hour and a half . . . maybe two," she guessed.

"You should have woke me up."

She grunted. "If they gave medals for effort, I'd have a chestful. You scared the hell out of me, Ethan."

When he met her eyes, she saw regret in his.

"You need to try to eat something."

"Hold that thought." He leaned over to the side and promptly heaved up a good portion of the water he'd just drunk.

He sagged back against the wall, spent from the effort. "Oops."

"Oh God." Blood seeped through the bandage in an ever-widening circle.

"What are we going to do?" Darcy quickly straddled his thigh. She centered the heel of her palm against the bandage, applied pressure. "If that little bit of movement started the bleeding again, there's no way you can walk out of here."

"No word from . . . Dallas? Or Manny?" His voice was weak. His breathing labored.

"Word?"

"Didn't we . . . didn't *I* contact them?"

"Contact? You have a way to contact them?"

He looked like he needed toothpicks to keep his eyes open. "Could have sworn I raised them on the SAT phone."

"You have a phone?" She didn't know whether to laugh or cry.

"Sweetheart, I've got everything but blood."

And then he passed out again.

"Hang on, Ethan," Darcy whispered. Of course he didn't hear her, but it made her feel better to tell him just the same. "Manny's on the way."

She'd found the SAT phone, figured out how to operate it. When she heard Manny Ortega's voice on the other end of the line, she almost cried with relief.

Manny had walked her through activating the GPS and had been able to get a fix on them.

"I'm not more than a click or two away," Manny had assured her. "Be there in half an hour."

Half an hour. Manny would get them out of here in a half an hour.

Darcy checked Ethan's watch. Not even five minutes had passed. It felt like hours.

And when, a few minutes later, she heard what sounded like footsteps above their little hideout, she almost ran out in the open.

Almost.

Until she heard someone speaking Tagalog.

Her heart picked up several beats.

Manny? Manny spoke Filipino?

Then she heard another voice. One she recognized. And it wasn't Dallas.

She scrambled to get to the M-4. Before she could reach it, an AK-47 shoved aside the tangle of roots. The business end of the weapon was pointed right at the center of her forehead.

"Up. Up!"

Darcy recognized the voice ordering her to lift her hands above her head. It was one of the ringleaders of the rape squad. Standing at his side was a faint glimmer of hope.

"Ben," she said, an appeal in her voice.

"Quiet!" the other man yelled, and kicked the M-4 out of her reach.

He said something in rapid-fire Tagalog and spit at her feet.

Darcy didn't need to know the language to interpret what he said. But she did know. And that made it worse.

He blamed her for the death of his Abu Sayyaf brothers. And what he said next stopped her breath.

"Patayin mo na siya!" he ordered Ben. *Kill her.* *"Patayin mo na siya!"*

Ben's eyes grew large. He didn't want to do it. Darcy could see it in his dark eyes. In the way his Adam's apple bobbed jerkily when he swallowed.

"Gawin mo na o akong nang bahala nito!" *Do it or I will!*

Ben's gaze locked on hers in apology as he slowly lifted his weapon with shaking hands.

Everything became surreal then. Like watching a movie—without the popcorn and the cushy seat.

She was going to die. This boy was going to kill her.

Ben sighted down the barrel of the rifle.

Ethan was going to die. And it was all her fault.

Ben looked into her eyes.

Fixed his finger on the trigger.

And swung the gun away.

He fired three rounds dead center into the terrorist's chest.

Darcy flinched with each round.

And realized she was still alive.

Heart jackhammering, she looked in disbelief from Ben to the terrorist. Watched in stunned silence as the man looked down at himself, dropped his weapon with a clatter, and clutched his chest.

He just stood that way. It seemed like hours before he lifted his blood-drenched hands and stared at her as if he couldn't believe he was dying and not her before slowly lifting his faraway gaze to Ben.

There were tears in the young man's eyes as he watched his fellow soldier fall to the ground.

For the longest moment, Darcy felt numb. She couldn't speak. Couldn't breathe.

And then the realization set in. Instead of killing her, Ben had killed *for* her. Because of him, she was alive. Because of him, Ethan was alive. She had no doubt he would have been next.

"Ben," she said in a thready voice. "Oh, Ben."

He forced his gaze away from the dead man. Searched her eyes like he was lost and was counting on her to show him the way.

"Thank you," she whispered as he slowly lowered his weapon.

A tear slid down his cheek. "I . . . so sorry, miss."

"No, no. It's okay. You did right, Ben. You did the right thing."

"I . . . I want to . . . to go home."

She felt tears form in her own eyes for the boy who had wanted to be a man for all the wrong reasons but who had just become a man for all the right ones.

"Come here." She held a hand out to him, unable to quell the involuntary trembling. "Come sit by me. Someone's coming. He'll help us both get home."

16

"I'VE GOT 'EM."

"Thank you, Jesus." Dallas pressed a thumb and forefinger to his eyes as he listened to Manny on the SAT phone.

"Darcy contacted Manny," Dallas told Amy in an aside.

His relief didn't last all that long. Frowning, he held up a hand when Amy started to ask him for details.

He listened as Manny filled him in.

"Yeah. Wait. Let me get it turned on." Dallas snagged his GPS tracking unit, flipped it on. "Okay. It's on. Yeah. There it is. I've got a signal."

Manny broke the rest of the news about Ethan's wound and blood loss.

"The hell you will," Dallas said. "I'm on the way." He disconnected and started gathering gear.

"What? What's happened?"

Dallas looked up into Amy's anxious eyes. "Ethan took a round in the thigh. He's lost a lot of blood. Evidently he passed out for a couple of hours, got a little disoriented. Anyway, Darcy figured out how to use the SAT phone—once she knew he had one—and made contact with Manny."

"Is Darcy okay?"

"Yeah. Yeah, she's fine. Ethan, though—not so much," Dallas admitted, concern for his brother adding an edge to his urgency to get to him. "He's not going to be able to get out of there on his own power. And Manny isn't going to be able to carry him out." Not even with the help of the boy Manny had told him about.

He met Amy's eyes. They were more gray than blue and he knew she knew the score. Still, he pointed out the obvious. "You know I've got to go help them."

"I'll go, too."

He shook his head. This was going to be hard. "You need to save your strength for the rest of the trip."

"But—"

"You'd slow me down, Amy. I'm sorry. But that's the bottom line."

She gnawed furiously on her lower lip while he loaded up with extra ammo and tried not to think about how scared she was going to be waiting here all by herself.

"Look. You're going to be all right. You're well hidden—and this spot has already passed the tango test. But, just in case, I'm leaving this with you."

He handed her the M-4.

She shook her head. "You'll need that."

"I've got plenty of firepower and I'm not leaving you without it. Now let me show you how to use it."

Dallas walked her through the motions. "Got it?"

She gave him an absent nod.

"You're going to be all right," he insisted. "If I didn't think so, I wouldn't leave you here alone. Just lay low. Stay quiet and if any tangos chance by, keep your cool and they'll never spot you. You know that, don't you? Tell me you know that."

Another slow nod.

"I'm sorry. I'm really sorry, but I've got to go. Anything you need, it's probably in there." He nodded toward his ALICE pack. "Help yourself."

He checked his handgun. The 9mm Berretta was military issue and he'd been damn happy to get ahold of it. "Don't look for us until later in the afternoon. Probably closer to dark. It's going to be a long, rough trip."

Dallas's SAT phone rang just as he was strapping on his knife.

It was Nolan calling from Zamboanga. "I've got a fix on Ethan on the GPS."

"Yeah. I was just about to contact you. Manny's just located him. He's with Ethan and Darcy now. Problem is, they're a couple of hours from away from me."

"Is there like a rule that you guys can't say within four Ks of each other?" Nolan sputtered.

Ignoring his brother's grumbling, Dallas filled Nolan in on Ethan's condition. "Better see if you can scare up an IV. We're going to need to rehydrate him. Maybe pump some blood."

"Yeah, sure. Why don't I get a triage team while I'm at it?" Nolan said, heavy on the sarcasm. "Who the hell do you think I am: Superman?"

"Yeah," Dallas said. "I do. He's in a bad way, Bro. Do what you can."

"Okay, right. I'll see what I can do. We adjusting the pickup time?"

"Negative. We're not staying on this mosquito-infested island a minute longer than we have to."

"Roger that. I'm outta here." Nolan hung up.

Amy's eyes were round and scared when Dallas turned to her. He felt a gut-deep urge to draw her into his arms, hold her close, and reassure her that everything was going to be okay.

But he knew what would happen if he touched her. At least he'd thought he knew—until she tentatively reached out and covered his hand with hers.

That simple, minor gesture damn near tore him up. He knew from encounters of the closest kind how she felt about physical contact. At least the male–female kind of contact. And he figured he knew she had damn good reason to be scared to death of the touch of a man.

That she would reach out, breach that divide with him, without coercion, without even necessity, undid him.

He covered her hand with his, looked into her eyes for any sign of discomfort—and found nothing but trust.

There were a lot of things he could have said to her then. There were a lot of things he wanted to say. Things like, *Another place . . . another time . . . if your life wasn't so screwed up . . . if mine wasn't just the way I like it.*

Well . . . there were just a lot of things he wanted to say.

None of them appropriate. None of them wise. He didn't want her getting attached to him. Didn't want her to start thinking she meant any more to him than seeing her safely out of here. Because she didn't. She absolutely didn't.

And even if she did, he wouldn't let things go anywhere between them anyway. Present situation excluded, his life was nice, neat, and orderly, just the way he liked it. If he ever decided he wanted a woman to be a part of it, her life would have to be nice, neat, and orderly, too.

Amy Walker didn't have a prayer of nice, neat, and orderly for a very long time—if ever. She'd live with and struggle with and be tormented by what had happened to her in this jungle for the rest of her life.

No. Nothing neat and tidy there.

"Look," he said when he realized he'd been sitting here working damn hard on convincing himself of something that should have been a no contest. "Don't come out for anything. I'll give you a signal when we arrive so you'll know not to shoot us," he added with a grin, hoping to get an answering one from her.

"A signal?" she asked with that too serious face and those too worried eyes. "What kind of signal?"

"Don't worry." He'd do enough of that for both of them. "There won't be any mistaking it's me."

He rolled to all fours. "Stay strong. I'll see you later." Then he backed out of their cover and hightailed it out of there after his big brother.

For the first hour after Dallas left, Amy sat with the M-4 cradled on her lap, her finger poised on the trigger. A bird landed on the tangle of orchid vines and Amy startled, jerking the gun to her shoulder and taking aim before she settled herself.

She hadn't any more than drawn a steadying breath when some forest creature skittered through the jungle brush and had her flicking off the safety again.

This has to stop.

She'd have a heart attack or shoot herself in the foot if she didn't get a grip.

She hated being so jumpy. Was so tired of being afraid. So weary of becoming someone she didn't know and couldn't control.

She'd always been a solitary person. She was comfortable with herself, didn't need the presence of other people to make her happy.

But that was before. Before she'd spent almost six months with a 24-7 guard. Six months with a demented pack of animals who . . . who . . .

She became aware of a high, keening sound. Finally realized the sound was coming from her.

She forced herself to pull away from the memory of the things they'd done to her. Because if she let them, the memories became real time, like the pain, and that's when she lost who she was.

She shook her head free of the thoughts. Concentrated on the sweet sound of the slowly trickling stream. Felt the sunlight filter down and kiss her skin through the canopy of trees and the netting of vines and orchids. And she thought of Dallas Garrett with the gentle blue eyes and the way he made her feel safe—when she'd never thought she'd feel safe with a man again.

She didn't think about the fear. She wouldn't think about the fear.

But she had to do something. Something . . . to keep herself busy. If she didn't, she'd drift back toward that place where she was so paralyzed by fear she lost her bearings, came close to losing her mind.

She looked around their hideout. Spotted the bulky backpack Dallas had left behind.

Anything you need, it's probably in there. Help yourself.

Setting aside the M-4, she scooted closer to the pack. And for the next several hours lost herself in something other than fear.

• • •

Darcy thought the wait until Dallas arrived was endless. By the time they transported Ethan to the rendezvous point, however, she knew what endless really was.

She'd thought she'd known what stubborn was, too. Ethan showed her yet another definition of the word.

"I'll get out of here on my own steam if I have to crawl."

"See? There's no reasoning with him." With Ben at her side, Darcy appealed to Manny and Dallas to talk some sense into Ethan. With the exception of last night when Ethan had shown up at the terrorists' camp, she'd never been so glad to see anyone in her life.

"Okay, fine, big talker." Dallas ducked his right shoulder under Ethan's arm and latched onto his wrist. Manny did the same on his left side. "You're in such goddamn good shape, carry us out of here."

"You're as funny as a rubber crutch, you know that?"

"Look. Just because you were able to take on a little fluid and some protein, and just because the bleeding stopped, it doesn't mean you're ready to fly solo."

Earlier, while Darcy had explained Ben to Manny— who had heard the gunfire and come tearing into the makeshift shelter like an avenging angel—Ben had scouted around in the jungle for something to stop the bleeding.

He'd come back with leaves and roots and sugarcane, then mashed it into a paste that he'd applied directly to the wound.

So far, so good. The bleeding had stopped to the point where Manny had been able to adjust the tourniquet and redress the wound.

And now it was time to leave. Provided Dallas and Manny could get the superhero to admit he needed some help.

"Okay, fine," Ethan finally conceded when he took a step and almost went down. "Let's just do it."

Darcy breathed a sigh of relief as, suppressing a wince, Ethan bore as much of his weight as he could on his good leg while Dallas and Manny wrapped their inside arms around his waist and headed out.

She felt useless as she followed along behind the three men. Despite her insistence that she could at least carry the ALICE pack, Ben had strapped it on. Ben also carried his AK-47 and Ethan's M-4 as they began the exhausting trek that would get them that much closer to their ride out of this jungle and away from any terrorists still on the hunt.

Carrying Manny's rifle, Darcy worried over Ethan every step of the way. Over tree roots. Over logs. Over rocks and streams and through bogs and jungle brush so thick it took Ben's machete to whack their way through.

It was endless, agonizing hours of trudging through the heat and the bugs. When the sun didn't fry them, the rain came down in torrents. And then they mucked through a slippery sweat bath, not only breathing the air but also wearing it.

The only thing that saved her was that they had to make frequent stops to let Ethan rest. He was holding up through sheer force of will. She couldn't believe he was still conscious.

When at last, an hour or so before nightfall, they stopped and Dallas said, "It's just over that last ridge," Darcy sat down on the wet, muddy ground, buried her face in her hands, and expended what dwindling stock-pile of energy she had left to keep from weeping like a baby.

Dallas swore to God that Ethan had gained weight on the trip. He wasn't an old man at thirty-four, but he'd been a helluva lot younger last time he'd hauled a wounded team member out of a hot zone.

He was beat. His dogs and his knees were killing him. He wanted to do what he could about stabilizing Ethan. Then he wanted to flop.

But first, he wanted to see Amy.

"I'll go on ahead and warn Amy that we're here," he told the group before letting them go any farther. "I don't want to spook her and have her shooting first and asking questions later."

As he headed toward the hideout beneath the downed tree, he fought the notion that he wasn't really as worried about getting shot by her as he was worried *about* her. But the sad fact was, he'd worried about her way too much today. Thought about her way too much.

And it pretty much pissed him off.

It didn't compute. She'd lived through hell before they'd rescued her from that camp. She hadn't needed him to come through it alive. She'd managed that all on her own. So tucked away all nice and safe in their little hidey-hole, she could get along just fine without him for a few hours.

And yet he wasn't going to relax until he saw, with his own eyes, that she was okay.

He'd told her he'd give her a signal. Told her she'd recognize it when she saw it. He guessed his face in her face was about as recognizable as it got. It was also

about as creative as he was capable of getting after
hauling roughly two hundred pounds of half-conscious,
pissed-off man through the rain forest.

Besides. He didn't have time to get creative. He
wanted to get Ethan on his back, get some antibiotics
and more fluid into him, and get him shored up before
they headed for the coast in the morning.

But right now, Dallas wanted to see Amy.

Just because he wanted to make sure she was okay,
he told himself again. This was no *Hi, honey, I'm home*
crap.

The fact that it even crossed his mind to say exactly
that ticked him off even more.

Just get it over with.

He crept up to the hiding place, lowered himself
carefully over the log, and crawled straight inside.

Empty.

His heart slugged him several good ones dead center in the middle of his chest.

She was gone.

Amy was gone. So was the M-4.

The ALICE pack lay neat and tidy where he'd left it.

A bleak scenario slammed through his mind. The
tangos had found her. They'd taken her. Hurt her.
Worse. Killed her.

Pulse racing, he sat back on his heels and whipped
his boonie cap off his head.

"God damn it." He dragged a hand through his hair.
He never should have left her! He should have known
she couldn't defend herself.

He should have—

A sound grabbed his attention, setting the hair on
his arms on end like a shock from a hot wire.

He froze, cocked his head. Listened.

And heard it again. It sounded like . . . humming?

Revived and revved on an adrenaline burst, he belly-crawled soundlessly back out of the hideaway and listened.

There. The sound was coming from the stream.

Creeping on his belly, he peered over the lip of a bank that had been carved away by centuries of tropical rainstorms.

And saw her.

It was one of those couldn't move, couldn't think, couldn't believe what he was seeing moments.

It was Amy all right. Thank God it was Amy. Not hurt. Not dead. Not captive.

She was alone on her knees, facing him on the opposite bank of the stream. The M-4 lay in the sand by her side.

She didn't see him. And she looked . . . hell. She looked like a different person. She was . . . clean. Even her hair was clean. The snarls had been combed out. She'd pulled the wavy blond mass of it back from her face, fastened it in a long tail at her nape somehow.

There was a yellow orchid tucked behind her ear.

And she was humming.

Not that horrible, tortured nightmare of a sound that had oozed out of her like a slow seeping wound. This was . . . pleasant. Pretty even. Dallas didn't recognize the melody, but he recognized the mood: peace.

He didn't feel peace.

On the heels of a load-leveling, grateful relief, what he felt was a swift, consuming rage.

He launched himself off the embankment. Landed midstream in front of her with a splash and a snarl. "What in the hell are you doing?"

17

AMY JUMPED, GRABBED THE M-4, AND STUM-
bled to her feet. She'd hauled the gun halfway to her
shoulder when she realized Dallas was squared off in
front of her.

His face was still covered in paint, his fatigues were
dirty and ripped, and the floppy brim of his camo cap
hid his eyes in dark shadows.

Air cleared her lungs like a fire alarm cleared a building. "Jesus, Dallas. You scared the breath out of me."

Before she could even think to lower the gun, he
grabbed the barrel and jerked it out of her hand.

"Yeah and if I'd been a tango, I'd have killed you.
What are you *thinking?* What are you *doing* out here?
Out in the open?"

When her heart finally moved out of her throat, she
realized she was facing a man on the edge. He wasn't
just angry. He was fighting mad. And all of a sudden,
so was she.

A temper that had been terrorized, beaten, and bru-
talized into submission resurfaced like a struck match.

"Living," she said, lifting her chin. "What I'm doing
is living. On *my* terms."

"By making yourself a target?"

She took a step toward him, pinned him with her glare. "By doing something I want to do."

"I can't believe you'd be so reckless."

"I wasn't reckless."

"The hell you weren't!"

He swore under his breath and spun around toward the opposite bank. She grabbed his arm, surprising them both before he could stalk away.

When he turned and met her eyes, what she saw there took the bite out of her anger.

"I'm sorry," she said, finally understanding. "I'm sorry if I frightened you."

"You didn't frighten me." He bit out the denial like it was bitter fruit. "You pissed me off. Christ, Amy. You could have given us away. You could have been captured again. We could have walked into an ambush and we'd all be dead now instead of—"

He cut himself off. Wiped a hand over his face. Settled himself down. "Look. It's done. We need to get settled in. Ethan needs attention."

All that anger. All that fear—whether he'd admit to fear or not—and he pulled himself back under control.

She felt very guilty suddenly. And very grateful that Dallas was the kind of man he was. "I'm sorry. I didn't think about endangering anyone else."

He stuck out his chin, looked away from her. "Forget it."

But she couldn't forget it. "I . . . I needed to be clean," she finally said in halting explanation. She didn't expect him to get it. Didn't expect that he could possibly understand that until she'd washed six months of beatings and rape and degradation off of her body, out of her hair, she couldn't begin to heal.

But when he looked back at her, his blue eyes probing, then softening, she realized that he did. He *did* get it.

For a moment, she thought he was going to touch her. For a moment, she wanted him to. She wanted him to pull her into his arms and hold her against all his safe male strength.

But the moment passed. For him and for her. And the quiet that settled in its wake filled up with unsaid words, fractured emotions.

"I used your comb," she finally said inanely, touching a hand to her hair, then flushing red when she encountered the orchid she'd tucked behind her ear. She tugged it out self-consciously.

"I scrubbed my hair with sand." Her body, too, then she'd luxuriated with one of those premoistened wipes that made her think of the way a baby smelled after a bath.

"Yeah," he said, his blue eyes sweeping her hair before returning to rest on her face again. He smiled. "I can see that. Um. Look. I'm sorry I yelled at you."

She breathed her first full-fledged breath since he'd landed in the middle of the stream like an avenging angel.

"I'm sorry I scared—I mean, I'm sorry I made you mad."

"Yeah, well. We're a sorry pair."

And that made her smile. "Not so much," she said.

He gave her a long, searching look.

Then he turned without another word and headed up the bank.

Interesting man, Dallas Garrett, she thought, following him. Beautiful man with his dark hair and amazing blue eyes and tough, rangy build. Even through the face paint, she could tell that he was what her friends would call—well, they'd call him any number of things. A hunk. A hottie. A hero.

A cold bleakness came over her. She tossed the orchid to the ground. Too bad she hadn't met him six months ago. Six months ago when the thought of a long-term relationship with a man and the physical intimacies that came with a committed relationship were still a possibility in her life.

Six months ago, when the thought of sex with someone special had been a sweet dream instead of the nightmare it had become.

There were many moments Darcy would look back on and remember with clarity when they finally got off this island. Most would come in the night in the form of nightmares.

This moment, however, she would remember with awe.

It was the middle of the night. The treetops swayed gently above. Every once in a while, through the intricate netting of orchids and vines and vegetation of the shelter, the glimmer of a star would shimmer down from a sky bathed in the translucent light of a china moon.

The night was pleasantly cool. But for Amy and Ethan's restful, sleeping breaths on either side of her it was also blessedly silent.

Darcy felt no fear. For this moment, she felt no apprehension. Just gratitude and peace in the dark. A moment suspended from reality . . . until the moment ended when a shadow that she recognized as Manny drifted by the shelter of vines.

Reality slammed back swift and harsh. Manny was on watch. She'd heard Dallas wake him a while ago and take his turn catching some sleep. Before him, Ben had insisted on doing his part.

Only Darcy and Amy and Ethan had been relegated to the shelter. In truth, there was barely room for the three of them.

On her left, Amy slept. Darcy still couldn't get over the way Amy had looked when she'd climbed up that stream bank.

Thrilled to see Amy, Darcy had fallen into her arms.

"You made it," Amy said, hugging her.

"Barely." Darcy pulled back. Looked at her. "Amy." She watched as the sweetest blush stole over the younger woman's face and she caught a glimpse of an innocence so brutally stolen. "Look at you . . . you look wonderful."

Okay. So she didn't look wonderful, exactly. With her emaciated frame and cuts and bruises marring her face and body and the lingering effects of her fever, she looked far from wonderful. But she did look at peace. And Darcy could see all the signs of a beautiful woman that the pain and the snarls and the dirt had hidden.

"I'm glad you're here," Amy said, diverting the attention away from herself.

"So am I," Darcy confessed.

Apparently, Amy was glad that someone else was here, too. *Interesting,* Darcy thought, observing the way Amy watched Dallas with those haunted blue eyes. Even more interesting was the way Dallas watched Amy when he thought no one was looking.

It had been hours since they'd settled in. Hours

since Amy's joy had transitioned to horror when she'd seen Ben.

Even after Darcy had explained Ben to her, Amy had still been leery.

But now Amy slept. And for the moment, all was right with her world—if you confined it to this moment, this tiny window of time and the promises it held.

Tomorrow they would finally leave this place.

Because of Ethan.

Ethan.

He slept on Darcy's right. His breathing was regular and deep. A recent check with the back of her hand against his brow told her there was no fever. Not yet. Things were looking up a little. He'd even asked her to dig out his stash of Life Savers earlier.

She lay on her back, never more aware of another heart beating in the night. Never more aware that his was the heart of a warrior. A lesser man never would have made the grueling trip today. Ethan Garrett had never been a lesser man. Still, if he hadn't come on this operation well prepared, there was no telling what shape he would be in now.

Thanks to his foresight, both Amy and Ethan were on a regular regimen of antibiotics. Thanks to Dallas and Manny, who were both well versed in administering medical aid, Ethan had taken on enough fluid to retrieve some of his strength. Tonight before falling into a deep sleep he'd eaten as well. He wasn't out of the woods yet, but his chances for recovery had increased dramatically.

As quietly as she could, Darcy rolled to her side, facing him. Even in sleep, he looked fierce and commanding. Even in pain and weak from blood loss, he looked strong.

And even five years after she'd left him, she realized she still loved him. Loved the heavy roughness of his beard, loved the sculpted angles and planes of a face that still struck her as beautiful.

Loved the implicit trust he invoked, that he was a man who commanded that trust because he'd delivered on every promise he'd ever made.

Even when she'd left him, he'd made promises.

If you ever need me, I'll be there.

And one more time, Ethan had delivered.

A hot tear leaked out, slid down her temple, and trickled into her hair. She never should have called him. She never should have put him in such peril.

Yet she'd be dead now if she hadn't—and he might still die because she had.

How did she justify that? How could she ever justify asking this much of a man? Asking this much of *this* man?

And the bigger question. The one that kept her awake as the moon slowly drifted across the expanse of ink black sky to fade in the light of morning. How was she going to walk away from him again if they got out of this alive?

"I do— fu-in' li— —is."

"Say again!" Ethan yelled into the SAT phone the next day as Dallas's voice broke up.

With an M-4 wedged under his arm and a Life Saver stashed in his cheek, Ethan propped himself up against a coconut palm and tucked in against a rising wind that whipped up frothy surf and slammed it onto the beach.

Dallas was with Manny and Ben reconning the

shoreline, searching for a friendlier landing zone for Nolan and the Huey. Ethan had just called Dallas and broken the news that he'd been unable to raise Nolan.

"I repeat. Say again!"

"I said, I don't fuckin' like this!"

That came through loud and clear. Ethan grunted out a weary laugh as a palm frond flew past, flipping end over end across the sand. Where water met shore green coconuts bobbed around in the agitated surf. "Meaning there's something about this fiasco you *do* like?"

For the life of him, Ethan couldn't figure out what that would be. Thanks to the golden BB that had tapped him of more blood than a vampire's buffet, instead of leading the pack out of this bug-infested jungle today all he'd done the last thirty-odd hours was slow them down.

Instead of solving the problem, he'd become the problem.

And now this. The storm of the century was about to hit Jolo and they couldn't raise Nolan, who was supposed to have been here by now to haul them out.

Fuck.

It was his fault. Because of him, they'd rested until daybreak this morning. Yeah, he was stronger today. Yeah, he'd taken on enough fluid and protein to drag him back among the marginally functional. But it had cost them precious time.

Not to mention, it had pretty much depleted what was left of his pride. This morning, Ethan had had to let Manny and Dallas cart his sorry carcass through the jungle again, turning what should have been a six-hour hike to the beach into ten.

And now they'd finally made the rendezvous point and they couldn't raise Nolan.

Ethan squinted against the wind and knew they had less than a half an hour before the last ray of daylight surrendered to a towering bank of black clouds that boiled across the sky like a swarm of pissed-off hornets.

All hell was about to break loose on Jolo—and him without a pitchfork.

Beside him, Darcy and Amy huddled together, shielding their eyes with their hands as a wind gust Ethan clocked at about forty per bent the palms into rustling *U*s. Sand peppered their skin like pellets.

He rung off with Dallas and tried to raise Nolan again. "Come on, Nolan; answer the damn phone."

Nothing.

Double fuck.

Ethan squinted up and down the beach for a sign of the boys and contemplated the *if* factor.

If Nolan made it to Jolo and *if* the boys found a safe LZ and *if* Nolan could land the Huey in this storm *if* they did and *if* he could spin up again and *if* he could fly back to Zamboanga in this weather, then *maybe* they'd survive this yet.

Yeah, *if* was a helluva big word when your life hung in the balance. It wasn't his life he was worried about. It was everyone else's.

He wasn't exactly out of commission now, but he was less than half-steam. His leg throbbed like a bitch. He'd never admit it to them, but he was still as weak as a goddamn baby. And this ordeal was far from over.

He glanced at the women. Amy was hanging in there, but Darcy was the glue that held her together. Like she'd held him together yesterday until Manny had arrived.

He took in his fill of her. He hadn't lied. In a sweat-stained and beat-up T-shirt and shorts, with her hair plastered to her head, exhausted and miserable, she was still the most beautiful woman he'd ever seen.

And one of the strongest. She didn't know it, but she'd saved his life yesterday.

While he was passed out and headed for shock from blood loss, she'd done the tough work. She'd staved off infection by cleaning him up, dressing the wound, and stopping the bleeding.

Yeah. She'd saved his ass. Watched over him like a mother hen ever since and yet somehow managed to keep her distance. He understood. She'd contacted him for one reason. She was in trouble and she'd known she could count on him to get her out of it.

End of story.

And he'd be a fool to think there were any unread chapters to a book that involved him and her together after they got off this island.

If we got off this island, he thought again.

Ethan redialed Nolan. "Come on; come on." He yelled into the SAT phone to be heard above the wind. "Answer me, gawd damn it!"

"Keep your shirt on, big brother." Nolan's voice came through loud and clear. Finally. "As I said to my sweet lady the night before I left her, I'm coming as fast as I can, darlin'."

Ethan pushed out a grunt. "Damn, I was beginning to think you'd bailed on us."

"What? And miss all this fun? Nice to hear you're still among the living."

"Yeah," Ethan said, and left it at that.

"Fuck." Nolan's curse came from between clenched teeth as Ethan heard the growl of the chopper in the background. "I've never seen a storm come up so fast. What island god did you piss off, anyway?"

"Damn near every one of 'em from the looks of things." Ethan searched the sky for a sign of the Huey. "So what's your ETA?"

"ETA? Fuck that. I'll be there when I get there. *If* I get there," he added.

Yeah, Ethan knew they were still dealing with that factor.

"This is some bad shit," Nolan continued. "I don't know. I might have to deep-six this party and turn back, catch you when this sucker blows over. Can you hang on that long?"

It wouldn't matter if he could. No way was Ethan going to jeopardize the entire rescue on his account. "Hell yeah," he said. "I'm starting to like it here anyway. Sort of hate to give up this cushy spot on the beach."

"Well, before you lay down any cash for a time share, let me talk to Dallas."

"Be happy to, but he's not here." Besides, Ethan knew what Dallas would say. He'd tell Nolan that they needed to get him and his bloodless self a transfusion yesterday.

Ethan was about to tell Nolan to turn back to Zamboanga when he saw a blur of motion scuttle down the beach toward them.

He had started to wave the women back into the cover of the trees when he recognized Dallas.

Dallas was panting when he dropped to his knees beside Ethan on the beach. "We've got trouble."

"Hold on," Ethan told Nolan.

Dallas's head snapped up. "You got Nolan?"

When Ethan nodded, Dallas reached for the SAT phone. "Where the hell are you, Bro?"

"About to turn back and wait for this crap to break."

"That's a negative. Repeat. Negative. We're going to have company any minute and they aren't comin' for juice and cookies."

Ethan's grip on the M-4 tightened as he listened to Dallas's side of the conversation.

"You know that company of Philippine infantry you said might be on the hunt for Abu Sayyaf?" Dallas asked Nolan as Manny and Ben joined them. "We just spotted them—about a hundred strong. And if they keep on their current heading, they'll be hitting this section of beach in about ten minutes."

To a man, they all knew what that meant. If it turned out this was a left-wing faction of the Philippine military—and that was too much of a possibility—their purpose might be better served by killing the Americans and blaming it on the Abu Sayyaf rather than helping them get out alive. Politics on this side of the world played fast and loose with more than diplomacy.

Even if they weren't dealing with left-wingers, Ethan and the boys were here without U.S. or Philippine military sanction. It would be shoot first, ask questions later, and the soldiers wouldn't care if the women went down in the process along with the men.

"Yeah, things could get worse," Dallas said, evidently responding to Nolan's metaphoric question. "And they are. You're probably going to be spinning into a hot LZ. I repeat, it's going to be a hot landing zone here, Nolan. Providing you can land at all."

Ethan glanced at Manny, who was grinning and

shaking his head and, Ethan figured, thinking the same thing as he was.

The main rotor span on the Huey was about fourteen or fifteen meters. The beach where they were camped wasn't any more than ten meters wide. Didn't take a math degree to compute that sad equation.

Manny used his finger to draw the letter *F* in the sand.

Yeah. They were so fucked.

And just to make sure they knew it as a certainty, another vengeful island god joined the fun and let loose with the rain just then to remind them who was really in control. It was like someone poured a swimming pool against a wind tunnel fan as the rain beat down sideways and made hearing almost impossible.

"Negative!" Dallas shouted in response to something Nolan had said. "We don't have that much room! . . . Right! And no way can we make it the two clicks to a section of the beach that's big enough for you to set down! We're going to have to do a fast extraction!"

A fast extraction. Under fire.

Could it get any better?

"Roger!" Dallas yelled. "We'll be ready!" And he hung up.

"So." Manny turned his back to the pelting rain, and the faint sound of the Huey's rotor blades chopping through the wind reached them. "We're going on a suicide ride."

18

Darcy looked from Dallas to Manny and finally to Ethan as they gathered their gear in preparation for Nolan's arrival.

The men were worried. They didn't say it, but to a man the grim looks on their faces relayed the urgency of the situation. And it wasn't just the advance of the Philippine army that added an elevated level of gravity to an already grave situation. It was the weather.

"What's a fast extraction?" Darcy yelled to be heard above the deluge of rain and wind. At least the rain had settled the sand. Her arms felt raw where it had constantly peppered her skin.

The men cut dark glances to one another. Ethan finally answered her. "There's a winch fixed on the side of the Huey—just above one of the doors. The winch lowers a rope with harnesses. We clip onto loops and Nolan will haul us up and away. When he finds an LZ wide enough to set down the bird, he'll lower us to the beach. Once he lands we'll climb on board and get the hell out of here. Piece a cake."

Darcy squinted against the rain, scooped her sopped hair out of her eyes, and tried to absorb what Ethan had just said.

The picture formed in her mind of the six of them dangling from a rope over the whitecapped water in a blinding rain while a company of Philippine soldiers took potshots at them from the beach.

Piece of cake?

Ethan's hand on her arm shocked her back to reality—the other reality that was: how was he physically going to manage the extraction?

"It's okay," he assured her. "Nolan's a pro. And it's nothing the three of us haven't done before. We'll get you hooked up. We'll get you out of here."

Darcy nodded, but her teeth had started to chatter. Beside her, Amy slipped a hand into hers. Darcy squeezed it tight just as the chopper appeared offshore, dipping and dodging and bouncing around in the air like a cork in choppy water. A rope dangled out of the open door, its tail whipping back and forth like the tail of a tornado in the gale-force winds.

"Suicide ride," Darcy said aloud, thinking of Manny's grim statement.

Ethan leaned in, slung an arm around her shoulder—as much, she suspected, to help him stand against the force of the wind as to reassure her. "Don't mind Manny. He's afraid of heights."

She looked up. And Ethan was grinning.

Grinning.

"Just think of it as the ultimate amusement park ride."

"Probably be best if I don't think at all," she said, then dragged her sodden hair out of her eyes again as Dallas and Manny waded thigh-deep into the raging surf.

"Come on, No-man. Come on. You can do it." Watching from the beach, Ethan urged his brother on as the chopper swooped down, then lifted a full twenty feet as the wind slapped it around and made jockeying for position close enough for Manny or Dallas to snag the rope look like an impossibility.

"They are coming," Ben said urgently, and pointed behind them.

Shit.

Talk about your rock and hard place.

"Move the women down to the water's edge," Ethan said, hobbling over to their cache of weapons. "Get 'em ready to go."

He traded his M-4 for Dallas's with the M-203 grenade launcher attached. He didn't intend to engage unless they were fired upon, but—

The *chuck-chuck-chuck-chuck* of automatic weapon fire ended any debate on return fire.

"Go!" Ethan yelled at Ben, and shoved Darcy toward the surf.

From the corner of his eye Ethan saw Dallas make another grab for the rope and miss. Manny was right beside him. When the chopper swooped down again, Manny jumped and lunged, snagged a loop on the rigging, and hung on like a leech as the chopper lifted again. Manny flew out of the water like a torpedo, hung out over the choppy surf at about five meters, then rode it back down as the chopper dipped again.

Another round of automatic fire sprayed the sand several meters in front of Ethan's feet.

"Hook 'em up!" Ethan yelled, shouldering the M-4. "I'll give these guys a little something to think about."

The M-203 had a fifty-meter kill zone, so he sighted to a spot about sixty meters ahead of the boots closing in and fired. The explosion sent sand shooting in every direction and left a crater the size of a Jeep. He didn't want to kill anyone if he could avoid it. He just wanted to slow them down.

And he didn't want to get shot—again—or leave anyone on the beach. On the off chance they were taken prisoner instead of killed, it would be a little difficult to explain what they were doing there and why.

Can we say "international incident," boys and girls?

The warning round did the trick. The forces scattered back into the jungle brush and trees.

"Good thinkin', boys," Ethan said under his breath. "You all just sit tight back there until you figure out what you're up against."

With a little luck—okay, with a battleship full of luck—they'd be outta here by the time the Philippine CO came up with a plan of action.

Still wielding the grenade launcher, Ethan backed toward the surf, his thigh screaming in pain with each step. He ignored it and glanced over his shoulder. And his heart damn near sank into the deep.

They'd hooked Amy up to the harness. She was thigh-deep in water as Dallas snugged Darcy onto a loop about three feet beneath Amy. Dallas had just gotten Darcy secured when the wind sucked the chopper up again and jerked both women out of the water.

They dangled ten feet above the rocking surf, fully exposed to any crack sniper with his sights set on a trophy as the wind and rotor wash spun them like tops.

Ethan loaded another grenade and launched it in the general area of the withdrawn troops to discourage them from poking their heads up high enough to draw a bead on the women.

Behind him Ethan heard Manny swear and Dallas bellow for Ben to get his ass over there. Ethan chanced another glance over to see that the chopper had dropped down again. Nolan was doing his damnedest to hold a hover at about five meters, buying time to hook up Ben.

"Ethan, now!" Dallas yelled above the roar of the storm and staccato *whump* of the chopper blades.

Ethan loaded and launched one more grenade, tossed the rifle into the surf, and hobbled out to catch his ride.

Dallas reached for Ethan just as the surf sucked his good leg out from beneath him and took him under.

They both went down, fought for purchase, and finally came up spitting salt water and swearing a blue streak.

"Hurry," Manny urged, and dragged Ethan to his feet. "You're next."

"The hell I am!" Rainwater poured down Ethan's face as salt water sucked at his waist. "Get yourselves hooked up! Do it! We don't have time to argue!"

Because they both knew he was right and because they both knew he was a stubborn S.O.B., Dallas and Manny hooked on, calling Ethan everything but a son of God as they did.

They could call him anything they wanted. If he didn't make it, fine, but he'd be damned if he'd take them down with him. He'd brought them into this mess, he'd damn well get them out.

Finally, finally, everyone was secured. With the rope attached to him like an umbilical cord, Manny waded back to Ethan and fixed him into the last harness.

A monster wave rolled in just before Nolan lifted off, sucking Ethan under again. Salt water stung his eyes. His lungs threatened to burst from holding his breath. Seaweed and grasses grabbed at his arms, tightened around his throat.

Goddamn. This couldn't be it. And now he was pissed. He hadn't gotten this far just to drown in three fucking feet of water. He roared, dug for purchase with his good leg, and pushed—just as the bird lifted and wrenched him out of the surf at about five knots.

Air! He sucked it in. Coughing and spitting and swallowing as much rainwater as he had salt water.

They were airborne. Below him, the soldiers had resurfaced on the beach and were lined up, rifles at their shoulders, firing enough ordnance to launch WW III.

Nolan pushed the Huey and flew them out of range while they all dangled from the belly of the bird. Above him, Dallas, Manny, Ben, Darcy, and finally Amy clung to the hoist rope like monkeys.

The last line of an old military song drifted through Ethan's mind as dark descended.

The monkeys have no tails in Zamboanga.

The monkeys have no tails, he thought again as the adrenaline rushed out of his body—like the blood that was once again rushing out of his leg.

The monkeys have no tails in Zamboanga.

The song was still running through his head when the Huey hit a downdraft and dropped like a stone.

"Oh shit!" Ethan swore as the water flew up to meet him. He hit the whitecapped surf at about ten knots. It felt like he'd slammed into a cement wall at sixty miles an hour.

Pain exploded through his body. Water gushed through his nostrils, forcing his mouth open. He tasted salt and sea. Both assaulted his lungs, wracked him with spasms as the speed of the chopper dragged him along beneath the chop.

The monkeys have no tails in Zamboanga.

Over and over and over, the line played through his mind as he fought for his breath, fought for life, and knew he was losing the battle on both counts.

Darcy. Darcy was safe. At least he'd managed that.
The monkeys have no tails. . . .
Funny, he reflected as unconsciousness claimed him. He'd always figured his final thoughts would be a little more profound.

Darcy was clean. She was dry. She was cruising in the lap of luxury at forty-five thousand feet and she was well out of Philippine airspace. She was safe. At least for the time being. What happened next was anybody's guess, but she knew this wasn't over.

As she looked back, it all seemed like a movie to her now. A tragically senseless movie filled with violence and loss of life.

A heavy sadness engulfed her, weightier than the guilt and the residual fear that had latched on in the wake of her adrenaline letdown. She closed her eyes, turned her head on the pillow of the bed in the master cabin, and stared at the ink black sky.

But for the soft glow of courtesy lights, the cabin was dark. In the forward cabin of the luxurious Gulfstream G-5—which had been waiting on the tarmac at Zamboanga courtesy of Darin Kincaid, Nolan's billionaire father-in-law—Amy was stretched out sound asleep on the leather sofa. Darcy had checked on her not more than fifteen minutes ago. Manny and Dallas were sprawled in cushy reclining side chairs, passed out from exhaustion.

Darcy hadn't seen Nolan. He was probably up in the cockpit with the pilot and copilots. Maybe Nolan was sacked out in their quarters or finally taking his turn in the shower. It still amazed her that the jet had a shower and a master bedroom and had been stocked with clean clothes, food, and medical supplies.

She wished she could sleep like the rest of them. Wished she could stop thinking about Ethan and the way he'd looked when Nolan had finally managed to set the Huey down out of the worst of the wind on the east side of Jolo.

The picture of him lying there, morbidly still, deathly gray, still haunted her.

She closed her eyes, tried to block the grim looks on Dallas's and Manny's faces as they'd carried Ethan's lax body into the Huey.

Closing her eyes didn't work. Distance didn't soften. They'd been in the air over four hours and she kept seeing Ethan that way.

The cabin door opened with a soft snick. Muted light streamed in and fell across the double bed.

She looked up to see Nolan standing in the doorway.

"Hey," he said softly.

"Hey."

"Thought you'd like to know we've still got about six hours until we set down in Anchorage."

It had surprised her when they'd told her earlier their flight path took them to Anchorage, Alaska, for refueling and U.S. customs check before flying on to West Palm. She'd never guessed that would be the closest route. But then a lot of things had surprised her, from Nolan landing the Huey in a remote field outside of Zamboanga City to being met by a pair of club cab pickup trucks driven by unnamed friends of Nolan's who looked and acted suspiciously like Special Ops soldiers.

After handshakes and hugs, one of the trucks hauled Ben back to Manila and his mother.

The other truck drove them under the cover of the storm and darkness to the Zamboanga International

Airport. Once there, they'd simply driven onto the tarmac and boarded the private jet. It seemed nobody cared much who left a country these days. Officials were more interested in who came in, so customs wasn't even an issue.

The Huey was. That's why they'd ditched it. There wasn't any doubt that the Philippine military had gotten a bead on the bird and radioed ahead alerting major airports.

But that was behind them now. If it hadn't been for the storm, they'd have been airborne several hours before they'd been cleared for takeoff, no questions asked.

"How you doing?" Nolan asked gently.

She shook her head. Must have looked as lost as she felt, because he closed the door softly behind him and sat down on the bed. "C'mere."

She sagged into his arms. Allowed herself the luxury of clinging. And wondered why there were no tears. Maybe she was still numb. Maybe some part of *her* had died on that island.

"How can you be so nice to me? After . . . after what happened?"

Nolan's strong hands rubbed comforting circles on her back. "Just a sucker for redheads, I guess."

She sniffed against his broad chest. Of Ethan's two brothers, she couldn't decide which one looked the most like him. The blue eyes, the dark hair, the broad shoulders and narrow hips—they all had them. All three Garretts had that innate strength and vitality.

Or they had.

"I'm so sorry. So sorry I got him into this," she said.

"Hey. It's not like you held a gun to his head."

"Didn't I? I asked him to come. I *begged* him. I

knew he would. I knew he'd move heaven and earth to get to me."

"It was still his choice. No one told him what to do."

"Why are you talking about me like I'm dead?"

Darcy whipped her head around toward the man lying on the far side of the double bed.

Ethan was as colorless as the white pillowcase, as still as death, but his eyes were open as he tried to focus on her.

"Back among the living for a while again, are you?" Nolan stood, then leaned over his brother. "So, how are things in la-la land?"

But Ethan was already out again.

Darcy pressed her fingers to her lips.

"He's going to be fine," Nolan assured her as he checked the drip on the IV pumping fluids. "The round just nicked his femoral artery—"

"How do you know that? He hasn't regained consciousness for more than a few minutes at a time since you hauled him off the beach. That was hours ago."

"I know because if it had severed the femoral he *would* be dead. He'd have bled to death. You're going to be surprised how fast he'll recover once he gets another dose of blood in him. If I could have scored more than a pint, he'd already be barking orders and looking mean again. Kind of nice to see him so peaceful."

He was teasing. Darcy knew that Nolan was worried, too. And she was never going to forgive herself if Ethan didn't make a full recovery.

"Look, Darcy. He's strong. He's fit. Just let him sleep this off. I'll lay odds that he'll walk off the plane in West Palm under his own steam. And in a few days, he'll be good as new. In the meantime, you should get some sleep yourself."

"What about you?"

"Me?" He shook his head. "I'm too wired to sleep. Maybe later."

"Stay," she said when Nolan turned to go. "Talk to me for a minute."

"Okay." He sat back down on the corner of the bed. "What do you want to talk about?"

Anything sane. Anything that had nothing to do with the nightmare that was not yet over. Yes, she was off the island. She was free of the terrorists. But it was far from over. And she still hadn't figured out what she was going to do.

"Your wife," she said, grasping at straws. "Tell me about Jillian."

At the mention of his wife, a softness came over Nolan's face that was the closest thing to peace Darcy had ever seen. When she'd met both Nolan and Dallas several years ago, like Ethan they'd both been active military, Nolan a Ranger, Dallas a Marine, Force Recon. And they'd had the same intensity of purpose and self as Ethan.

"Jillian is amazing."

For the next few minutes, Nolan told her about his auburn-haired wife, how strong she was, how beautiful. He laughed about how they'd hated each other on sight when he'd been hired as her bodyguard when a deranged stalker was determined to kill her. How they'd fallen in love—fighting it every step of the way. But mostly he talked about how happy he was and how thrilled he was about the baby on the way in less than two months.

"Of course, it's a nice plus that she also comes from a little money."

Yeah, like that was really important to him. It was obvious that Nolan Garrett was deeply, wholeheartedly lost in love with his wife. Jillian could have been a pauper and he'd still be crazy about her.

"A *little* money?" Darcy glanced around the plush cabin.

He laughed. "Just a little. Kincaid is just about richer than God, I'd guess. We can thank him for funding this little adventure, not to mention the use of the plane and his pilots."

And that led them right back to territory she didn't want to tread. She averted her gaze to her hands, which she was surprised to find clenched tightly on her lap.

"Can I ask you something?"

When Darcy saw the probing look on Nolan's face, she knew what was coming.

"What happened? What happened between you and Ethan? I know. We only had that one opportunity to meet, but you two seemed so great together. And if I might make an observation, it's pretty damn clear you're still in love with each other."

She could have disputed his statement, but what was the point? She looked down at her hands again. "He never . . . never said anything?"

"No. Nothing."

She pinched her lips, looked over her shoulder out the porthole window.

"Okay. Look. Sorry. I was out of line. It's just—"

"I know. You care about him."

Nolan touched a hand to her shoulder, squeezed. "You, too, Darcy. I care about you, too."

"I know. I don't know how I'll ever repay you . . . for all you've done. You and Manny and Dallas. You could have been killed. You took so many risks."

"Okay, now you're just plain insulting us if you

think there was risk involved. Superstuds like us? Hell. This was a walk in the park."

She smiled because Nolan wanted her to.

He squeezed her shoulder, playing big brother again. "You need to stop thinking about this and get some sleep. And quit worrying about Ethan. He's strong as a bull. And he really is going to be okay."

Nolan dropped a kiss on her forehead and left, closing the door softly behind him. She sat there for a moment, thinking about what Nolan had said.

Walk in the park.

"A park littered with land mines maybe," she said into the silent cabin. Then she rose and checked on Ethan.

He seemed to be sleeping peacefully. His brow was cool. His color was good. She wished she could be sure that Nolan was right. But there was only one thing she was sure of.

She wasn't letting Ethan out of her sight until she was sure he was out of the woods. Or until it became necessary for her to leave him for his own protection.

Six hours to Anchorage. Maybe she should try to sleep. Feeling very weary suddenly, she walked to the other side of the bed and lay down facing Ethan.

And she thought of other nights in her bed when she'd lain awake in the dark and just looked at him. Just looked at him to assure herself that he was real and hers and because she simply loved to look at him. Loved to be with him. Could no longer imagine life without him.

They really had been good together.

So very, very good.

Until Tel Aviv. Then everything fell apart.

19

DARCY WAS BEAT. AND IT WAS ONLY MONDAY.

"Give me visa apps any day," she told Lisa England as she pushed away from her desk and grabbed her purse from the bottom drawer.

"Yeah. We live for bureaucracy." At the desk beside hers Lisa England shut down her computer. The pretty blonde—whose husband was an Air Force pilot stationed in Saudi—had joined the Tel Aviv embassy staff three months ago. She and Darcy had bonded over Big Macs and fries at a McDonald's where Darcy went once a month to remind her of home. Now they went there together and commiserated about the pitfalls of long-distance relationships.

"Okay. They may be boring," Darcy agreed, heading for the door, "but I'm not up for any more drama like this afternoon."

She must have considered two dozen applications for temporary visas in the morning, all of them with enough complications to slow the process to a crawl. Assisting the lovely couple from Colorado with the adoption of their infant nephew, whose Israeli parents had been killed in a car accident, had been a pleasure but a long, arduous process.

"You get those other folks taken care of?" Lisa asked, walking out of the office behind her.

"Finally."

"I missed most of the commotion. What happened anyway?"

Their heels clicked on the glossy tile in the hallway as they headed for the stairs.

"American tourists—from Manhattan, Kansas, no less—got stranded on the road to Jerusalem when their bus broke down. One of the women on board decided it was a great time to have an anxiety attack. She'd been certain they were going to get ambushed by the PLO or Hesbollah and damn near created an international incident by the time the bus driver contacted me."

Darcy shook her head as Lisa opened a stairwell door and they headed down. It had taken several calls, but Darcy had finally managed to contact an embassy staffer who by some minor miracle was within five minutes of the scene.

"Thank God John was in the area. I raised him on his cell phone and he drove over and put out the fire—at least until I made arrangements for overnight lodging."

"I can offer sympathy but not absolution. So no calling in sick tomorrow," Lisa warned with a grin when they reached the main floor. "I'm not going into the monthly staffing without you riding shotgun."

"Don't worry. I'll show up," Darcy said as she hit the front door—and stopped dead in her tracks when she stepped outside.

Ethan.

He was standing on the top step of the portico. In full dress greens. His beret settled smartly on his head.

He had one hand buried in his pocket. In the other, he held an open roll of cherry Life Savers.

"Want some candy, little girl?"

"Ethan. Oh my God! Ethan!" She flew into his arms. Held on tight as he swung her off her feet and hugged her so hard it hurt. She didn't care. She didn't want him to ever let go.

It had been six months since she'd left him in Lima. She'd been brokenhearted ever since. And she hadn't had a clue that he was coming.

His arms were strong and possessive and thrilling wrapped around her. And when he kissed her, she tasted everything from cherry, to longing, to misery, to joy.

"Okay," Lisa's voice reached her from a few feet away. "So, forget what I said about calling in sick. I've got a feeling you're going to have a problem getting out of bed in the morning."

Darcy finally broke the kiss, laughing. Ethan pressed his forehead to hers and without breaking eye contact with Darcy asked, "Who is this woman and why do I like her already?"

"Hello, *problem,*" Lisa said with a grin, and held out her hand. "I'm Lisa. And I'm jealous as hell."

Gathering Darcy close to his side with his other arm, Ethan returned her handshake. "You have a thing for my wife?" he asked, deliberately misunderstanding.

Lisa laughed. "Life might be simpler if I did."

Happy beyond belief, Darcy explained. "Lisa's got a flyboy hubby she hasn't seen in—"

"Three months, two weeks, and five days—if anyone's counting," Lisa informed them. "Nice to meet you, Ethan. Take care of her. The girl's had a bad day."

"It's about to get a whole lot better," he promised, and dragged her under for another deep, drugging kiss.

• • •

They spent the next several hours in bed in her apartment. Loving, talking, sleeping, catching up. Everything was perfect. Whatever problems had cropped up in Lima before she'd left were distant memories.

In the moonlit night, in the quiet, Darcy stared at their joined hands where they rested on Ethan's bare chest. She hadn't wanted to ask until now. Hadn't wanted reality to intrude.

But reality had. He'd just told her why he'd been pulled out of Peru. Sort of. Things had gotten too dicey for him to stay there any longer.

Ethan didn't elaborate. In a way, she was glad. Right now, she didn't want to know what had happened, how close he may have come to being killed.

"Where will they send you?"

"I don't know yet." He aligned the pads of their thumbs, danced them slowly back and forth. "And you know I couldn't tell you if I did."

Right. She had known that. She'd find out eventually, all the wives did, but it would be long after he was deployed.

"I hated leaving my team."

She knew that, too. A-teams worked, played, ate, slept, and lived like family.

But she didn't want him sad in this bed.

She pushed herself up on an elbow. "How long do we have?"

"Two weeks."

Two weeks. Fourteen days. And one of them was almost gone. She opted to show excitement over disappointment.

"I can work you over pretty good in fourteen days,"

she said, slinging her leg over his lap and sliding it back and forth seductively.

He laughed. "Do your worst."

"Oh, I plan to. I plan to."

She brought their joined hands to her mouth. Kissed his fingers. The pulse at his wrist. The inside of his elbow.

"I've dreamed of this," she whispered in the dark, and rising over him trailed kisses across his naked chest.

"I've missed you," she murmured, loving the warmth of him, the vibrant beat of his heart beneath her mouth. "How I've missed you."

He lay supplicant, letting her do what she would.

"Dreamed of touching you. Here. Tasting you. Um. Here."

She lingered over his left nipple. Licking, nuzzling, indulging in the taste of her man, in the power she felt over this warrior who could be so gentle, so giving, and, at the moment, so totally focused on what she was doing to him.

"I love you," she murmured, breathless and adoring the feel of his restless hands as they skated up her naked back, over her shoulders, and knotted in her hair.

"You're diving me crazy." His words came out on a strained groan.

"Oh yeah?" She smiled against his skin, rimmed his navel with the tip of her tongue, and glided her hand down past the flatness of his belly. Found his sex. Hard and pulsing and jumping in her hand.

"Oh God. Yeah." He arched his hips when she cupped his scrotum and gently squeezed.

"Then this is going to push you right over the edge."

As she'd teased her tongue around his navel, she

teased it around the glistening tip of his penis. Making him swear. Making him groan. Making him understand that she would do anything, *be* everything he needed her to be.

If need had a taste, it was him. If love had a sound, it was the one she made when she took him into her mouth and with deliberate sloth and gentle suction set out to drain him of his last slippery grasp on control.

He didn't last five minutes.

"Darcy . . . God, Darcy. Stop. Stop. I want to be inside you when I come."

She lifted her head, licked her lips, and he went wild. He reached for her, dragged her up the bed, and covered her mouth with his on a strangled moan. "I have to be inside you."

He flipped her to her back. Hooking both of her legs over his arms, he pressed her knees to her chest and drove deep.

The pleasure was cutting and sharp. Blinding. The speed and strength of her orgasm stole her breath as he pumped into her like a wild man, making her come over and over again in a stunning, staggering rush.

He came with a strangled moan that registered somewhere in the periphery of her mind while she rode heaving waves of sensation too huge to quantify, too intense to absorb.

"Darcy." He collapsed onto her, into her, burying his face at the hollow of her throat, and went boneless.

Good. It was too, too good. It took forever to catch her breath. And not nearly long enough to drift on the wake of pleasure.

She sighed his name.

He chuckled softly.

She smiled at the joy of it all, turning her face into his neck and thinking life had never been this good.

Too good, in fact, to be true.

The next day, she learned that it was.

"Have you given any more thought to requesting a stateside PCS?"

Darcy looked up from her breakfast. While Ethan had slept in—she suspected that more than jet lag had caught up with him—she'd arranged for the next two weeks off.

Then, wearing only his T-shirt so she could smell him anytime she wanted, she played hausfrau. She fixed a huge skillet of scrambled eggs with peppers and cheese, squeezed oranges for fresh juice, and brewed coffee—strong, the way he liked it.

He'd shuffled into her tiny kitchen in bare feet and boxers. His eyes heavy, his cheeks stubbled, his hair standing on end. She'd never seen anything so sexy. And when he'd drawn her against him, swayed with her in a dreamy little dance while her favorite CD played in the background, she'd never felt so happy.

"Packing heat, are you, soldier boy?" she'd teased when she felt his erection rise against her belly.

"Baby, I've always got fire for you."

Then he'd laid her down on her tiny kitchen table, buried himself deep, and blown the top of her head off.

"Oh, wow. And good morning to you," she'd laughed when her head cleared.

He'd only grinned. Cleaned her up. Cleaned up the table and asked, "What smells so good?"

That had been all of fifteen minutes ago. And with one question he'd broken the spell and the mood.

"Have you given any more thought to requesting a stateside PCS?" he asked again as he forked up the last of the eggs.

She reached across the table for his empty plate, then rose and refilled it from the skillet on her apartment-sized stove. "Let's not have this discussion, okay?"

She smiled. Set his plate back in front of him, then headed for the coffeepot. "Not today."

When she returned to the table, he'd leaned back in his chair. Her playful lover was gone. And she could see that he wasn't going to let this drop.

She met his eyes with a stubborn stare. "Please," she said finally. "Don't spoil what little time we have together."

"And what about spoiling it for me? Darcy, most men can look after their wives. They're there for them. With them. Protecting them. Looking out for them. I can't be one of those men. I don't know how else to protect you without getting you out of harm's way."

She set down the coffeepot and went to him.

"Ethan," she pleaded, sitting down in his lap. "I am perfectly safe here."

"Safe? Jesus. Don't you read the newspapers? Watch TV? People get blown up every day here."

She played absently with the hair at his nape. "No one has any reason to hurt me."

"You're an American. To a radical Palestinian extremist that's reason enough."

"You're looking for reasons to worry."

Instead of wrapping his arms around her, he planted his fisted hands on the table. "I'm being realistic."

"No." She pressed a kiss to his furrowed brow. "No, Ethan. You're not."

"You don't understand."

"I'm trying." She pulled back, rested her hands on his shoulders. "I'm trying to understand, but you don't give me much to go on. Tell me what's really bothering you."

He worked his jaw, refused to look at her. "Forget it." He stood abruptly, dumping her to her feet. His chair scraped on the floor and almost toppled over. "I'm going to take a shower."

She didn't try to stop him. She just watched him walk away. She'd hoped . . . she'd so hoped that they'd left this argument in Peru.

But obviously, they hadn't. And during the next several days it came up often, hung between them like a curtain the rest of the time they had together.

They laughed, yes. They loved, absolutely. But the easy grace was gone. He seemed obsessed with worry over her, was overtly critical of the extra steps she took for her American citizens. Constantly made noises about her playing it safer, maybe even considering another career.

She tried not to let it get to her. Tried not to let it affect their precious few days together. But he made no attempt to guard his words while she worked overhard to guard hers. She didn't want to fight. She just wanted to love him.

A few nights before he was due to leave for the panzer unit in Stuttgart where he would redeploy, they went out dancing. She'd just wanted to let off a little pent-up tension. Let her hair down.

And the unthinkable happened.

SOMEWHERE OVER THE NORTH PACIFIC
PRESENT

Ethan woke out of a sound sleep. "What? What's happening?"

A soft, sleepy voice steadied him in the dark. "It's okay. We just hit an air pocket."

Darcy. Air pocket. What the—?

Oh yeah. He wasn't dead. Wasn't drowned.

But the monkeys still had no tails in Zamboanga.

He turned his head on the pillow . . . and saw her. She was raised up on an elbow beside him. Her hair was a mess. Her eyes were heavy with sleep and concern. And he had a vivid memory of the many times in their brief marriage he'd awakened and seen her looking at him in exactly this way.

An ache that had nothing to do with the throbbing in his leg settled heavy and deep.

"Hey, babe," he said, wanting to erase some of her concern and because if he didn't say something he was going to beg her to kiss him. "How's it shaking?"

She smiled. Then yawned. "It's shaking just fine. How are you doing?"

"I think maybe I'm back among the living. Got the headache to prove it."

"I'll get you something."

He reached out, wrapped his fingers around her arm when she started to get up. "No. Don't. It's no big deal. Just . . . just, ah . . . little muzzy yet, I guess. It's fine. Where are we, anyway?"

She checked her watch. His watch, actually. She must have taken it off of him and decided to hold on to it for safekeeping. "It's about four a.m. Pacific. And we're about four hours out of Anchorage," she said on another yawn.

"Yeah?"

"Yeah."

"So. Present company excluded, it all went off without a hitch."

"Present company excluded," she agreed.

He closed his eyes and had almost drifted off again when he heard her voice, tearful and tortured in the dark. "I thought you were dead."

The tremor in her voice told him just how dead she'd thought he was. "Not a chance. Didn't want to miss this cushy plane ride."

"Ethan, I am so, *so* sorry I got you into this."

Okay. She wasn't going to lay out any cash to buy his "no big deal" shtick. But he wasn't going to let her invest any deeper in the guilt.

He turned his head to look into her eyes. Her beautiful green eyes. "And what if you hadn't?" he asked, leveling the playing field. "What if you hadn't called me?"

They both knew the answer to that. She *would* be dead. Amy, too.

He figured Darcy didn't want to think about the alternative outcome any more than he did. But he had to know. He'd put off asking long enough.

"Why you, Darcy? What did they want with you?"

She shook her head, looked away. "I don't know."

Interesting. There were still things he hadn't known about her. Like the fact that she was a lousy liar. And like why she thought she had to lie to him now when she'd never lied to him before.

"It's the body that's running on empty, babe, not the mind. You know what they wanted. You called me. Said you thought you were in trouble."

"It . . . it was just a feeling." She still wouldn't look at him.

"A feeling?" he echoed, making sure she understood that he didn't believe her.

"Yeah. I . . . I don't know. I just sensed that I was . . . being followed."

"Big trouble," he said, throwing her own words back at her. Words that had tied him in knots until he'd found her alive. "You said you thought you were in big trouble. That doesn't equate to a sensation of being followed to me."

She lifted a shoulder still looking guilty as hell. "I don't know what else to tell you."

"I think you do," he accused, but was hit by a wave of fatigue that slapped him down like a lightweight. "And I think it has something to do with Amanda Stover's *hit-and-run* not so accidental death."

Her gaze snapped to his. "How did you know about Amanda?"

Frustrated with both her and the fog settling over him, he ignored her question. "Someone tossed your hotel room. And your apartment in Manila. Nolan checked. It was trashed, Darcy. So was Amanda's."

Even in the pale cabin light, he could see her face drain to chalk.

"You want to tell me now why I took a bullet and you would have rotted in that jungle if we hadn't found you?"

All the horror of her captivity showed in her eyes—along with guilt for placing him in harm's way. And yet she held her silence.

"Darcy, we both know that it wasn't an accident you ended up in the Abu Sayyaf camp," he stated, his voice as hard as his eyes. "Now, for God's sake, tell me what's going on. Who ordered the abduction? What were they looking for? What do you have that they want?"

"I . . . don't know," she said so softly he could barely hear her. "I don't . . . know."

He swore. "You lie for shit, babe."

She looked hunted. And very weary. "Go back to sleep," she said softly. "We'll talk about it later. You need to rest now."

The bitch of it was, she was right. He was fading fast.

"We . . . will . . . talk."

But not now. Suddenly he felt like he'd run the twenty-seventh mile of a twenty-six-mile marathon. He sensed more than felt that she was going to leave the bed.

"Don't . . . go. Stay . . . stay with me."

He had no sense of how much time passed before he felt the mattress shift, felt the warmth of her body as she lay back down beside him.

"I'm not going to leave you." Her whisper filled the dark like a promise.

I'm not going to leave you.

The words floated in from a distance. Through a dream. As he drifted. Drifted deep into sleep again. Drifted back to a time when the words got garbled, twisted, and butted up against the stark reality of another place, another time, when *I'm not going to leave you* became a tearful *I have to leave you* and all he could do was let her walk away.

20

DARCY WANTED TO DANCE, SO ETHAN TOOK her dancing. It wasn't his cuppa, but it was hers and he'd do anything for her. Including stop badgering her for one night about requesting a transfer back to the states.

"I promise," he'd said just before they'd left the apartment and she'd begged him to just enjoy the evening. "No pressure."

She'd gone up on tiptoes and kissed him.

And he set his mind to making sure she had fun. Yet all night it ate at him. Crippled him with worry for her.

If she'd just use her head. But whether she was on assignment in Peru or here in Israel, he knew her MO. She was always sticking her neck out a little too far, taking reckless chances to help U.S. citizens abroad. And if she didn't stop, she was going to get hurt. Or worse.

It was the worse that ate at him like a cancer.

The song ended and he dragged himself back to the woman in his arms.

The night was balmy, the music rockin' and loud, as he took her hand and led her off the crowded dance floor. "Let's get out of here."

"But I want to dance with you some more," she protested, dragging her feet. Her eyes danced with deviltry as she tried to tug him back toward the dance floor beneath dozens of paper lanterns hanging from the crisscrossing lattice suspended above the outside bar and restaurant.

He didn't budge. "Tell you what, twinkle toes, let's go home and we can do a little dancing that doesn't call for an audience."

She laughed and fell against him, draping her wrists over his shoulders and kissing him full on the mouth. "You mean dirty dancing?"

His gorgeous wife was not much of a drinker. She had a misty glow going and it had loosened her up enough that he'd recognized it was time to take her home. Before she kissed him like that again and talked him into a quickie in the bushes.

He'd already nixed that idea once tonight and not for lack of interest on his part. While the club was nice and many of the patrons were embassy staff and Israeli professional types, he didn't like the neighborhood. And he didn't want to get caught with his pants down—literally—if some of the seedier elements he'd seen on the streets on the cab ride over decided he was an easy mark.

"Or how 'bout a little mattress dancin'?" she purred, and rubbed up against him.

He groaned. "Come on, woman. I am definitely taking you home."

With her tucked under his arm, he snagged her purse from the table and herded her toward the street.

"It's so nice out. Let's walk," she suggested, wrapping both arms around his waist and snuggling close.

"It's a thirty-minute cab ride," he pointed out. "I

don't think you're up for walking quite that far. And I know I'm not."

"We could dance that far," she said brightly, and on a laugh pulled away from him to execute a wobbly pirouette.

"You are so smashed," he said on a chuckle as she did a really awful ballerina spin, dancing and twirling in front of him with a childlike joyous smile on her face.

God, she was something. It made him ache just looking at her. Her red hair flew around her bare shoulders. Her short little strapless emerald green dress hugged her lean body like a glove. The dress was just tight enough to make him wonder if—

"I don't have any panties on, you know," she informed him, reading his mind, as she floated in close and danced a circle around him, angel turned devil.

"You are really determined to get in trouble with me tonight, aren't you?"

She giggled when he made a grab for her hand and missed. "Catch," she said, kicking off one black shoe that wasn't much more than a high heel and a slim strap across her arch.

He caught the shoe as it flew by his head, caught the other when it came sailing at him, too. "You're turning me into a girlie man," he accused as he stood there, holding her purse and now her shoes.

"Just so you're *my* girlie man," she assured him.

"Hokay. That does it. I'm hailing a cab."

"Spoilsport."

Walking backward away from him, she put a fair amount of lip into a pout. He was just about to tell her he had better uses for those luscious lips when he spotted the man stepping out of the shadows of a building.

"Darcy!"

Too late. The creep had already lunged for her.

Which made him as good as dead.

Ethan cleared the fifteen feet between them in a single heartbeat. It was over in less than that.

With one merciless lethal blow to the neck, the thug went down like a rock, his gun clattering into the gutter.

Stunned sober, Darcy stood there, hugging herself, her eyes wide with terror.

"Did he hurt you?"

Her gaze darted from Ethan to the still figure sprawled facedown, his head at an unnatural angle to his shoulders.

"Did the fucker hurt you?" Ethan roared, and pulled her hard against him.

"No . . . no," she stammered.

"Come on," he said. "Let's get out of here."

She pulled away from him. "But . . . don't you think we should call for help? He may need a doctor."

"He's dead, Darcy. There's not a doctor in the world who's going to fix that."

Her eyes widened in horror. "Dead?"

Ethan's jaw went tight.

"Oh my God, Ethan."

As her gaze shifted from him to the body of the man he had just killed to protect her, the shock in her eyes transitioned to something that would haunt him for the rest of his life.

"He'd have killed you," he said flatly.

He wasn't going to defend himself beyond that. Didn't have to. And he sure as hell didn't have to watch her stare at him as if he were some kind of a monster who could have pulled his punch. Could have taken the worthless piece of shit down without taking him out.

No, he didn't have to watch her look at him. Not that way. Because when she looked at him that way, he saw himself a little too clearly.

Everything changed between them that night. As hard as she tried to hide it, every time Ethan met her eyes he saw it. Uneasy speculation. Confusion. Even a little fear.

Fear. Of him.

It ate at him that she'd seen his darker side—the trained soldier, the emotionless killer—but it had been kill or be killed, so he'd killed for her.

And if he told himself often enough that he hadn't had another choice, he thought grimly, he'd begin to believe it.

Darcy walked out of the bedroom, gathering her hair at her nape and securing it with a gold clip. She stopped when she saw him. "Why aren't you ready to go?"

Ethan didn't look at her. He sat on the tiny balcony of her apartment wearing only a pair of black cargo pants, his bare feet propped on the iron rail. He took another pull from the half-empty bottle of beer he'd been nursing for the past half an hour. They were supposed to meet some of her friends from the embassy for dinner.

"Ethan?" She joined him on the balcony, leaning her hips against the rail, her back to the street and facing him.

He looked her up and down. She was wearing that little black number she'd been wearing the first time he'd seen her. His gut tightened at the memory.

"Go on without me," he said, and stared at the traffic bustling by two stories below. "Just make sure your cab delivers you right at the restaurant door."

"Don't you feel well?" Her voice was filled with concern as she stepped into him, pressed her soft hand to his forehead.

"I'm fine. And you're not my goddamn mother," he growled, and pushed her hand away. "I don't need you to take care of me."

He could count the seconds between heartbeats as she stood there, stung, confused. He felt like the biggest prick on the face of the earth. Because he was. And he couldn't get himself to say he was sorry.

"What's going on?" she asked in a small voice.

"Nothing." He rose and shouldered by her, a big, bad, surly sonofabitch. He hated himself for it. "I just don't feel like going out, okay?"

"Then we'll stay in," she said simply.

Only there was nothing simple about it. For the last two days since she'd been attacked outside the dance club, they'd tried to pretend that nothing had changed between them.

He knew different. Everything had changed. *Everything*.

And the tension humming between them was driving him nuts.

"Look, just go without me." He dug into the refrigerator for another beer. "You'll be safe at the restaurant."

"I don't want to go without you," she said from the kitchen doorway. "I want to be with you."

"Well, maybe I don't want to be with you right now."

Jesus. He twisted the top off the bottle, tipped it up

for a long, deep swig as the self-anger built and gorged on itself. So, of course, he took it out on her.

"Maybe," he said, turning to face those wounded eyes that had been messing him up for two days, "maybe I don't want to see you looking at me like that for just two goddamn hours! Is that too much to ask?"

He yelled the last of it. Swore again, then turned away from her. And felt tears . . . *tears* sting his eyes, for chrissake.

Perfect. Just fucking perfect.

On a roar, he hauled back and hurled the beer bottle at the wall.

It hit with a shattering crack. Splinters flew in every direction. The stink of beer filled the tiny kitchen, as bitter and sour as the taste in his mouth. The taste of raw anger and frustration and pain.

The silence echoed. And then he heard her footsteps. The creak of the pantry door opening, then closing.

"Leave it," he said when she walked past him toward the broken glass with a dustpan and a broom.

She started sweeping.

"I said leave it!"

She whirled on him, good and pissed now. And hurting with it. "Fine. Clean it up yourself."

She shoved the broom into his chest, slammed the dustpan on the floor at his feet, and all but ran from the kitchen.

He tossed aside the broom and tore after her. Caught her by the arm and spun her around toward him before she could get to the bedroom.

"Leave me alone!"

He dragged her flush against him. Slanted his mouth down hard over hers.

She pushed against his chest and broke the contact of their mouths. "Go to hell!"

He would. He had no doubt he would. If not for what he'd done, for what he was about to do.

He lifted her off her feet. Carried her into the bedroom and dumped her on the bed. When she started to scramble away, he dived down after her, landed flush on top of her, and captured her mouth again.

She bit him. He swore, then pinned her hands above her head and, using his body for leverage, reached up under her dress and ripped off her panties.

He was sweating. Breathing hard as he shoved down his pants, then wedged a knee between her thighs.

She cried out. Not in pain. Not in fear. But in total, unequivocal disbelief.

It shocked him back to himself.

Jesus. *Jesus.* What was he doing?

What the hell was he doing? Punishing *her* for *his* sins? Making her pay because he couldn't live with himself?

Feeling sick to his stomach, he rolled off of her. Sucked in air, then sat on the edge of the bed with his elbows propped on his thighs and buried his face in his hands.

"Christ, Darcy. I'm sorry. I'm so sorry."

She was everything good in his life. And he'd been about to use her in the ugliest, cruelest way possible.

He could hear her ragged breaths leveling out behind him. Waited for her to tell him to get his badass self out of her sight. It was what he deserved. He was scum. He was—oh Christ. He was crying.

Bawling like a baby.

And then she was there. Her soft hands soothing. Her warm arms enfolding. Her own tears hot and wet on his shoulder as she pulled him back against her. With gentle persuasion, her words laced with pain, she laid him down beside her, pressed his face against her lush breasts, and shushed him like a child.

"It's okay. It's okay. I love you, Ethan. I love you. We're okay."

She murmured those words over and over again, pressing kisses to his face, to his damp eyes, to his mouth, when he rolled her beneath him and entered her with the gentlest of care.

For a while, he believed what he felt. Believed what she said. They were okay. Everything was okay when he was inside her sweet, healing warmth.

"We're okay," she whispered again when he'd spilled himself inside her.

It was a lie.

And they both knew it.

So they lay in the dark the rest of the night, holding each other close, afraid to let go because they knew they would have to face the truth in the morning.

That tonight was the beginning of the end between them.

ANCHORAGE, ALASKA, USA
PRESENT

Darcy looked up as Nolan entered the bedroom. They'd landed less than five minutes ago and the plane had just taxied to a stop on the customs ramp.

"What's happening?" Ethan asked.

He'd awakened the same time Darcy had. The chirp of the wheels connecting with the tarmac had startled them awake.

"Nothing yet," Nolan said. "We're waiting for instructions."

Beside her, Ethan pushed himself up against the headboard so he could sit up. Darcy could see the effort cost him. "What's the plan?"

"To make it past customs without causing a stir."

"But I don't have my passport. Neither does Amy." Darcy looked from Nolan to Ethan. "So how's that going to happen?"

She'd been worrying about that since they'd boarded the private jet at Zamboanga. Wondering how they were going to get back into the U.S. without ID. Not to mention she'd been hoping to keep her return quiet until she could figure out whom she could trust and where to go from here. And more and more she was worried that it might not be only her life that hung in the balance, but anyone who associated with her.

"Your passports are the least of our worries," Nolan said. "We just staged an unsanctioned paramilitary action under the nose of a foreign government. Trust me, we'd just as soon keep you under wraps."

"Like that's going to happen with the local army showing up in force," Ethan pointed out.

Nolan grunted. "You can bet the Philippine press will get wind of the unidentified individuals who rode out under fire in a military chopper—especially when they find the Huey and put together that it was the chopper in question."

"Won't be long before the international press tunes in, too, does the math, adds your abduction into the mix," Ethan said, nodding at Darcy, "and they start looking for answers. They'll have 'em if you and Amy are found aboard this plane."

What a mess. Darcy had known there could be far-reaching implications, but this . . . God.

"You could all be facing criminal charges," she said, feeling guilt tighten inside her. "Not to mention Darin Kincaid and the pilots who are in this up to their necks, too."

"Darcy," Ethan said, "you put your trust in us on the island. Don't give up on us now. We're not going to let it get that far.

"Now what's the plan?" he repeated, looking toward Nolan.

"We're going to take on fuel and food here at the FBO. While we wait, Jim—the head pilot—will leave the plane, declare everyone but Amy and Darcy on board, and present our passports to the customs agent to stamp."

"The agent won't board the plane?"

Nolan shrugged. "Yeah, he'll board but according to Jim, he probably won't go past the main cabin."

"Probably? But what if he does?"

Nolan tugged on his ear. "That's where it gets a little dicey. I'm banking on him not bringing the dogs, but if he does a full search, we need a back-up plan." He shot Darcy a grim smile. "How do you feel about tight, dark places?"

Oh, God. "How tight? How dark?"

"We'll have to hide you and Amy in the baggage compartment," Nolan clarified with an apology in his voice. "The agent would have no reason to believe a corporate royal barge like this one would be smuggling in stowaways. He'll do a cursory search—probably out of curiosity more than anything, just to see how the other half flies—and when he's gotten an eyeful, he'll call it good."

"And when will we know if it's door number one or door number two?" Darcy asked.

She jumped when a knock sounded on the bedroom door.

With a quick lift of his finger to his lips warning Darcy to be quiet, Nolan cracked the door open.

Dallas poked his head inside. "FBO just called. Jim and the agent are about to board."

"Closet?" Darcy asked, her gaze cutting first to Dallas, then to Nolan.

On a deep breath, Nolan nodded. "Just to be safe."

"I'm worried about Amy handling it." The concern on Dallas's face said exactly how worried he was.

"She'll be okay," Darcy said. "She'll be strong. Let me go talk to her."

"Better make it quick," Nolan warned. "We've only got a few minutes."

And thankfully, it was only a few minutes that Darcy, holding Amy tight, had to spend in the closet. A few minutes that seemed like hours while Amy shook in her arms, while Darcy whispered reassurances and prayed Amy could hold it together.

When the closet door opened and light flooded inside, followed quickly by Nolan's, "All clear," Darcy realized that Amy hadn't been the only one struggling to keep it together.

"That's it then?" Darcy asked, hearing the tremor in her voice and recognizing it as a mix of panic and relief as Nolan walked with her back to the bedroom and Dallas shepherded Amy back to the sofa in the main cabin.

"That's it," Nolan said brightly. "Even though we overfly Canada, since we're clearing customs in Alaska, we're good to West Palm. And since we cleared customs at a point of entry into the U.S., we don't have to clear again."

"We just caught a huge break, babe," Ethan said. "I think this calls for a treat."

She rolled her eyes as Ethan produced a roll of Life Savers.

"Smile," he said, popping one into his mouth. "You're almost home."

Dallas closed the door and walked back into the main cabin. Nolan stayed in back with Ethan and Darcy. Manny was evidently up front with the copilots shooting the shit.

Only Amy remained in the main cabin. She was lying on her side on the sofa, covered by a blanket, sound asleep again.

Dallas stood over her, frowned in concern. He suspected that her fever had returned but was hesitant to check, afraid he'd wake her.

She looked so frail and childlike lying there, her fists knotted tight under her chin, her blond hair spilling across the bone-colored leather of the sofa. Her lashes were thick and long and lay like pale tawny fans against her sunburned cheeks. Her bruises had changed color yet again—smudgy purple being the most predominant.

He dragged his gaze away, looked out the window where the ground crew was in the process of refueling the jet. And he reminded himself that Amy wasn't frail. After what she'd been through, she sure as hell wasn't childlike, either.

She could take care of herself. And she would. When she got healthy. Until then—God he was a fool—until then, he was going to make sure she didn't have to recover on her own.

He forked his fingers through his hair. When he'd come to that decision he didn't exactly know. And why in the hell he thought it was his job to take care of her was an even bigger mystery. He knew he could turn her over to Eve. And that's what he should do. But Eve was basically still a newlywed. She and Mac were in the process of building their new house.

Some excuse, a sarcastic voice needled him. *You'd use any excuse to ensure that you were the one taking care of Amy until she got back on her feet.*

Jaw tight, he buried his hands in his back pockets and turned back to her—to see that she was awake now and watching him. Blinking like a little bird, with only her head out of the covers.

"Hi," he said, and cleared his throat when it came out gravelly.

"Hi," she said in a voice so soft he could barely hear her.

"How you feeling?"

She pinched out a smile. "Good. I feel good."

"Yeah. And I'm Spiderman."

"Yeah," she said, her smile real and spontaneous this time, "you are—well, maybe not Spiderman but a superhero just the same."

Okay. That wasn't good. She was splashing all kinds of color on a canvas that should be nothing but black on white.

"I told you . . . I came on this op kicking and screaming. I was just saving my own hide out there— you happened to reap the benefits."

"And he's humble, too."

He shook his head. Was going to set her straight but could only stand in silence when her eyes fluttered shut again and she drifted back off to sleep.

An unwanted tenderness filled his chest as he tucked the blanket around her feet.

He stood there. Not liking what he was feeling. Not feeling what he should.

And he didn't have a clue as to what to do about it.

21

CHARLES HATED THE FUCKING PRESS. JACK-als and scavengers. That's all they were. And every one of them was trying to pick his bones clean as he walked from the complex to his waiting car.

"When we have more information," he said smoothly, addressing the half a dozen or so reporters swarming him, "we will notify you."

He didn't give a fuck if they couldn't hear him above the questions the members of the foreign press corps shot at him like bullets.

He paused before climbing into the backseat of the limo. "In the meantime, rest assured, we are doing everything in our power to locate Ms. Prescott. I have every confidence that she'll be found hail and hearty. Now, please excuse me. I have a meeting and I'm already late."

He smiled his best ambassadorial smile, waved magnanimously, and ducked into the limo.

"Fuckers," he muttered under his breath as the car sped down the street.

They just wouldn't let it die. All right. Fine. It stood to reason that when a U.S. Embassy employee went missing it would cause a stir—even on the international level. And yes, as the U.S. Ambassador to the Philippines he was bound to be the one they'd turn to for answers.

But this fuss had better, by God, die down soon. Hell. It would have already been as dead as Darcy Prescott if that nosy desk clerk at the Garden Orchid Hotel in Zamboanga hadn't blabbed to anyone who would listen about the beautiful young American who had disappeared from his hotel.

Even worse, the loudmouth was circulating the report that her room had been ransacked after she'd turned up missing.

Bumbling fools. Charles worked his neck beneath his shirt collar, tugged on his tie to loosen it. That's all he had to work with. Bumbling fools. Yes, he'd instructed Legaspi to have his people search for the missing tape, but he'd expected a little finesse for chrissake.

He reached into his breast pocket when his cell phone rang.

"Gatlin."

A red-hot rage boiled through him as he listened to his connection in the Philippine government, Santillan Legaspi, tell him that Darcy Prescott was alive. Not only alive, she'd been rescued and flown off Jolo.

Charles closed his eyes. Felt his heart expand in his chest. Felt a need to hurt someone.

"How did this happen?"

Rage built to a fever pitch as he listened to excuses about how a handful of what appeared to be American commandos managed to snatch Darcy Prescott away from a bloodthirsty band of terrorists—who were on his payroll, he might add—*and* a company of Philippine army infantry.

"Who knows about this?" he asked, amazed at the

calm in his voice when he felt like all of his blood vessels were about to explode.

Okay, he thought when he'd heard the worst. Only the military knew. And they were currently too embarrassed to release the story since it appeared that one of their own helicopters had been stolen out from under their nose and used in the rescue.

"See to it that it stays quiet. No one else is to know about this, understood? I don't care how much money it takes to buy their silence, no one is to know. Just goddamn take care of it!

"I'll talk to you any way I want to, you colossal fuckup! Christ—our entire operation could be in jeopardy because of you! This was your plan! Your decision! Well, I'm making the calls now and so help me, if you screw this up again, Legaspi, you're a dead man."

He had to consciously settle himself down. He drew a deep breath. Then another. "Now find her. I don't care how you do it."

He dragged a hand across his face. "Jesus. Do I have to do everything? Figure it out yourself. She's got to have family. Friends. Someplace she would feel safe. See if there's a boyfriend. Connections to people who would know how to pull off a rescue like that. Just find her! And find that tape. She cannot be allowed to make it public."

Both men knew far too well the far-reaching repercussions if the information on that tape got out.

Charles snapped the phone shut. Felt sweat roll like oil from his forehead.

And knew he'd have a stroke or a heart attack if he didn't get himself under control. He reached into the side compartment of his briefcase with a trembling hand. Uncapped the engraved silver flask he carried there.

Two deep hits settled his hands. The third finally slowed his heart.

He stared straight ahead as tears stung his eyes. Why had he made that tape in the first place? Because he'd wanted some leverage over Amad, that's why. The weasel was always making noises about backing out of the deal. Well, Amad couldn't go anywhere with the incriminating tape as a bargaining chip.

Only you don't have the damn tape, do you?

Darcy Prescott had it and now he was up shit-creek. What in the hell was he going to do?

Okay. First things first. He would not, could not, panic. There was still time. Darcy Prescott was a smart woman. She had to know by now that her kidnapping was no random, run-of-the-mill terrorist attempt to extort money. That meant she knew she was as good as dead if she opened her mouth to the wrong person about that tape.

No, he thought, breathing his first breath of relief since his cell phone rang. She wouldn't talk. Not yet. Not until she found someone she could trust with the information. And that might take her a while.

He swore under his breath. Careless. He'd been so stupidly careless when he'd given the tape to Amanda Stover by mistake. One stupid, uncalculated misstep after years of dodging potholes and pitfalls and he'd fallen into the biggest hole of all.

He'd gotten too greedy. And that had made him stupid.

Amanda Stover had had to die of course. After he'd discovered that he still had the tape containing the weekly staffing he'd given to his secretary to transcribe, he'd realized his mistake. Instead of the staffing tape, he'd given her the tape he'd made of his conversation with Amad about their latest deal.

The one that was supposed to be his insurance. Christ. Some insurance. If the contents of that tape got out, he was a dead man.

He felt cold now. Through the sweat, he felt cold.

The blonde, Amanda, whom he'd handpicked because she *was* blond and appeared to have the intellect most of the free world associated with blondes with breasts, had been smarter than he'd thought. Smart enough, evidently, to pass the tape on to someone who would know what to do with it. Not smart enough to keep herself alive, though.

Well, Darcy Prescott didn't have what it took to outsmart him, either. No one did.

When they found her—and they would—he wouldn't rely on Legaspi and his derelict goons to get the job done this time.

He had connections all over the globe. Had lined enough pockets forging his alliances to fill the Taj Mahal. If he went down, so would several others. And they'd all go up in flames with him.

So, yes, wherever Darcy Prescott was hiding, they would find her. Find the tape. He would see to it that she turned up dead this time.

And life, as he enjoyed it, would get back to normal.

WEST PALM BEACH, FLORIDA
PRESENT

"Thank you," Darcy said as she let the nurse out of Ethan's town house in West Palm. "We really appreciate this."

"Just doing my job." Gina Cleveland, the private nurse Darin Kincaid had hired to care for Ethan, was tidy and tanned in her white pants and navy blue tunic top. "Call now, if you run into problems, but I really don't expect to hear from you. He's doing just fine."

Darcy closed the door behind Gina. On a weary sigh, Darcy leaned back against it, looked toward Ethan's bedroom—and, against all odds, felt like crying.

She pushed away from the door with a self-effacing shake of her head. "*Now* you feel like bawling. When the worst is behind you."

She was safe—at least for the time being. Ethan was recovering as everyone had promised her he would. With an open invitation from the Garretts to join E.D.E.N. anytime he grew weary of the Boston P.D., Manny had headed back to his job. Nolan was back with his pregnant wife, and Dallas . . . well, Dallas seemed to be clocking a lot of time playing guardian angel over Amy, who was resting at Jillian and Nolan's, where Jillian had insisted she stay until the Kincaid family physician declared her recovered. From all indications, Amy was resting comfortably after brief treatment in the hospital where Nolan and Dallas had taken her shortly after they'd set down.

That had been twenty-four hours ago.

Like every other day since this nightmare started nine days ago, the last day had also gone by in a blur. This morning, Darcy felt as if everything they'd been through was catching up with her.

Raking a hand through her hair, she walked into Ethan's kitchen—a neat and spotless, almost sterile space done in stainless steel and commercial appliances. She poured herself a cup of coffee.

Moving to the set of sliders, she slid one open and walked out onto a balcony furnished with serviceable white patio chairs, a small glass and chrome table, and little else. Like the kitchen and the rest of Ethan's town house, it was very male, very stark. Like the man, it was acutely efficient.

"If you squint and use a little imagination, you can occasionally see a mast on a sailboat slipping along the Intracoastal. At least that's what the realtor said. Seemed to place a lot of stock in that as a selling point."

Darcy didn't turn around at the sound of Ethan's voice. Didn't bother to ask what he was doing out of bed. She'd only get the same answer he'd given her the last four times she'd fussed: "I'm not sick."

No. He wasn't sick. He was only recovering from a gunshot wound that had required ten stitches, a regimen of injected antibiotics, and two additional pints of blood.

The doctors said that if they hadn't made it back when they had, Ethan could have lost his leg. He could have died.

She forced herself to not think about what could have happened to him. She sipped her coffee instead, enjoyed the warmth of the midmorning sun against her face and the sweetness of a mild breeze that carried the faintest scent of the ocean.

At least she would have enjoyed it if she hadn't been so aware of Ethan limping up behind her. And if she hadn't felt so entangled in the domesticity of it all—waking up in the same house, sleeping under the same roof.

That was the hard part. In the three short years they'd been married, their opportunities to share morning coffee together had been precious and few. Each one was an indelible memory. It would be easy, so easy, to weave present and past together and make the grave mistake of confusing them with now.

Then, they had been married. Then, love had been enough.

Now . . . well, Darcy was very confused about now.

And she couldn't afford to be. She had to figure out where she went from here. Something much more important than just *her* life hung in the balance.

"I'd take a cup of that."

She looked over her shoulder, watched as Ethan eased himself into a patio chair.

He was wearing only a pair of loose-fitting tan cargo shorts. And God, he looked incredible. Stronger. Not yet fully recovered but definitely recovering and yes, she admitted, if it weren't for the fatigue that still claimed him and his limp, it would be hard to imagine what he'd gone through.

His abs were flat, his chest broad, his face—no longer pale and strained—clean-shaven. His blue eyes were clear and void of pain. His dark hair fell around his face. If he'd combed it, he'd used his fingers—and the effect was stunning.

"Um, Darcy? I'd take a cup of coffee . . . if it's no bother," he added, making Darcy realize she'd been staring.

Disgusted with herself for losing her focus, she dragged her gaze away.

She was disgusted with him, too. He was so good at that. Good at insisting he could take care of himself— *thank you very much*—when anyone offered a hand, then somehow managing to make her feel indispensable. At least he tried to make her think she was indispensable to him. She hadn't figured out yet why he felt the need.

"Still take it black?" she asked, setting her cup on

the patio table. Rising, she headed for the kitchen, playing his game.

"If it ain't black, it ain't coffee."

"Never knew it could taste so good."

Since Jolo, there were a lot of things Darcy would never take for granted again. Like clean clothes, showers, shampoo. And toothpaste. Lord, had she missed toothpaste.

"Thanks." He gave her a sleepy smile when she set the coffee on the table beside him. The kind of smile he used to give her when their love was fresh and innocent and new. *And enough,* she reminded herself.

"Sit with me," he said when she hesitated.

She'd like to run for the hills. He must have seen it in her eyes. But since they both knew she had no place to go and pretty much nothing to do, she sat.

"It was nice of Mr. Kincaid to send the nurse," she said inanely.

Ethan nodded. "Well, it would be a little difficult to explain a wound from an automatic weapon to an ER staff. They'd have to report it to the police. There'd be an investigation." He lifted a shoulder in a negligent shrug. "We could work around it, but, frankly, I'm relieved to have avoided the hassle."

"And how did they explain Amy when they checked her in at the hospital before transferring her to Nolan's?"

"If need be, admissions in the Darin Kincaid Wing of the hospital don't require explanations. Or insurance," he said easily.

"Why is Kincaid so generous with us? He doesn't even know me or Amy."

Ethan smiled. "Before Nolan married Kincaid's daughter, Kincaid had hired him as Jillian's bodyguard to protect her from a stalker. Without going into the entire ugly mess, suffice it to say that Jillian's alive because of Nolan. Kincaid's gratitude—especially once his princess fell in love with and married the commoner—extends to the entire Garrett clan."

He gave a go-figure shrug. "He likes us. And I think maybe he's a closet adventurer. When we needed funds to get you out of Jolo, he couldn't open his checkbook fast enough. I think that if he hadn't known he'd jeopardize the mission, he would have joined us."

"Well," she said, constantly overwhelmed in the face of Kincaid's generosity, "I don't know how I'll ever be able to repay him."

"You'd insult him if you even tried."

"Still—"

"You'll get your chance to thank him sometime," he assured her. "Have you called your parents yet?"

Her stomach took a dive. She shook her head. "No. Not yet."

And she couldn't call them. She couldn't let them know she was alive and well until she figured out what to do. And she couldn't figure out what to do until she figured out whom she could trust. Until then, she needed to keep her presence in Florida quiet and her whereabouts unknown or her parents could be in danger, too.

"I imagine they're thinking the worst by now," he prodded gently. "Don't you think you should be contacting them?"

She pinched her lips between her teeth and nodded. And hated herself for the torture she was putting them through. But calling them now would be too risky. No matter how much they suffered now, she couldn't drag them into this.

"Darcy."

She couldn't look at him.

"Darcy . . . whatever is going on, you've got to tell me. I can't help you if you won't tell me what you're up against."

It was pointless to deny she was still in trouble. He hadn't bought her lies on the plane. Wasn't going to buy them now.

"My trouble almost got you killed once. I'm not going to risk it again. I'll work this out on my own. I just need a couple of days to think it through."

"For God's sake—"

"No," she said. Closed her eyes. Touched her fingers to her temples. "No. You've done enough. Beyond enough. I've got to handle this myself. That's just the way it's got to be." When she glanced at him, his expression was stormy. "Look. You're doing better. Maybe it would be best if I just leave now."

He snorted. "And go where? You don't have any clothes. You don't have any money. Hell, you don't have a driver's license or ID. How far do you think you'd get?"

Yeah. There was that. She had a small bank account that she'd always kept in D.C. along with her post office box. Without an ID, however, she couldn't access her account. Without money, she couldn't get to D.C. and the PO box. Both were critical if she was going to survive this.

"Don't you know people? People who could take care of getting me an ID? A driver's license?"

"Since I'm not allowed to help you anymore, I guess those are rhetorical questions, right?"

"You wouldn't be helping me," she argued. "You'll just be putting me in touch with them."

"The hell I will."

She glared at him, accepted the truth. She was no longer a captive of a group of barbaric terrorists, but she was a hostage of circumstances just the same.

She had to think. And she couldn't think about anything but the way he looked, the way he looked at her, when she was this close to him.

"I'm going to take a shower."

"Fine. You do that. And while you're at it, think about this. I'm the only game in town, Darcy. You knew it when you called me from Zamboanga and you know it now."

22

AMY HAD BEEN STAYING WITH NOLAN AND Jillian a little over two days. She was doing fine. Dallas knew that and he'd told himself he'd just stop in for a few minutes and check on her. That had been two hours ago.

"Well," he said, figuring he should leave so she could rest and wondering why he really didn't want to go. "I've left Eve holding the fort long enough. I should get back to the office."

They'd been playing gin most of the time. Hell. It had seemed safe enough. She'd looked so lonely and unsettled when he'd found her sitting on the lanai playing solitaire. So he'd stayed.

Any old excuse.

"Absolutely," Amy said. "You . . . you should go. I feel guilty taking so much of your time."

"What you should feel guilty about is beating me out of fifty cents."

She grinned, which was what he'd wanted, and gave back as good as she got. "Fifty-six. It was fifty-six cents."

"The world hates a gloater," he teased, encouraged

by this little bit of foolishness after everything she'd been through. "And if I wasn't so rusty, you'd be into me for a helluva lot more than chump change."

Yeah. He liked seeing her smile. Liked it a little too much. And he liked seeing her bruises healing and a healthy glow returning to her skin.

She was wearing a long-sleeve silk blouse and pants. Both were blue. The color of her eyes.

They were Jillian's clothes, he imagined, and even though Jillian was a slim woman when she wasn't seven months pregnant, the outfit still hung on Amy. But in a good way, he realized, just a little too intrigued by the drape of the silk over her breasts.

Don't even go there, he told himself. Amy Walker carried a cargo bay full of baggage on her back. None of it would fit in his closet or his life.

"I'm already into you for more than I'll ever be able to repay," she said, sobering. "You. And your brothers. Jillian. My God. She and Nolan have treated me like a queen."

They'd better, Dallas thought, or they'd have him to answer to.

And where the hell was that coming from?

"Are you getting enough to eat?" Better to concentrate on her health than why he felt so protective of her. Rehydrated and on the way to clearing up the infection caused by her numerous cuts, she actually looked like she'd put a few pounds on. "To hear Nolan tell it, Jillian's not much in the kitchen department."

"So she says. But she's got a heck of an array of gourmet restaurants programmed into her speed dial. And Nolan knows his way around a grill. I've never eaten so well."

"Good," Dallas said, wondering about where Amy Walker had come from and where she would eventually be going. "That's good. You'll be back to fighting weight in no time."

She nodded, too, a tight smile tilting her lips. "You'd . . . um . . . you'd better go," she reminded him.

Yeah. He'd better. But for some odd reason, he felt a kernel of trepidation take root at the idea of leaving her. "You'll be okay, right? Until Jillian gets home? You've got my cell number if you need anything?"

"I'll be fine. Thanks. And yes. I've got your cell number."

"Well. Okay then." He turned to go.

"Dallas."

He paused in the doorway. Turned around slowly.

Her blue eyes searched his for a long time, sober, thoughtful, before she forced a smile. "Thank you. Thank you for . . . everything."

He looked at her long and hard. Couldn't shake the feeling that her thank-you sounded a whole lot like something else. Something like good-bye.

"I'll see you later," he said, and waited for her to nod. It took a long time until she finally did.

"Yeah. I'll . . . I'll see you later."

Dallas thought about the look on Amy's face all the way across town as he headed for E.D.E.N.'s suite of offices. And wondered why he thought about her so much. Wondered why, later that afternoon, he spent the better part of three hours running a search on Amy Walker.

He'd held off doing it until now. It hadn't felt right. Like he'd be adding insult to substantial injury if he invaded her privacy after all she'd been through.

If she would just talk to him. But she wouldn't. And

he'd have felt like a bully pressing her. So he'd given her time.

Now he felt like he was running out of time. And after leaving her today, it felt like the clock was ticking faster and faster.

What he uncovered told him why. The information he found was puzzling and incomplete. When they were back on Jolo, Amy had told him she didn't have a family. That there was no one waiting for her back here in the states.

She'd lied.

She had a mother. He didn't turn up anything on Amy's father, but he'd found a grandfather. And what he found was beyond disturbing.

Evelyn Walker, sixty-two, was a longtime resident of Pleasant Manor Mental Institution in upstate New York.

And Edward Michael Walker, eighty-two—Amy's grandfather—had a last-known address in Manila, the Philippines.

Where Amy had been abducted.

Dallas broadened his search on Edward Michael Walker. The name popped up several times linked to some damn spooky stuff. One item in particular made Dallas's blood run cold.

"Jesus," he swore, slumped back in his desk chair, and stared at the screen on his laptop. He reached for the bottle of water. Took a long deep pull.

"Jesus," he swore again.

PARC-VRAMC was a nonprofit organization set up to educate the public about sadistic abuse, ritualized torture, and invasive nonconsensual mind control experimentation.

Edward M. Walker was referenced several times on
the site, along with a list of Nazi scientists and physi-
cians who had found refugee after World War II in any
number of countries—the U.S. included—and had
been granted funding to conduct "medical" research.

*Invasive nonconsensual mind control experimenta-
tion.*

This was *Manchurian Candidate* shit.

Maybe it was a mistake. Maybe this Edward M.
Walker wasn't who Dallas thought he was.

"And maybe the sun don't rise in the east," Dallas
muttered, reaching for his cell phone, understanding
now why Amy might have felt the need to lie about not
having family.

"Jillian. Hi, it's Dallas," he said when his sister-in-
law answered.

"Hey, Dallas, what's up?"

"I was just calling to check on Amy."

Silence, then surprised. "Isn't she with you?"

Dallas felt his gut tighten; his heart started to pound.
Damn it.

Goddamn it!!

He'd known something was up when he'd left Amy.
He should have trusted his gut. He should *always* trust
his gut.

"Dallas? Amy's with you, right?"

"No. She's not with me," he said, and listened with
half an ear while Jillian told him she'd come home
from shopping an hour ago and Amy had been gone.

"I thought maybe you took her out for some fresh
air," Jillian continued. "Maybe . . . maybe she went for
a walk. She's bound to be restless cooped up all day."

"Yeah. That's probably it," he said, but he knew,

deep in the gut that he'd trusted too late, that Amy
Walker had gone for more than an afternoon stroll.

She was gone.

Gone.

He felt . . . hell. What did he feel?

He rose, walked to the window, and absently rubbed
the heel of his hand up and down along the center of
his chest where a dull ache had settled.

She had no business out there on her own. She
wasn't well. She hadn't fully recovered. And what he'd
found out about her family . . . Jesus.

Okay. He needed to step back a few feet here. He
was drawing semi-sized conclusions with a Matchbox
truck full of information.

Yet, if he was wrong, why had she felt the need to
leave like this? He glanced back at his computer,
where he'd bookmarked page after page of information
on Edward M. Walker.

. . . *sadistic abuse . . . ritualized torture . . . nonconsensual mind control experimentation* . . .

And her mother was in a mental institution.

Dallas wiped a hand over his jaw, let out a long
breath.

"What did he do to her, Amy? What did he do to
you?"

And why did he feel such a huge, yawning hole inside him knowing that in all likelihood, he'd never
know?

Because he knew, bone deep, that in all likelihood,
he'd never see Amy Walker again.

By the next afternoon, Ethan had had it.

He and Darcy had been tiptoeing around each other

the past two days since they'd been holed up in his town house like they were walking barefoot over needles.

There was so damn much about this entire situation that pissed him off. Starting with the slow return of his physical strength and ending with Darcy's stubborn determination to protect him from who was after her by refusing to tell him what was going on.

And that's what she was doing, he thought grimly as he hobbled into his den where his free weights and bench were set up. She was protecting him. In her misguided process, she was tying his hands from protecting her.

Well, he had all the time in the world. He'd wait her out, damn it.

Feeling surly and restless, he straddled the weight bench, tinkered with the bars until he had a set of thirty-pounders, and started to curl.

He worked up a sweat in five minutes.

"Fuck." Angered by his physical weakness, he pushed himself harder. Pushed until his bad leg, which he had to use for leverage, screamed. Pushed until his muscles burned. Until he was drenched in sweat.

And then he curled some more.

"What are you doing?"

He didn't turn around at the horror in Darcy's tone.

"Minding my own business," he grunted, and started another set of fifteen reps. Implied, but not said, was, *Now go away and mind yours.*

But he was lying to both of them. He didn't want her going anywhere.

Christ, he could smell her through his own sweat. She must have just gotten out of the shower. Eve had supplied Darcy with a shopping bag full of shampoo, lotions, soaps, powders, creams . . . you name it, his sister had brought it. From the scent of Darcy—floral and musk and citrus—she had taken full advantage.

He wouldn't, he told himself, and set his jaw. No matter how badly he wanted to, he would *not* take advantage. Darcy may be tough. Mentally she might be one of the strongest women he knew, but emotionally she was fragile right now.

Plus, he'd seen the look in her eyes. The one she tried to hide when he caught her watching him. She was as aware of him as he was of her.

And he wanted her.

Yeah. He wanted her, but not until they figured out what was happening between them. And what had gone so wrong.

He'd been thinking about that, too. If there was a fix for them, he wanted to make it. The question was, how? She wouldn't even confide in him about the trouble she was still in.

"Do you think this is a good idea?"

Her voice startled him. He'd thought she'd left the room.

"Well, darlin', seems I'm all tapped out of good ideas." And because he was feeling mean suddenly over any number of things—from her secrecy, to wanting what he couldn't have, to this damnable weakness—he took it out on the closest target. "I'm also damn tired of being treated like an invalid."

"No one is treating you like an invalid. You're recovering from a gunshot, for God's sake. You lost most of your blood."

"Yeah, and now I've got it back. I need to do something other than lie around and take up space. I need to build up my strength. So unless you've got a better idea on how I can do that, just back off, okay?"

Silence.

He expelled a deep breath. Bowed his head and finally leaned down and set the dumbbells on the floor.

"You didn't deserve that."

More silence.

"I'm sorry," he said, finally looking back over his shoulder.

He immediately wished he hadn't.

She was wearing a silky short jade green robe over a matching gown. Eve's doing again.

Lust coiled in his gut like a spring under about ten tons of pressure.

Her hair was wet. Her legs were long. And smooth, and, Jesus, he wanted her. Hadn't stopped wanting her since she'd left him five long, empty years ago. Since he'd spotted her on the ground in the jungle with her wrists bound and her eyes bleak.

He turned away from her abruptly. Then he lay on his back on the bench, his head beneath the big bar loaded with a lousy 120 pounds of free weights when he was used to working out with 250.

He lifted the bar off the base and started pressing. And immediately got in trouble. All the blood that was supposed to be in his bicep and shoulder muscles had gone south.

After the fifth lift, his arms started trembling.

And not entirely from muscle fatigue. He could still smell her. Couldn't stop thinking about the silky skin beneath the silky gown. Couldn't block the memory of how she tasted, how she felt moving beneath him . . .

And then she was there. Standing behind his head. Her hands clamped beside his on the bar, lifting with him as he pushed and finally helping him settle the bar on the cradle.

The hem of her gown brushed the side of his face.
Her bare thigh was less than an inch from his mouth.
Aw God.

She was so close, he could feel her heat. Smell her
woman scent mixed with bottled scents. She was so
damn tempting, his belly muscles clenched like he was
in the middle of a lift.

"You shouldn't do this with . . . without a spotter,"
she said, the huskiness of her voice telling him more
than he wanted to know. More than he should know.

The fact that she didn't move—not one fraction of
an inch—told him even more. She seemed as frozen as
he felt, standing above and behind him, her fingers still
wrapped around the bar beside his.

Their eyes met.

He didn't know how long they stayed that way. Him
on his back. Her standing behind him. Their eyes
locked in a haze of smoky heat.

Neither did he know who made the first move. He
only knew that one minute he was dying to touch her
and the next their fingers brushed. Then twined together, clutched.

And then nothing mattered but the need to be inside
her. Under her. Surrounded by her.

It was wrong. He no longer cared. She was vulnerable. He didn't give a rip. He physically hurt with the
need to make love to her.

"Kiss me. For God's sake, Darcy . . . kiss me."

It was all sensation then. Soft, soft lips. Warm wet
tongue as she walked around the bench and bent over
him, offering her open mouth and, at his urging, strad-
dling his lap, pressing the giving heat of her core
against his erection.

He gorged himself on the tastes he had never forgot-

ten. On the kitteny sighs he'd heard in his dreams. Felt
like he *was* dreaming as he reached for the loose belt of
her robe and untied it. He dragged it off her shoulders,
let it slide across his legs to the floor as he lifted the
slip of green silk up and over her head.

She was so outrageously beautiful. She felt exactly
as he'd remembered . . . supple and alive and on fire
beneath his hands. Her nipples, sweet Lord, her nipples. They were a velvety, dusky brown until he surrounded her ribs with his hands, drew her down to his
mouth, and sucked her in. Velvet turned to diamonds
against his tongue.

She cried out as he devoured her, braced her hands
on the barbell above them, and, suspended like that,
arched her breasts into his mouth as he reached down,
clamped her hips in his hands, and rubbed her hard
against his erection.

He turned his head to her other breast, frantic to
taste more of her as he lifted her hips, fumbled with his
shorts, and freed himself.

He groaned in absolute mind-numbing pleasure
when he guided the swollen head of his penis into her,
clenched his jaw to keep from coming when she took
him home, took him deep, settling herself slowly down
on top of him.

Her eyes were closed when he summoned the presence of mind to look at her. Her hands were still
clamped on the bar above his head; her beautiful
breasts swayed close to his face. Her mouth was tightened in concentration as she strove to hang on to every
nuance, every intense, heated stroke of her body on his.

He felt the tension coil tight in her, sensed the moment she surrendered to the power. He was right along
with her when she came on a deep, lush cry, her inter-

nal muscles convulsing around him like a greedy, clutching fist, and he couldn't . . . couldn't hold back . . . couldn't hold on . . . couldn't breathe for the need of her.

Couldn't imagine anything—*anything*—better in this life than the feel of spending himself inside her snug, gloving heat.

If you were going to make a mistake, it might as well be a big one, Darcy thought when she finally came back to herself.

There you go. Blame it on an out-of-body experience.

Oh God. How could she have been so stupid? This never should have happened. And she had only herself to blame.

"Don't." Ethan wrapped his arms around her when she made to move off of him. "Just . . . don't," he whispered, softer this time as she let her cheek rest back against his chest. "Don't think about it. Don't analyze it. Don't be sorry about it."

A tear leaked out, hot and fast and unexpected. Perfect. This was just perfect.

She squeezed her eyes shut, refusing to cry.

She had to get off of him. Had to get out of here.

"I . . . I'm getting cramps . . . in . . . in my calf," she lied.

He immediately let her up. But he wouldn't let go of her hand. Without a word, he rose and, slinging an arm over her shoulder, walked her to his bathroom.

She met his eyes when he turned on the shower. Shook her head. She couldn't do this again. She couldn't take this brand of intimacy and not want more. She couldn't . . . she just couldn't.

"I got you all sweaty. And besides, I need your

help," he said simply. Then he smiled with just enough mischief and mayhem that she folded.

"You play dirty, Garrett," she said, and held him steady as he stepped into the tub.

"Yeah, well," he dragged her under the spray with him, "whatever works."

23

THEY HADN'T MADE LOVE IN THE SHOWER. Well, not in the traditional sense. Darcy really was worried about Ethan's strength. Even more worried about ripping his stitches.

For all the good her worrying did her. And whatever happened to her resolve?

Gone. Like soapsuds down the drain, evidently, because when she woke up several hours later, she was still naked and still wrapped in his arms.

At least this time they were both horizontal. And that's the way she wanted him. Not for sex, though Lord knew sex with Ethan had always been incredible.

No change there, she thought with a tingling sense of satisfaction.

But after—after, she'd wanted him resting. And he had. So had she.

She yawned as she stretched an arm over her head and caught a glimpse of his bedside clock.

It was almost 9:00 p.m. Amazing. She'd slept the day away right alongside him. Evidently, she was still in recovery mode, too. Recovery from the abduction.

Now she had another recovery to make: recovery from him.

She threw her arm over her forehead and stared at the shadowed ceiling. Before all this had happened, she'd really thought she'd put Ethan Garrett behind her. Okay, in sporadic and infrequent moments of abject *denial* she'd thought she'd put him behind her.

But as she lay here in his bed again, wasted and spent, bombarded by a glut of emotions, loving the familiar feel of him, the scent of him, she recognized what a liar she'd become—at least she'd been lying to herself. She'd never stopped loving him.

And to what end? What good would come of it? Nothing had changed. The same issues that had driven them apart would keep them apart.

She thought back to that final year of their marriage. The year after the incident in Tel Aviv. While she'd been concerned before then—about his unreasonable demands that she quit her job or at least go stateside, about his inability or unwillingness to talk to her about what went on inside his complicated, intelligent head—everything changed between them that night.

Beside her, his chest rose and fell as she remembered the confusion. The strain. The concern. Most of all, she remembered the hurt.

She'd known he'd been trained to kill. But seeing what he was capable of doing—even in defense of her. It had been a little unsettling.

Okay. She sighed into the night. It had scared the hell out of her.

Her warrior husband was programmed to protect and defend, and yet what Ethan had done to that man that night . . .

She shivered at the memory, despite the warmth of Ethan's body against hers. It had eaten at her—just as her safety had eaten at him.

After that night and in the few days they'd had left together, she'd seen way too much of the dark side of her husband. A side that made him quiet sometimes. Withdrawn. Angry.

She'd been hopeful that he would open up to her. That'd he'd grow to trust her with that part of himself that he must have felt she wouldn't condone.

But he never had. And Tel Aviv proved to be the beginning of the end of them.

The next two years still seemed like a blur. She'd expected something as cataclysmic as the death of their marriage to be earth-shattering. Universe altering. But over time, it just sort of faded away.

Somehow, it was more painful for the ease of it all. Ethan had even quit badgering her about leaving the State Department, she realized in retrospect. He quit caring. A year drifted to two, and the chasm between them grew to a yawning hole of uncertainty and chilling silences.

Since she hadn't had him in any real sense of the word for longer than she cared to acknowledge, she finally asked for a divorce. Missing him, missing what they'd never found in each other, but too tired to fight to hold things together any longer.

She was still tired, she realized as she rose slowly from the bed so she wouldn't wake him.

She headed straight for the guest bathroom that was adjacent to the guest bedroom where she'd spent last night. Pulling the hair back from her face with her hands, she stared at herself in the mirror—and saw a fool.

The worst kind of fool.

A fool in love.

Love hadn't been enough before, she reminded herself as, wide-awake now, she wandered into the living room. And she couldn't put herself through the pain of thinking love was enough now. Not with a man who either wouldn't or didn't know how to be a half of a whole.

"Just in time for the summer travel season, the price of crude oil has risen yet again, surpassing an all-time high established last summer. OPEC officials blame the . . ."

Ethan tuned out the sound of the cable TV news anchor. He leaned a shoulder against the doorjamb that opened to his living room and watched the profile of the woman who continued to complicate his life.

He hadn't been surprised to wake up and find Darcy gone from his bed. Just like he wasn't surprised to find her sitting in front of the TV in the middle of the night engrossed in the ten o'clock news.

From what he could figure, this was how she'd spent the bulk of last night, too. Flipping from one cable news channel to another.

He stood in the dark, watching her, the images on his plasma screen the only light in the room. She didn't know he was there. And he wasn't sure why he was. Except that making love with her had changed everything between them.

At least he wanted to think that it had.

But then, sex had never been their problem. It was everything else that had screwed them up.

"On the international news front, the story out of Manila in the Philippine Islands concerning the fate of U.S. Embassy employee **Darcy Prescott** remains uncertain."

The newscaster lent immediacy and reality to the moment and drew Ethan's attention back to the TV.

"As we reported in our live exclusive from Manila earlier," the anchor continued, "Ms. Prescott, who served abroad in the vice consul's office, went missing several days ago when she failed to return to her hotel in Zamboanga City following what a hotel employee referred to as an evening walk."

Ethan darted a glance back at Darcy.

Curled up on one end of his sofa, she sat perfectly still. If her heart was beating as hard all over as the pulse jumping at the base of her throat, she wasn't nearly as cool and collected on the inside as she was on the outside.

She hadn't been cool and collected earlier. He could still see her moving above him on his weight bench. Could still feel her skin, slick and soapy, her hair soaked and cascading around her face as she'd gone down on her knees in front of him under the spray and taken him in her mouth. Destroyed him.

He dragged his attention back to the newscast.

A photograph of Darcy that appeared to have been taken from a personnel file appeared on the screen.

Ethan watched Darcy closely as all of her focus was concentrated on the TV. She watched it in intent but impassive silence until the camera cut to an impromptu interview with a man getting into a limo.

She gasped and her mouth tightened in the next instant.

Ethan jerked his gaze back to the TV when the anchor announced, "As you can see, we're rolling some footage shot two days ago when our reporter caught the U.S. ambassador to the Philippines, Charles Gatlin, leaving the embassy in Manila."

"Mr. Ambassador," a reporter called out from off camera, "what can you tell us about Ms. Prescott's disappearance?"

Ethan studied the man who was the center of attention and had caused such a pronounced reaction from Darcy.

Charles Gatlin looked to be sixty-something but well preserved. Tan skin. Two-hundred-dollar haircut. Expensive, tailored suit. Crisply knotted tie. Overall, as slick and polished as a new recruit's boots.

"When we have more information," Gatlin was saying, smiling into the camera but still managing to look properly concerned, "we will notify you. In the meantime, rest assured, we are doing everything in our power to locate Ms. Prescott. I have every confidence that she'll be found hale and hearty. Now, please excuse me. I have a meeting and I'm already late."

The ambassador ducked into the backseat of the limo, graced the press with a politician's smile, a dismissive wave, and shut the door behind him.

"Bastard," Darcy swore in a harsh whisper.

Ethan reached down and turned on a table lamp. "Not boss of the year material?"

She jumped. Her head swiveled around so fast he was afraid she'd sprained her neck.

"You scared me half to death. God, Ethan." She dragged her hair back from her face with both hands. "How long have you been standing there?"

"What's the story with Gatlin?" he pressed, ignoring her question and resisting the urge to calm her.

The truth was, Darcy was too calm as a rule. Too collected. Maybe if he kept her a little rattled, she'd let down her guard and talk to him.

No such luck. She visibly settled herself. "Well, he's not Al Hayden," she said evasively.

Ethan knew, he just knew, there was a lot more to what she was saying than a personality comparison to a man they had both known and loved but who had, sadly, died from a stroke shortly after Darcy had left Peru.

"How long are you going to play this game?" Ethan was pissed now. Good and pissed that she wouldn't come clean.

She picked up the remote and flicked off the TV when the anchor moved on to a train derailment in Australia. "I'm sorry if the TV woke you."

So, we're playing the "ignore the question" game.

She rose from the sofa, wrapping her robe around her. "I'm going to turn in."

He snagged her arm when she walked by him. Glared at her when she squared off in front of him. He ignored the feel of green silk against the back of his hand where it pressed against her ribs. Ignored the woman scent and heat of her and bullied his way on.

"You're international news, Darcy. So far, for whatever reason, it's being kept quiet that you're no longer a hostage. That's fine with me, but whoever's pulling the strings on this deal has to be in the know."

She'd already considered that. It showed in her eyes. Just like it showed that she was in denial. He pressed his advantage.

"Think about it. They have to know that you were sprung. Christ, a company of Philippine infantry witnessed your great escape.

"You think they didn't capture some of the Abu Sayyaf cell members?" he asked pointedly. "You think they didn't figure out a way to make them talk?"

He made sure she knew she was fooling herself if she did. "The military knows. They know you were on Jolo and they know that you escaped. And whoever wants you gone or dead knows it, too. Most likely they've known it for over forty-eight hours, according to the news footage we just saw. It won't be long before they find you again. And when they do, I'd just as soon know what we're up against."

She looked stricken.

"For God's sake, Darcy," he pleaded, at the end of his patience. "Talk to me. Who's after you? Who wants you silenced? And what have you got that they want?"

Tears glittered in her eyes as she slowly shook her head. "I don't want to place you in any more danger."

"And I don't want to see you dead!" he roared back.

She wet her lips, rubbed at her eyes as if she were so weary she couldn't think. Then she steadied herself. "Look. This was a bad idea—my staying here."

He pushed out a disbelieving laugh. "You think staying is a bad idea? Try leaving."

With his fingers clamped firmly around her upper arm, he walked her back toward his bedroom.

"I don't think sleeping with you is going to solve anything," she said, stopping at the guest bedroom door.

"I don't really care what you think." He pulled her the rest of the way into his bedroom. "Until this is over, you don't breathe without me feeling it against my skin. You don't brush your teeth without me handing you the toothpaste. Just consider me your very own personal bodyguard for the duration, sweetheart, because you're not getting out of my sight. And you're not getting out of touching distance."

"When did you become such a bully?" she grumbled, sitting down hard on the bed and glaring at him.

"About the same time you became so bullheaded. So I'd say that makes us even."

The drapes in Ethan's bedroom were open to catch the cool night breeze. The light from a quarter moon hanging low in a night sky dusted with stars was enough to let Darcy see the face of her ex-husband sleeping beside her.

Sleeping beside her.

The implications and confusion that reality brought to light were too numerous and complicated to even contemplate.

What wasn't complicated was the urgency she felt about getting away from him.

What choice did she have? Ethan was right. If the story of her escape had been out for over forty-eight hours, Gatlin had had plenty of time to launch an organized search for her. He'd probably already dug into her personnel file, found names and the addresses of her family and friends. And when he ran across the fact that her ex-husband just happened to be former SF, it wouldn't take long for Gatlin to piece together who was responsible for rescuing her from Jolo.

In fact, Gatlin had probably already figured it out. Ethan's town house might well be under surveillance right now. Which meant that when Darcy left she'd lead them away from Ethan.

And right now, that's all that mattered. She did not want to be with Ethan when they found her. Every moment she spent with him placed him in further jeopardy.

She'd feel guilty about the money she planned to lift from his wallet later. And about the fact that she needed to "borrow" his car. For the time being, it couldn't be helped. She needed to hole up somewhere away from Ethan to sort things out, to figure out whom she could trust. Whom she could contact with her information. And she needed to retrieve the tape she'd mailed to the PO box she kept near D.C. so she could find out exactly what was on it and why Gatlin had no qualms about killing to get it back.

And it didn't stop there. Once she figured out whom she could trust, she had to get an investigation rolling on the ambassador. One that she was beginning to suspect would launch a scandal and a probe of historic proportions. Oh yeah. And she also had to keep herself alive in the process.

Piece of cake, she thought grimly but with no less determination.

She stared at Ethan's hard, clean profile in the night. And finally admitted another truth. She needed to get away from him for reasons other than his safety. She needed to get away from him for *hers.* Despite surviving an abduction by terrorists, she wasn't sure if she could survive Ethan Garrett again.

Look what had already happened. She'd made love to him. Couldn't stop wanting to make love to him. Despite how angry she was at him for bullying her, it was all she could do to keep her hands off of him.

Five years she'd been without him. And she'd never stopped craving his touch. Never stopped . . . loving him, she admitted finally. *Not for a second.* And the longer she was with him, the more she realized that for her, loving him was not an option.

She'd always loved him.

She always would.

And that was reason enough to leave.

Ethan was deeply asleep now. And Darcy couldn't put it off any longer.

His alarm clock said it was 12:35 a.m. when she eased out of bed. She dressed quietly in the dark and with a quick glance over her shoulder lifted some folded bills out of his wallet.

She was almost to the door when a hand clamped over her mouth at the same time an arm as strong as tempered steel caught her around her waist.

She was hauled back against a body she knew all too well.

"Don't make a sound," Ethan whispered in her ear, then slowly let her go.

She turned around, mortified at being caught, confused over the urgency she saw in his eyes.

"Someone's trying to break in," he whispered close to her mouth. He lifted his hand, touched a finger to his lips. "Stay quiet. And stay here."

Heart pounding, Darcy watched as he reached into his bedside table and withdrew a sinister-looking handgun. Regardless of his leg wound, his bare feet were silent on the carpeted floor as he walked to the bedroom door with the speed and the stealth of a man who had years of practice at both.

She hadn't even heard him get out of bed and yet he'd heard someone outside the town house.

He nosed the door open with the barrel of the gun, peeked into the hall, then quietly eased out of the room.

Stay here? she mouthed silently as she crossed the room. *I don't think so.*

Tiptoeing and staying close to the wall, she followed the route he took down the hall. The town house was light enough that she could make out shapes and shadows. A table lamp by the sofa. The dark bulk of the entertainment center against a far wall.

And oh God . . . the shadow of a man easing open a slider from the balcony. When he slipped inside, she dropped to a crouch, holding her breath, afraid to call out to Ethan and warn him. Afraid not to.

She saw the flash of fire from the muzzle of a gun before she heard the sharp blast, then the crack of shattered glass.

A rapid series of answering shots drowned out her gasp. Then came more breaking glass. The crash of a lamp as it was knocked to the floor. The muffled grunts and sickening smack of fists against flesh and bone.

It seemed like hours when only seconds could have passed when Ethan swore.

The scrape of the slider on its rail rang through the night as Darcy looked up and caught a glimpse of a man's back as he raced out of the town house and disappeared over the side of the balcony rail.

And then she heard nothing but silence.

24

"ETHAN?" DARCY'S FRIGHTENED WHISPER cut through the pounding in Ethan's ears.

He pushed himself to his feet with a grunt. "Thought I told you to say put."

"Thank God you're alive." Her relief, evidently at finding him alive, was quickly outdistanced by a frantic, "Are you hurt?"

He heard her take a step toward him in the dark. "Stop. Don't come in here. There's broken glass all the hell over the place. Sonofabitch!" he swore, and picked a splinter of glass out of the bottom of his foot.

"Are you hurt?" she repeated.

"No," he grumbled. Hell yeah, he was hurt. Mostly his pride. The only thing that took the sting out was the knowledge that he'd put a round into whoever had broken in with a big bad Glock. And if there was a God, the bastard wouldn't be feeling so great right now.

He'd also be reporting back to his boss the first chance he got.

Ethan made an instant decision.

"Go get a towel and toss it to me so I can wade out of here without slicing my feet to ribbons.

"No. Stop right there. Just toss it to me," he said

when Darcy rushed back into the living room with the towel.

"Throw a change of clothes for both of us into my duffel—it's in the closet on the top shelf. And no lights. We're getting the hell outta here."

Fifteen minutes later, Ethan was still wired. The adrenaline was still pumping when they slipped up the on-ramp and eased into traffic on I-95 heading north. He had no idea where they were going. He just knew he had to get her out of West Palm. And they didn't have a helluva lot of choices on their mode of transportation. Without ID for Darcy, they were pretty much stuck with his wheels.

He needed to contact his brothers but decided it could wait until he had more answers.

Shifting a Life Saver from one side of his mouth to the other, he glanced in the rearview mirror of his SUV, fairly well satisfied that the jumbled route he'd taken through town would have shaken anyone who might have had a notion to follow him.

"For the record," he said, his voice hard, "if my hands weren't full of steering wheel, I'd throw you over my knee right now and whale the daylights out of your pretty, sexy ass."

He glanced sideways at Darcy, where she sat beside him in the front seat.

His thigh throbbed. His shoulder burned where the sonofabitch had clipped him. He felt about as mad and as mean as a junkyard dog and he was tired of playing patty-cake with his ex-wife and pandering to a lingering weakness from the blood loss that hit him at the damnedest times.

"Care to tell me why you thought you had to sneak off like a thief? Oh, wait. I forgot. You *are* a thief. How far did you think five hundred bucks was going to take you?"

She stared dead ahead. "I was going to pay you back."

"Tough trick when you're zipped into a body bag wearing nothing but a toe tag."

Jaw hard, his eyes dead ahead, he shot through traffic. "In case the significance of that little scene was lost on you, whatever misguided notion you had of taking me out of the mix just got shot all to hell. You're too smart to think that was a random break-in. Whoever's after you knew you were there with me.

"They found you once, babe. It won't be long before they find you again," he added.

He let her think about that for a minute, then started in again. "Face it. It's time to give it up. I'm a big boy. I know how to play big-boy games."

She hesitated for several more moments. But he could tell by the defeated droop of her shoulders that she knew she'd played this out at far as she could.

"Why don't you start with Amanda Stover?" he suggested with a little nudge to help break the ice. "Something tells me her death is at the heart of all of this. You knew her, right?"

From the corner of his eye he saw a single tear trickle down Darcy's cheek. He clenched his jaw against the ache her pain caused in his chest.

"Yes. I knew her." She lifted her hand, wiped the tear away with her index finger. "She was just a kid. Nineteen. Manila was her first PCS."

"What did she do at the embassy?" he prodded when Darcy lapsed into silence again.

"She was clerical staff that exclusively served the ambassador's office."

"Ambassador Gatlin," he stated, figuring he was finally getting somewhere. "He's got something to do with this, doesn't he?"

Another protracted silence. Then a bitter, "He has everything to do with it.

"Amanda came to me the day before she died," Darcy went on after a moment in which Ethan could see a new resolve straighten the set of her shoulders.

Atta girl, he thought. She was pissed now. And she wanted justice for Amanda. Resolution for herself.

"She told me she had a tape she wanted me to listen to. Insisted that it was important."

"What kind of tape?"

"One she'd gotten by mistake. It was supposed to be a tape of a staff meeting Gatlin had given her to transcribe. The problem was, there was no staff meeting on the tape."

"What *was* on it?"

Darcy expelled a deep breath. "I don't know exactly. Amanda never finished telling me. She got all spooky. Shoved an envelope into my hand, told me the tape was in there along with a note of explanation."

She shook her head. Her eyes filled with tears again. "Amanda was . . . she was kind of a cliché, you know? Blond. Built. Oh, she was sweet, but she . . . she had a flair for drama and she always seemed a little thickheaded."

Darcy plucked at the hem of her white linen shorts. "We never could figure out why she was assigned directly to the ambassador's office. For that matter, I never figured out why she latched onto me. Maybe because we were both from Ohio. God, I don't know. We sure didn't have anything in common. But she was a little homesick, so I mothered her when she needed it.

"And she needed it a lot. She was always crying over a relationship, certain someone was trying to get her fired."

Darcy touched her fingers to her forehead. "Anyway, when she gave me the tape, I just considered the source. Took it to placate her. Basically, I blew her off . . . told her I'd listen to it right away and get back to her."

"But you didn't."

She shook her head, guilt evident on her face. "No. I didn't. I was swamped that day. Had to catch a plane right after lunch. If I'd have taken her seriously, taken the time to listen to the tape right away—or at least read the note—I might have been able to help her."

"You're not the bad guy in this."

"Tell that to Amanda's parents."

"Tell me what you know about the tape," Ethan said gently, knowing she had to work through her guilt in her own way, in her own time.

"I threw it in my briefcase and took it with me to Zamboanga thinking I'd have an opportunity to listen to it then. I never got the chance. Before I was able to round up a tape player, someone called and told me about Amanda's death."

"The hit-and-run."

She nodded. "I knew right away something was off with that story. That's when I finally opened the envelope. Along with the tape was a note she'd written, begging me to listen to it. The note said the tape was of Gatlin talking to some guy with a heavy Middle Eastern accent. Said she had a hard time understanding it, but she was certain that Ambassador Gatlin was up to something . . . something bad with this guy."

"Evidently, she was right." Darcy stopped, sighed. "Dead right."

"How did he make the connection that you had the tape?"

She looked out the window, shook her head as if she couldn't believe what she was about to say. "I got to feeling guilty, even a little concerned, that I hadn't listened to it before I left for Zamboanga. So I called Amanda that night. She wasn't home."

Because she was probably already dead, Ethan thought, and figured Darcy was thinking the same thing.

"And you left a message," he concluded. Gatlin's goons had trashed Amanda's apartment, according to Nolan's sources. No doubt they listened to the message and it led them straight to Darcy.

"And since back-to-back hit-and-run deaths of U.S. Embassy employees might prompt more than a little suspicion," he went on aloud, "you got door number two and Gatlin gave orders to have you abducted."

"So it would seem. As soon as I heard about Amanda, I read her note. Then I called you and got rid of the tape."

He whipped his head her way. "You destroyed it?"

"Mailed it to a post office box I keep near D.C."

He couldn't help it. He grinned. "Smart girl."

She leaned her head back against the seat rest, closed her eyes. Lights from oncoming cars and trucks flashed across her face. "Yeah, I'm so smart I managed to get abducted right after I dropped it at the post office."

Which explained something that had been eating at Ethan since this all started. He'd never understood what she'd been doing out on the city streets by herself at night.

He flipped open his cell phone and dialed.

"This better be good," Nolan grumbled, his voice gravelly with sleep when he finally picked up on the sixth ring.

Ethan grunted. "Little brother, you don't know the half of it. Call me back on a secure line."

He disconnected. And waited for his cell to ring. When it did, he filled Nolan in on everything he knew at this point, including where they were headed.

"Holy shit," his brother said.

"That pretty well sums it up, yeah. Now here's what I need you to do."

"No," Darcy said simply as they traveled north, still on I-95 and two hundred miles closer to D.C. than they'd been three hours ago. "I'm not telling you."

So Ethan was mad. *Too bad,* Darcy thought as he sat in a surly slump beside her in the passenger seat while she took a turn at driving.

"I want the post office address, your box number, and the combination to the lock."

"So you can tuck me away somewhere safe while you take all the risk retrieving the tape? I don't think so."

He heaved a breath heavy with impatience. "So if something happens to you, someone else will know how to get to it."

"Sorry," she said. "No sale. When we get there, we'll go together."

Let him brood. He could get as mad as he wanted. She wasn't telling him. She was going with him when they went after the tape.

"Are they following us, do you think?" she asked, trading one sour subject for another.

"They'll do their damnedest. It'll be a little harder for them, since the GPS transceiver I found attached to the undercarriage of the SUV is now in a trash can outside that motel near Daytona."

"That's why we stopped there?" She'd thought he'd been taking a restroom break.

"It'll take 'em a while to figure out we're not bunked down there for the night. It won't stop them, but it'll throw them off for a while. Gatlin must have a helluva network if he found you this fast. And he must have a helluva secret if he doesn't blink an eye at murder."

"Whatever is on that tape has to be huge," Ethan added, his face stone sober. "I figure we can cross skimming and bribes off the list of possibilities. That's small potatoes in the real world. He'd have attempted to cut Amanda in on the action first if that was the case instead of going right for the kill."

"Espionage of some kind?" she suggested.

He lifted a shoulder. "We'll know soon enough. In the meantime, tell me what you know about Gatlin."

"Not that much. Like I said, he isn't Al Hayden. Gatlin's an industrialist with interests all over the globe. Steel, I think. He was appointed around fifteen years ago under President Clark. Word was he always had a lot of heavy-duty lobbyists camped out on Capitol Hill, was a major contributor to Clark's political campaign."

"Which explains how he bought his appointment."

"Sadly, yes."

"Who can you trust?" he asked after a lengthy silence. "Who were you planning on going to with the tape? And what was going to happen to it if you hadn't made it out of Jolo alive?"

The last question was easier to answer than the others. "I have a friend who lives in Richmond. If . . . well, if I'd ended up dead, she knows about the PO box. She has the combination and drives up and cleans out the junk mail for me every six months or so."

"Does this friend have a name?"

"None that I'm willing to give you. You'd just call your brothers and have them coax the info out of her."

"It was worth a try."

"Do you think my family is being watched?" she asked, dreading his answer.

"Let's just say you were wise not to let them know you're stateside. If this is as big as it's starting to look, even my family's phones are probably bugged."

Darcy felt another stab of guilt for placing them all in this danger. "I hate it that your family got dragged into the thick of this."

"My brothers can take care of themselves. So can Eve and the folks. Now, who can you trust?" he repeated.

"I don't know," she said honestly. "And I've thought about it a lot. Aside from Gatlin's hookup with the terrorist network, he obviously has connections with the Philippine military—probably with the government, too. Otherwise, why wouldn't my rescue be news by now? He may even have the media in his pocket."

She flipped on her turn signal to pass a pickup. "As far as someone in the State Department . . . who knows how many layers up this runs—whatever *this* is?"

"Well," he said, slumping farther down in the seat and closing his eyes, "until we get that tape in our hot little fists and take a listen, I guess we're still stuck with more questions than answers."

He was tired. Darcy could hear it in his voice. Just the fact that he'd let her take over driving was telling. So she was relieved when he let his head fall back against the seat and he closed his eyes.

"Wake me up in a couple of hours. And keep your eye on the rearview."

"What am I looking for?" she asked, glancing into the glare of headlights shining in the mirror.

"The bad guys, babe. The bad guys."

"They'll be carrying signs, right?"

One corner of his mouth tilted up in a weary grin when she glanced his way. And then he was asleep.

MANILA, PHILIPPINES

Next to her discretion, what Charles liked best about Magda was her amazing mouth. He moaned with pleasure and decided he'd pay her double for tonight.

My God! The woman was a magician when it came to working him.

He lay back on a lush pile of thick red pillows, watched in the gaudy gilt-edged mirror that hung over the bed as she knelt over him, her head bobbing up and down on his lap.

He'd needed this, he thought as he watched her fall of ink black hair drift across his thighs, her round, pale ass tilted skyward, as she sucked him like a Hoover.

He'd needed it bad.

"Harder, baby." He fisted a hand in her hair and guided her to move faster, take him deeper. "Yeah. Oh yeah."

That did it. He shot into her mouth with a groan of satisfaction, then floated on the high as she let him go with a long, lush glide of her tongue and crawled up his body to snuggle.

Had Marion ever been this sweet? This slutty?

His cell phone vibrated, then skittered around on the bedside table where he'd set it with his pocket change.

He'd started dreading answering that fucking phone.

And with good reason.

His blood ran cold as he listened to Legaspi make excuses about yet another bungled attempt to do away with Darcy Prescott.

He shot to a sitting position, shoving Magda away.

"I don't want to hear your excuses. What the fuck is it going to take to make you realize what's at stake here!"

When he heard the hysteria in his voice he forced himself to settle down. But his blood pressure spiked again when Legaspi informed him where Prescott and her superstud ex-husband, Ethan Garrett, were headed.

Washington.

Son of a fucking bitch.

"And you know this how?"

He listened. Breathed a small breath of relief. At least they'd done something right. Garrett had found the GPS device that had been planted as a decoy. He hadn't, however, discovered the secondary unit or listening device.

"All right," Charles said, shoving Magda's hands away from his flaccid cock as she worked to distract him. "All right," he repeated, his mind back in rational mode.

This wasn't all bad news. Prescott didn't know what was on the tape. Christ, what a break. No one alive but himself and Amad knew.

And, according to the conversations that had been monitored in Garrett's SUV, no one but Darcy Prescott knew where the tape was stashed. The woman was smart; he'd give her that.

"Relay instructions that neither Prescott nor Garrett is to be intercepted until they retrieve the tape from her precious post office box. Then I want them dead, you understand? But for God's sake, make sure they don't take them out in broad daylight or make a spectacle doing it. . . ."

He sighed in disgust. "Okay. I'll spell it out for you. Discretion is imperative, do you understand? There's more security in Washington these days than politicians. If there's even a hint of a disturbance, blue-and-whites will come out of the woodwork. And I—make that *we*—can't take a chance on that tape being confiscated. . . .

"I don't know," he growled. "We're talking about one woman and one man who you tell me has been laid up with a hole in his leg, for chrissake. You've got the numbers. Take advantage. Just make sure they get the tape, then kill Prescott and Garrett without a fuss, or so help me, more heads than theirs will be on the line."

He snapped the phone shut, tossed it on the table. On a deep breath, he lay back down. "Carry on," he told Magda when she sat back on her knees, her almond eyes questioning and eager to please, her pointy little breasts standing at attention.

With a sultry smile, his little whore bent over him again.

"Harder," he snapped when his cock just lay there, wilted and unresponsive.

After fifteen minutes of vigorous and unsuccessful manipulation, he pushed her angrily away.

This was all Darcy Prescott's fault. The meddling bitch. He was going to dance in the streets when she was finally dead.

And then he was going to fuck Magda blind.

25

"YOU'RE NOT REALLY GOING TO START UP again, are you?"

They were in Arlington, Virginia, just outside D.C. Ethan glared at the mule-headed woman behind the wheel as they slowly circled a three-story building with a façade of large black stone slabs that housed, among other things, the post office where the tape sat in Darcy's post office box.

"Just tell me the damn box number and combination," he restated between clenched teeth as he scanned the street from the passenger seat, looking for a place to park.

"We go in together or we don't go," she insisted, and started another circle around the block when the parking spaces were all filled.

God *damn* her, she was stubborn.

And he was dead beat. They'd driven straight through, raced like hell to get here in fifteen hours to make sure they made it before the post office closed at 4:30. They had about a half an hour to spare. Neither one of them had caught more than a few hours' sleep during the past thirty-plus hours, and that had been in the SUV.

Ethan was running on adrenaline and the really bad coffee they'd picked up at some fast-food joint along the way. He didn't know what was keeping Darcy awake. His stitches were pulling, and he felt like he could mainline another gallon of blood and still come up short.

And his sixth sense was warning him that they had a tail.

Had he missed something? Unfortunately, it was entirely possible. He cursed the dumb luck that had landed that round in his thigh and knocked him off his game. He felt as sharp as a basketball.

"I'm not going to find a spot on the street this time of day," she said. "Everyone's rushing to beat the windows closing."

She whipped the SUV around the corner and nodded toward a parking garage. "Okay?" she asked.

"Nothing about this is okay, but it's not like we've got a lot of choice."

She pulled in, finally found a spot on the fourth floor of the garage, and parked.

Ethan reached into the glove compartment and pulled out his Beretta. He shoved it into the waistband of his cargo pants, tugged his black T-shirt over it, and opened his door. Then he gave Darcy one last beseeching look.

She ignored him and joined him outside the SUV.

"Stay alert."

With his hand clamped tight on her elbow, they left the ramp's elevator. Working to stall a limp, Ethan steered her outside and across the street.

"If I say run, you haul ass, understood? No questions. No hesitation. Just run."

"You really think they might have found us?"

He tugged open the heavy glass double front door of the building. "Let's just say I'm not willing to take any chances. If something happens and we get separated, Nolan's and Dallas's numbers are programmed on the speed dial," he added, reaching into his pocket. He pulled out his cell phone and handed it to her.

"Ethan—"

"Just call them if we run into trouble, okay?"

"Okay, fine," she grumbled, and led him through a lobby done in white marble and plate-glass windows.

Ethan studied the face of every person they met as they turned a corner and passed a bank of elevators. He checked out their clothes, looking for loose shirts that could conceal a piece.

"This way," Darcy said, pulling open another set of glass doors.

He checked their six as she walked through the door, didn't spot anyone who looked out of place, and followed her through into the post office lobby.

Rows of post office boxes filled the wall to their left. Half a dozen people were in various stages of retrieving their mail. To the right, uniformed clerks manned windows, assisting with the lines of individuals waiting with outgoing mail or cards telling them they had packages too large for their box. A long, narrow counter ran down the middle of the lobby between the service windows and the wall of mailboxes. The counter was occupied by a dozen or so people filling out address labels and looking up zip codes.

Nothing looked out of place. It appeared to be normal, peak time, business as usual.

And it made him as nervous as hell.

"Over here." Darcy started toward the boxes.

He tugged her back toward the door, made a show of pulling her into his arms and kissing her.

"Easy," he whispered against her lips, smiling as if he were telling her lover's secrets. "Let's not tip our hand just yet."

He lowered his head to her neck, nuzzled, and positioned them so he could watch the room. "Laugh. Like I just told you something that shocked you."

"Like my life hasn't been one unexpected shock after another?" she said after pushing out a credible laugh.

Doing a damn fine job of diversion and driving him crazy in the process, she wrapped her arms around his neck. Playing with the hair at his nape, she whispered in his ear, "Do you see anyone suspicious?"

"Nope. And that's enough to set my teeth on edge." So was the way her hips were pressed against his belly, but he kept that little tidbit of trivia to himself.

He let out a tight breath. "Okay. Let's do this."

Arms around each other's waists, they walked casually to the boxes. He shielded her body with his as she bent slightly to work the combination.

"What's taking so long?" he asked under his breath as he continued to scan the lobby.

"My hands are shaking."

"Deep breath, babe. You can do it."

"Finally," she said, her voice breathy with relief.

He glanced around to see her withdraw a number of current-box-holder-type advertisements—and a small, padded manila envelope that she quickly tucked between all the junk mail.

"Got it," she said.

He relieved her of the stack of mail so quickly she didn't have time to react. With his back to the main lobby, he worked the envelope open, slipped out the tape, and tucked it into the pocket of his cargo pants.

"Let's go." Without drawing any attention, he tossed the empty envelope and junk mail into a trash can when they walked by.

"So far, so good," Darcy said.

And just that fast everything went to hell. They'd just stepped outside when Ethan realized they were in trouble.

A man in a pair of jeans and a loose, open shirt over a white T-shirt came out of nowhere and walked up beside them. He wore a Patriots football cap and a pair of Oakleys—like an average Joe sports fan who just happened to carry a gun with enough firepower to down an elephant.

Ethan recognized the feel of a Glock when it was shoved into his kidneys.

"Keep walking," the guy ordered.

Before Ethan could react, another man, similarly dressed—this one an Eagles fan—joined them, flanking Darcy on the left.

"Ethan," she squeaked, her eyes widening in panic.

"Just be cool," Ethan said as the pair of guns walked them down the sidewalk toward the curb.

"Good advice, hero. You're smarter than you look."

"Look, if it's money you want," Ethan said, stalling for time as he scoured the street for a possible way out of this, "just take the wallet, pal."

"I'm not your pal. And you know what we want."

Yeah. Ethan knew. Just like he knew what he wanted. A miracle.

Damned if he didn't get one.

An Arlington PD cruiser pulled up at a stoplight.

"Don't even think about it," Oakley warned, shoving the business end of the Glock deeper into Ethan's back.

Ethan laughed. "You're fucked, *pal*," he said, and, tugging Darcy hard, lunged toward the black-and-white.

"Officer!" he yelled. "Hey . . . can you give us a little help here?"

Oakley and company stood frozen on the curb behind them, their firepower mysteriously disappearing.

The uniform looked everyone over before his gaze landed back on Ethan. "What's the problem?"

"Our ride is in the garage," Ethan said, with a jerk of his head over his shoulder, "but my battery seems to be dead. We were just asking these guys who to call for a jump—we're from out of town," he added with an aw shucks grin, "but I can tell they're in a rush. I hate to hold them up.

"Thanks, guys," he added for effect, turning to Mutt and Jeff with a dismissive wave as he walked right up to the cruiser, pulling Darcy close. "Appreciate the help, but we've got it covered now."

The hired guns had little choice but to push out pained smiles and walk on down the street.

Beside him, Darcy was deathly pale.

"Hop in," the officer said. "I'm about to go off-duty. Let me check in with dispatch and then I'll jump you. I've got cables in my trunk."

"That's great." Ethan couldn't open the cruiser's back door fast enough. "You're a lifesaver."

"Yes," Darcy said, her gaze meeting Ethan's. "A real lifesaver."

• • •

"Because I knew they weren't going to take a chance of creating a scene in broad daylight," Ethan said when Darcy asked him how he'd known the two men who had jumped them wouldn't just shoot them.

"Gatlin is bound to have given orders to handle this discreetly," Ethan continued as he inserted the key card into the lock on the door of the room he'd rented amid a string of motels along the I-95 corridor.

The best feature of the motel was that it was six blocks away from the multistory Holiday Inn where his SUV was currently parked in an underground garage. And where he hoped Oakley and his buddy were currently settled in, waiting for them to hop in the SUV and leave.

"Blasting us in front of a cop," he explained, "wouldn't exactly fall under the heading of discretion. And it would still leave them without the tape."

"Why didn't we just tell the cop what was going on?" Darcy walked directly to the bed and flopped down on her back, flinging her arms above her head.

Ethan felt a pang of sympathy. She was beat. And no doubt terrified, although she rarely let it show. Her body had endured one too many adrenaline spikes and letdowns in the past week.

But she was tough, he thought with pride. An hour after their last close call, and she was still hanging in there. And her absolute willingness to follow his cues during their last brush with Gatlin's goons spoke volumes for her self-control.

"We didn't tell the cop for the same reason we haven't told the feds. Because it would play out something like: the local law enforcement would contact the feds, who would contact the State Department, and since we don't know who in the department is involved in this, we can't take the chance. Not until we get a better handle on what's going on with Gatlin and the tape. And not until we hear back from Nolan and Dallas with whatever help they've been able to turn up."

She seemed to think about that as he walked to the drapes, glanced out the window to identify an escape route if they needed to make a fast exit from their second-floor room, then pulled the drapes shut against the summer heat of a sun dropping past six o'clock.

"How did they find us so fast?"

That's the part that pissed Ethan off. "There has to be a secondary GPS attached to my SUV somewhere. I must have missed it when I found the other one. Which was probably the plan."

"They planned for you to find something they planted?"

He nodded and, locating the TV remote, removed the batteries. "It was probably a decoy so I'd figure we were clean and wouldn't look any farther," he said, fishing the tape out of his pocket. It fit perfectly where the batteries had been.

"I'm thinking there's a listening device of some kind somewhere, too," he added, replacing the battery cover. He tossed the remote on the dresser, hiding the tape in plain sight in the event they had uninvited company. "Most likely in an air-conditioning vent. I should have caught that, too."

"And you would have done this when?" She pushed herself wearily to her feet and headed for the bathroom. "We were out of your town house within two minutes of the break-in. I'm amazed you found the first one," she said above the sound of running water.

"They were counting on me not taking time for a thorough search." He set his gun on the bedside table, fished his cell phone out of his pocket, and set it beside his gun. "I played right into their hands." He lay down on the bed, feeling weary to the bone.

"How big is this?" she asked, walking out of the bathroom with a wet washcloth pressed against her forehead.

Her expression was bleak. It hurt him to see the worry in those gorgeous green eyes—yet he had nothing to give her to take it away.

"Soon, babe," was the best he could do. "Now that we've got the tape, we'll find out soon."

He reached for the phone, dialed guest services and finally schmoozed someone into sending up a cassette player. When he hung up the phone she'd disappeared into the bathroom again.

The sound of her retching behind the closed door made his chest knot. Exhaustion and tension and running on the edge were taking their toll on her. He'd been there. He understood fully that nerves had finally gotten the upper hand.

"Better?" he asked gently when she returned to the room a few minutes later.

She lay down beside him. Closed her eyes. Her skin was pale in the shadowed room. "I want this over."

"Hang in there." He rolled to his side, touched a hand to her hair. "We're getting there.

"You know," he said, propping his head on his palm and watching her face, "my personal experience tells me that sex is a great way to relieve tension."

One corner of her mouth tipped up at his nonsense. "My experience tells me that in *your* experience sex is pretty much the answer to everything."

"You picked up on that, did you?"

Another small smile did strange things to his heart-beat. "Go to sleep, Garrett. I'll get the door when they bring the tape player."

Two deep breaths later, he was relieved to see that she'd fallen sound asleep. And as he lay there, watching the face that he had never stopped loving, the woman with the spirit that had never stopped haunting him, he swore to himself that if they got out of this alive, he wasn't letting her leave him again.

"Jesus," Ethan said twenty minutes later as he sat at the table in the corner of the room and turned off the tape player. "Jesus H. Christ."

Beside him, wide-awake even though her brief nap couldn't have done much to revive her, Darcy looked shell-shocked. "He's trying to broker a deal for enriched uranium? How can this be happening? And why would Gatlin tape something this incriminating?"

Ethan grunted, wiped a hand over his lower face. He needed a shave. He needed sleep. He wasn't going to get either any time soon.

"Why tape it? Most likely for insurance against his partners in crime. How can it be happening? You take your basic multibillionaire, give him a God complex and a position of power. Place him in a fairly benign post in a region adjacent to any number of enemies of democracy and dangle the gilt-dipped carrot. Power to assholes like Gatlin is not in political appointment but in the control that money can buy."

And apparently, he was in the process of working a deal with the devil. The tape clearly revealed that Gatlin was in league with at least two minor but determined rogue governments to broker a deal for enriched uranium that, Ethan was certain, wouldn't end up within a country mile of an electrical power plant. No. There was only one use for material of this nature, and the application was more suited to nuclear warheads and dirty bombs than creating an alternate power source.

"I wonder who he was talking to on the tape?"

Ethan shook his head, still mired in the repercussions if this deal actually went down. "If he's on the government's watch list, they should be able to do voiceprints and get a match.

"Christ," he said. "No wonder Gatlin was able to track us down so quickly. He's got to have sources all the hell over the place. I figure that when we finally make the right connection and start the ball rolling on an investigation, this is going to make the oil for food scandal look like chump change."

"About that right connection," Darcy said. "Where can we possibly go with this information? What's to say the path doesn't lead directly to the top? Gatlin must have any number of government officials tucked deep in his pockets if he's managed to have them turn a blind eye to this."

Yeah. That was the sixty-four-thousand-dollar question. Where *could* they go with it and not end up dead for their efforts?

On a deep breath, Ethan flipped open his cell phone and dialed Dallas's number.

"It's me," Ethan said, and hung up.

A few seconds later, his cell phone rang. It was Dallas calling back on a line that couldn't be monitored from either end.

"Get Nolan and Eve," Ethan said. "I don't want to have to tell this twice."

While he waited, Ethan set his cell phone to hands free so Darcy could hear both ends of the conversation. A few minutes later, his brothers and sister were assembled and listening on speakerphone.

"For the love of God." Nolan's voice came through loud and clear after Ethan filled them in on the contents of the tape. "The asshole doesn't believe in small-timing, does he?"

"The way I figure it, Gatlin's been working his way up for years," Ethan said. "He probably started with a little exchange of military technology, graduated to illegal arms procurement—whatever. This is by no means a starting place for him."

"But we've got to make it a stopping place," Dallas said with grim determination.

"And keep you two alive in the process," Eve added.

"What have you been able to dig up so far?" Ethan asked. Not quite eighteen hours had passed since he'd called Nolan from the road on the way to D.C. in the middle of the night, so he wasn't hoping for much.

Nolan's voice came back on the line. "The word still isn't out on Darcy's rescue, but my sources in Zamboanga confirm that the military knows but has been ordered by unknown government officials to keep it quiet."

"Okay." Ethan dropped his head into his hand and rubbed his forehead. "Who have we got on the inside that we can trust uncategorically?"

"Eddie," Eve said as if she'd just thought of it. "Eddie Jackson."

"Eddie Jackson?" Darcy's eyes narrowed in puzzlement. "I know Eddie. He's a communication specialist at the embassy."

With his eyes on Darcy, Ethan said, "Someone want to explain things to her?"

"Darcy," Eve said, "Eddie's a spook."

"What? Eddie's CIA? Whoa. I mean, I know the CIA has operatives undercover in all the embassies, but . . . Eddie? I never would have guessed it."

"That was the idea," Eve added. "I knew him when I was with the Secret Service. We had to work together a couple of times."

"Okay," Ethan broke in. "You sure you can trust him?"

"With my life," Eve stated without hesitation.

"Good. Because you're going to be trusting him with ours. Reach out and touch him, Eve. Find out what he knows, if anything, about this. More important, find out who, in D.C., we can trust with the tape. We've already dodged several bullets and we've got to make a connection soon. I don't have to tell you our time is running out."

"Where are you now?" Dallas asked, his voice brittle with concern.

Ethan gave them the address of the hotel. "We'd be on the move again in a heartbeat, but I'm ninety-nine percent certain my SUV is bugged."

"Okay. Sit tight. We'll get back to you as soon as we have something."

"Dallas," Darcy cut in before they broke the connection. "How's Amy's doing?"

The silence on the other end of the line was sludge thick.

"Amy's gone," Dallas said finally, his voice hard.

"Gone?"

"Yeah." Nolan filled another lengthy and uncomfortable gap. "Evidently she felt it was time to move on."

Another heavy silence passed before Nolan spoke again. "Look, watch your six, okay? We'll get back to you ASAP."

Darcy stared at Ethan's cell phone long after the connection was broken. "Amy's gone." She said it as if she couldn't believe it.

"So it seems."

"What do you suppose she was thinking?"

Ethan rose, stretched his arms above his head. "The big question is, how is Dallas taking it?"

"Yeah," Darcy said. "I got the feeling he might have had some feelings for her."

"Been there. Done that," Ethan said, too tired to bank the flare of anger that suddenly swamped him. "I know exactly how it feels to have the woman you love walk away."

26

SHE COULDN'T DO THIS, DARCY THOUGHT, studiously avoiding Ethan's dark look. She couldn't handle going there. Not now. Maybe not ever, although in between a few minor other bumps in the road—like abductions and guns and hanging out of helicopters and running for her life—she'd found herself thinking about could-have-beens way too often. Could-have-beens and would-have-beens and should-have-beens.

She cleared her head and told herself again, she could *not* do this now. Now she had to figure out how to get through this without getting killed. And without getting Ethan killed in the process.

"I think I'll take a quick shower. Maybe it'll wake me up."

"Yeah," Ethan said. He was watching her closely. "Do that. I'll order room service. I'm running on empty. You must be, too."

"I could eat," she agreed, walking toward the bathroom. Although she wasn't really sure that she could. But he was right. She needed to eat. She just hoped that when she did, she wouldn't end up upchucking it.

"What do you want?"

"I don't care. Anything," she decided, figuring everything would taste like chalk anyway.

Before hitting the shower, she dug into the duffel she'd hastily packed and came up with clean underwear and a pair of white slacks and a red silk blouse. Between Eve and Jillian, she'd ended up with the loan of some pretty classy threads.

Feeling marginally human again after showering, she dressed and took advantage of the lotion and hair dryer the motel provided. When she opened the bathroom door, the smell of food made her stomach growl and roll at the same time.

"At least try," Ethan suggested when she frowned at the burger and fries filling the plate he pushed across the table toward her.

The first bite was the worst. After that, she was surprised to find it actually tasted okay. She'd nearly polished off her sandwich when Ethan's cell phone rang.

"Yeah," he answered before the second ring.

Darcy's nerves jumped as she waited and listened to his side of the conversation. A new, refined tension grew as she watched the grim set of his uncompromising jaw, the dark intensity of his blue eyes. And it had nothing to do with the threat facing them.

He needed a haircut. He needed a shave. He needed about a week of bed rest, she realized with another flare of guilt. Yet despite the dark circles under his eyes and the disreputable look of him, inside of her, woman low, he made her ache. Made her yearn and remember what it had felt like to be his.

She rose from the table abruptly, turned her back to him, and wrapped her arms around herself. It was never going to stop, was it? The regret? The sense of loss?

And the unavoidable, undying hope that somehow, someway, they could find their way back to each other?

More than once it had been on the tip of her tongue to ask him if he ever thought about trying again. And a time or two she'd sensed he'd been on the verge of broaching the subject, too.

Yet when offered the opportunity—as he'd offered one just a few minutes ago—she turned away.

Fear did that. Fear of opening up old wounds. Fear of carving out new ones. Fear of not recovering this time.

"Darcy."

She spun around, surprised.

"Where'd you go?" His cell phone was closed and sitting on the table. His expression was puzzled.

"Sorry. Zoned out. What's happening?" she asked, bringing herself back to the here and the now that required she think about life and death, not life and love, when neither was certain in her immediate future.

"What's happening is that Eve reached Jackson," he said.

"And?"

"And he didn't say as much, but Eve sensed that Eddie wasn't at all surprised to find Gatlin's name linked to your abduction and to the possibility of some shady dealings."

"Shady dealings? He thinks the brokering of a potential sale of material that could produce dirty bombs qualifies as a mere shady dealing?"

"Okay. Back up. My words. Not his, okay?"

She calmed herself down. "So what now?"

"Now we wait."

She dropped her chin to her chest. She didn't know how much more waiting she could take. "Wait for what?"

"For the wheels to start turning. Eddie's going to make some calls, set up a meet, then plunk his magic twanger and get us the hell out from under this."

She let out a deep breath. "Okay. Okay, fine. We wait," she said without enthusiasm. She felt so tired suddenly that she could hardly hold her head up.

"Get some sleep." Ethan touched a hand to her arm, then squeezed. "I'm going to hit the shower."

"I don't think I'll ever sleep again."

Then she walked to the bed, fell face-first on the quilt, and passed out to the sound of the shower running in the bathroom.

When Darcy woke up, the glaring red numbers on the digital alarm clock on the table by the bed read 10:05 p.m.

She rolled to her back, her thoughts muzzy, her mind numb. It took a while to do the math. She'd slept almost four hours. It felt like she had just lain down.

She closed her eyes against the sliver of light spilling into the room from the slightly open bathroom door.

Quiet. It was so quiet, she thought drowsily, then felt a sharp stab of unease. Her eyes snapped open.

Ethan. Where was Ethan?

She rolled to her side.

And there he was. On his back. Sound asleep beside her.

If the relief had been sweeter, she'd have gone into sugar shock. Almost went into another kind of shock when his voice, gravelly and gruff, broke the silence of his breathing.

"Tell me something," he said, his arms crossed behind his head, his eyes still closed.

"I thought you were asleep."

"I was. Now I'm not." He turned his head toward her on the pillow.

And Darcy knew, she just knew, what was coming next.

"Why did you quit on us?"

She looked away. Rolled to her back and, like him, laced her hands beneath her head. Maybe this wasn't the time, maybe this wasn't the place, but she was tired of avoiding this conversation. More tired of avoiding it than she was afraid of facing it.

As they lay in the dark, with the threat of the present hanging over them and the ghosts of their marriage haunting them, maybe it was time.

"I wasn't the one who did the quitting," she said simply.

He pushed out a disbelieving snort. "Babe. You left me," he pointed out.

She heard the hint of anger. It didn't begin to match hers. "And you let me."

He lifted up on one elbow, reached across her to turn on the bedside lamp. He pinned her with his gaze and she saw the hurt there. The confusion. "What was I supposed to do? You told me you wanted a divorce. You ran away from our marriage."

"Yeah. I did. I ran so you'd realize what you were throwing away. I ran so you'd follow me." She sniffed, rolled a shoulder. "But you didn't. You let me go. Just . . . let me go."

She felt the pain of it as if it had been yesterday. And suddenly she couldn't lie here beside him any longer. If they were going to have this discussion, she needed to be on her feet. Where she felt stronger. Steadier. A lot less likely to cry, because she'd be damned if she'd let that happen.

She pushed up on her elbows. And got exactly nowhere. A strong hand clamped around her arm and tugged her to her back again.

"I let you go," he said levelly, "because you wanted it to be over."

She shook her head, willed back those damning tears. "No, Ethan. What I wanted was for it to *start*."

The bewilderment on his face told her he didn't get it before he said as much. "What are you talking about?"

"I'm talking about you being there."

"Wait. Just wait a minute. You knew when you married me that I'd be gone at a moment's notice."

"I'm not talking about *physically* being there. I'm talking about *emotionally*. You were never invested in us."

"That's not true."

"And I was supposed to know that?" She turned her head on the pillow to look at him. "Tell me, Ethan. Tell me how I was supposed to know that. You never talked to me. You never confided in me. Every time things got a little intense, you shut yourself off. You would never let me in."

"I *loved* you," he all but roared, then physically settled himself down.

He wiped a hand over his face, rolled to his back again. "God, I killed for you." His voice broke and, if possible, he looked even more weary than before. "I always knew I'd end up killing for you. What more did you want from me?"

Her heart hit her ribs so hard she felt the bed bounce.

Stunned by what he'd said, she stared at his grim profile. At the way his jaw had tightened, at the grief in his eyes. At the guilt laced with accusation.

I always knew I'd end up killing for you.

Oh my God. There it was. The answer she'd always wanted to a question she'd never known was on the table.

She suddenly understood. Was devastated with understanding.

"You blamed me?" she pressed, so softly and with so much amazement she could hardly get the words out. "You blamed me for what happened that night in Tel Aviv?"

Silence.

Telling silence.

Ethan couldn't answer her. For some reason, he couldn't say the words. Blame her? Hell no. He didn't blame her for anything.

So why don't you tell her? Why don't you flat-out, no bones, deny it? Tell her she's crazy. Tell her . . .

Tell her what?

He didn't know why his heart was racing. Didn't know why he wanted to shout out a denial and yet the words stuck in his throat like a fish bone.

The ring of his cell phone sliced into a tension that was mud thick and made him jump. He snagged it from the bedside table, grateful for the reprieve. Grateful that he didn't have to wrestle with why he felt relieved over the opportunity to avoid wrapping his mind around Darcy's question. Around the implications if she was right.

"Yeah," he answered, rolling to a sitting position

when he heard Dallas's voice on the other end of the line.

Behind him, he felt the bed shift and knew Darcy had sat up, too.

"Wait a sec," he told Dallas when his brother started rattling off an address. "I need to find a pen and paper."

When he turned around, Darcy was already scrambling toward the desk at the far side of the room. He thanked her with a glance and sat down at the table when she set several sheets of motel stationery and a pen in front of him.

"Okay, shoot."

Darcy's eyes were wide and round when he hung up several minutes later. All of her energy appeared to be focused on the immediacy of the here and now. Their unfinished business would have to wait.

Hell, it had already waited five long years. And what faced them yet tonight couldn't wait another five minutes.

"What?" she asked. "What's happening?"

Ethan wished there was some way he could take her out of the mix. Wished he could just leave her here and get this done without her, but he didn't dare leave her alone.

"We've got to make tracks," he said, hoping he'd figure out some way to take her out of the line of fire on the fly. "I'll tell you on the way."

"I'll pack the duffel."

"Leave it." He grabbed the TV remote and dumped the tape into his palm. "We don't have time."

Then he rifled through the bureau drawers until he found a phone book. He ripped out the D.C. city map and headed for the door and what he prayed wasn't a colossal fuckup.

• • •

Cloak-and-dagger. It wasn't Darcy's cup of tea. Not that she hadn't known that from the get-go, but as Ethan filled her in on the plan of action as they hurried to his SUV, the gravity of the situation hit her with the force of a baseball bat.

Okay, fine. She could do this. She'd made it this far. She was not going to let herself or Ethan down now.

"When Jackson got back to Eve," Ethan was saying as they crossed an access road from one motel parking lot to another, "he confided that the State Department has had the CIA watching Gatlin for some time now, just waiting for him to make a slipup. Eddie Jackson wasn't the only spook on the block."

"You're not serious? There were other CIA operatives on to Gatlin?"

He nodded and grabbed her arm, stopping her when she would have walked out in front of a car.

"If they were on to him, why hadn't they done something about it? And what does this mean to us?"

The possibilities already running through her mind were numbing—and as endless as the string of traffic they dodged to get to the parking garage. Darcy knew how it worked when the CIA decided they needed to take a "stand back and wait" approach. She could end up in protective custody or even in a witness protection program. Both possibilities were unacceptable.

"Relax," Ethan said, evidently reading her mind. "The content of that tape is more than enough to move out of monitor mode and into resolution."

He gripped her elbow and pulled her closer as they walked the stairs down to the lower level of the parking garage. Their footsteps echoed in the poorly lit chamberlike stairwell.

"So they're going to arrest Gatlin?"

"In good time. First, we've got to get the tape into the hands of someone who knows what to do with it."

"And that's where we're headed now? To meet this person?"

When they reached the stairwell door Ethan opened it. "Yeah. That's where we're headed."

"Turn here. Left," Ethan said, squinting up from the map to the well-lit street. He rattled off an address.

"There it is," Darcy said when she spotted a purple façade painted with bold pink lettering and a spotlight aimed at the shop's name. "Sweet Tooth."

The ice-cream shop was located at the end of a block and boasted Georgetown's best homemade ice cream. It was also a popular summer tourist spot and one of many businesses that catered to the summer crowd by staying open until midnight on hot summer nights. It was 11:05 right now.

"Pull into that parking spot across the street," Ethan said. "We're twenty minutes early, but we'll wait inside."

"You sure we can trust this guy with the tape?"

"Ted's been with the company for as long as I've known him," Ethan said. "That doesn't mean something won't happen to screw things up. The minute we stepped out of that motel room, we became vulnerable again."

Darcy parked and on a deep breath stepped out of the SUV. Ethan was waiting for her by the driver's side door. For a man with a bullet hole in his leg, he could sure move when he decided he needed to.

"Remember." Ethan dipped his head close to her ear

as he walked her across the street. "Do exactly as I say. Exactly."

Darcy nodded and waited for him to open the door for her when they reached the shop's entrance. An old-fashioned bell tinkled when the door closed behind them.

Given that her heart was pounding so loud the sound of each beat flooded her ears, she was amazed she'd been able to hear it. She could feel every pulse beat in her fingertips, too, not to mention her legs felt like rubber.

God, let this be over soon, she prayed silently. Let everything go exactly as Ethan had told her in the SUV on the way to Georgetown: "We'll meet Ted. We'll turn over the tape and he'll hustle us off someplace to lay low until they pick up the nice men we met outside the post office this afternoon."

Simple, Darcy told herself now as she looked around the inside of the shop to get her bearings. The place was small. A dozen white wrought-iron ice-cream tables covered with red-and-white-checkered oilcloths sat to the left of the counter. Half of them were occupied by what appeared to be students or tourists.

"Made up your mind yet?" Ethan sounded annoyingly cool and collected as he stood behind her studying the ice-cream selection written in Magic Marker on the left side of the mirror covering the top half of the wall behind the counter.

Another night, another time, she'd have found the scribbled menu charming and nostalgic. Tonight it barely registered.

"Vanilla," she said.

Ethan grunted. "Oh, come on. They have ninety-nine flavors. Go for something exotic. Live dangerously."

Live dangerously?

He was actually grinning when she glared up at him. Against all odds, she smiled—which was exactly what he'd wanted her to do.

"Vanilla will do just fine," she said, then tensed all over when the bell above the door announced that someone had entered the shop.

She glanced up at the mirrored wall directly in front of her—and swallowed a gasp when she saw the two men, one wearing a pair of Oakleys and a Patriots cap and one wearing an Eagles cap—enter the shop.

Oh God. Oh God, oh God.

So close. They'd been so close.

"Easy," Ethan whispered in her ear. "Just take it easy."

27

As casually as possible and keeping one eye on the men in the mirror, Ethan positioned himself directly behind Darcy and squarely in the line of any fire that might break out.

He took stock of the way the two men sauntered in as bold as brass, Oakley leading the way.

Confident as hell, aren't you, asshole? Ethan thought with a quick glance at the freckle-faced kid behind the counter.

By this time, asshole number two had joined his partner and crowded up close behind Ethan.

"For you, sir?" the kid asked Ethan, tucking the towel he'd been using to wipe the counter beneath the register.

His eyes still on the Patriots cap, Ethan smiled like he didn't have a care in the world. "I'll have a double pistachio topped with a cache of semiautomatic weapons, please."

And that was all she wrote.

When the clerk's hand reappeared, it was full of firepower. And it was pointed dead center at the middle *t* in Patriots.

Ethan dodged left, taking Darcy with him. He dived

for the floor, covering her body with his. At the same time, six stools scraped against the white tile floor as the CIA agents planted at the tables rushed the pair of would-be assassins and took them down without firing a shot.

"You knew about this?" Darcy railed as Mutt and Jeff were taken away in handcuffs.

"Eat your ice cream before it melts," Ethan said, as much to settle her down as to distract her. He'd personally gone behind the counter and scooped up a cone for her when her first one had gone sailing. "Are you okay? No bruises from hitting the floor?"

"You knew the place was planted with CIA agents and you didn't tell me?" She glared at him, ignoring his concern.

God, she was mad. He understood. It was a helluva lot easier to explode in anger than in tears when you were as proud as this woman, and Lord knows she had more than enough reason to lose it. "I didn't want to tip our hand."

"I wouldn't have tipped our hand!"

"Darcy, I'm sorry, okay?" He tugged her aside when one of the CIA operatives walked past them toward the back of the shop to pick up some equipment. "If it'll make you feel any better, it was them, not me, who wanted you out of the loop."

"It makes me feel just dandy. When I saw those two guys come in here, I thought . . . I thought . . ." Her voice broke. She swallowed.

"You thought we were goners. I know." He drew her against him. "And again, I'm sorry."

She heaved a huge breath and pushed away, hanging on tight to her arms to keep herself together.

"Now if you want me to, I'll fill you in."

With a clipped nod, she let him steer her toward an ice-cream chair and set her down.

"*Everyone* in the shop was a CIA operative?"

It was all he could do not to laugh at her pouty look. "Just listen, okay?"

"Fine," she conceded as he pulled out a chair beside her.

"All right," he began. "Once Eddie contacted his superiors in D.C. they went to work. First thing they did was stake out my SUV. Turns out it *was* bugged."

"So you were right."

He nodded. "As long as we were in my SUV, Gatlin's goons were able to eavesdrop on every word we said once we left West Palm."

"Which explains why they were waiting for us at the post office this afternoon."

"And why they knew exactly where we were going tonight."

She blinked up at him, confused. "If the CIA knew your SUV was bugged, why didn't they debug it . . . or whatever it is they do?"

He grinned. "They didn't *debug* it because they were using us for bait. The idea was to draw out those two hired guns, hoping they'd scramble like hell to follow us and intercept the tape before we turned it over to Ted."

"Oh yeah. The nonexistent Ted."

"Oh, he exists. It's just that he was my freshman science teacher. Haven't seen him since I graduated."

She was not amused. But she was putting it together. "So that's why you were repeating the address of the shop and the street names on the way here. You were feeding them information."

"Dishing it up with a shovel. Fortunately, they ate it up and walked directly into the trap."

She finally took a lick of her ice cream. "Now what happens?"

"Now they'll be questioned, shaken down, and threatened within an inch of treason. Now *there's* a word that'll put the fear of God into a man. With luck, they'll roll over fast—not that we figure they were taking direct orders from Gatlin, but it won't take long for the minor monkeys to fall out of the tree and drag the king ape with them once they start talking."

"And what happens to us?"

The freckle-faced ice-cream scooper, who looked like he should be playing pickup basketball on a neighborhood court instead of taking down bad guys, walked up to their table and answered her question.

"Ms. Prescott. Mr. Garrett. If you could both come with me, please, I'd appreciate it. Oh," he added with a polite smile, "and I'll take that tape now, if it's no imposition."

Ethan fished the tape out of his pocket and handed it over. "With my blessings."

OFFICE OF THE SECRETARY OF STATE, WASHINGTON, D.C.
THREE DAYS LATER

It was nearing 3:00 p.m. as Darcy waited beside Ethan in a small vestibule to the rear of Secretary of State Hugh Morgan's office.

She'd met the secretary only moments ago. He reminded her of Al Hayden. And she'd felt an immediate sense of security in Morgan's presence.

Even so, her pulse thrummed in anticipation as she crossed her legs, then smoothed a nervous hand over her hair.

"Easy, babe," Ethan said with an approving nod. "You look amazing."

Darcy composed herself, gave him a tight smile, and looked away from the truly amazing picture he made sitting there on a green silk brocade wing chair identical to hers.

Today was the first time she'd seen him since they'd been driven from the ice-cream shop to the State Department Complex three grueling days ago.

She'd fought missing him. Every minute, every hour, she'd fought the good fight.

Just like she was fighting her reaction to finally seeing him again today.

He'd shaved. Gotten a haircut. And evidently, like her, he'd been allowed a quick shopping trip—on Uncle Sam's tab. His summer-weight suit was a stunning charcoal blue, and though there couldn't have been time for tailoring, it looked as if it had been designed to fit his tall, athletic body. His shirt was white; his tie was an understated stripe of navy, gray, and red.

To say he was impressive was to say the president was the most powerful man in the world. It was a new look for Ethan—at least in her experience. And just sitting there, not touching her, not saying a word that might indicate he'd been missing her, too, the power he wielded over her was stunning.

"Like the suit," he said, the same way he might have said, *Nice day.*

She wasn't normally the power suit type. At least it was a power suit in cut—the skirt was short and slim, the jacket fitted and sleek. And red.

The occasion had called for red.

The past three days she and Ethan had been separated and grilled and required to write down to the last microdetail everything they could remember about the Abu Sayyaf cell, their location, their members and weaponry . . . everything. Many things she'd just as soon have forgotten.

Amy remained a huge question mark but, it seemed, a benign one as far as the CIA was concerned. Ambassador Charles Gatlin, however, had a lot of questions to answer.

Darcy heard the murmur of voices in the secretary's office and her pulse jumped again.

"Almost showtime." Ethan shot her an encouraging grin.

"Yeah." She wiped damp palms on her skirt, refused to give in to the urge to reach out her hand to him, and focused on what was to come. She forced a brittle smile. "Almost showtime."

Charles Gatlin flicked a speck of lint from the sleeve of his six-thousand-dollar raw silk suit that he'd had tailor-made the last time he'd been in Paris to attend a state dinner. He paced in restless anticipation around the anteroom outside the secretary's office, shot his cuffs, squared his shoulders, and congratulated himself on a job well done.

In fact, he felt smug as hell that he'd been called back to D.C. for an audience with the Secretary of State. It continued to amaze Charles just how ineffective the "machine" that ran the government was. How little anyone knew about what happened in the real world. And how easy everyone was to deceive.

Take the Amanda Stover–Darcy Prescott episode. Although he'd had a few anxious moments, in the end, handling that little problem had almost been too easy.

But that was all behind him now. He breathed a satisfied breath, then checked his watch. He had an hour to make his next appointment. Should be plenty of time. Once he finished here, he'd make the scheduled meet and retrieve the tape that had added a few gray hairs. At this stage of the game, he didn't trust the transfer to anyone but himself.

That's why he was where he was today. Because he knew how to get things done. And that's why he'd been called back to the states. Ambassadors weren't pulled away from their posts unless there was something major on the horizon. Something like a commendation.

And why not? He'd earned it. Relations between the U.S. and the Philippine government had remained status quo under his ambassadorship—no easy feat in today's international climate and with the threat of global terrorism.

Of course he was appreciated. Of course he was due for some sort of recognition for his hard work.

And of course they didn't know about his extracurricular activities, he thought with a smug smile.

The door to the secretary's inner sanctum opened with barely a hint of sound.

"The secretary will see you now." A pinch-faced, matronly support staff stood like a sentry at the door.

Charles walked into the office with a spring in his step. "Secretary Morgan," he said with a hearty smile, and extended a hand as Morgan looked up from his massive antique cherry desk.

"Have a seat."

When Morgan rudely dismissed Charles's offer of a handshake, a nuisance kernel of unease drew his brows together in a frown.

"It's good to see you, sir," Charles said, feeling his

way carefully and wondering why he suddenly sensed a need to proceed with care.

Okay, he thought. *Okay.* Maybe he'd been wrong. Maybe this command performance wasn't about a commendation. Maybe it was about Darcy Prescott after all. There was bound to be concern. Bound to be a little wrist slapping over losing two embassy employees. Yes. It should be expected.

"I hope you're well," Charles continued, and told himself he wasn't groveling. He would not grovel to anyone.

Morgan's expression remained unchanged as he opened a drawer, drew out a tape recorder, and set it on the desk's glossy surface.

Charles didn't have time to swallow back the alarm that sent bile shooting to his throat before Morgan pressed the play button.

"What . . . what's this about, Hugh?" Charles squirmed in his chair.

Morgan pinned Charles with a look that commanded silence.

And then Charles heard his own voice resonate from the recorder. He felt the blood drain from his face just as the earth dropped out from under him.

This couldn't be happening.

This couldn't fucking be happening.

He'd received word from his man in D.C. three days ago. Word that his "problem" had been taken care of. That Prescott and Garrett were out of the picture. That the tape was secured.

Charles was peripherally aware of a door to the left of the secretary's desk opening. He flicked his gaze in that direction—and almost swallowed his tongue.

He stood shakily. Backed up a clumsy step, stumbled when he bumped into his chair.

Darcy Prescott.

"How?" he mouthed inanely.

"Hello, Ambassador," Prescott said as a tall, hard-edged man joined her.

Garrett. Charles knew without a doubt it had to be Garrett.

"You look a little surprised to see us," Garrett said.

There was no longer any reason for pretense. It was over. "That's because you're supposed to be dead," he said flatly.

"Money isn't the only thing that buys loyalty," Garrett said with a smug look. "You should be more careful who you hire to do your dirty work. Some men will say anything, tell any lies—oh, say like lying about Darcy Prescott being dead when, as you can see, she's very much alive."

Charles sank back down on the chair, dropped his head into his hands. He was ruined.

All he'd worked for. All he'd risked.

"I hope you rot in a cell for the rest of your life for what you did to Amanda. For what you tried to do to me. For what you were doing to your country."

Charles lifted his head, met Darcy Prescott's eyes, saw the hate, the disgust—and worse, a measure of pity—that punctuated her words.

He looked away. Heard another door open. Two pairs of uniformed legs appeared in front of him.

"I want a lawyer."

"Get him his lawyer," Morgan said. "But first get him out of my sight."

"Are the handcuffs really necessary?" Charles made

an attempt at a sympathy bid as the officers snapped on the cuffs.

But the secretary had already turned away.

"I want to thank you again, both of you," Morgan said as he extended his hand first to Darcy, then to Ethan. "The nation is in your debt. And so am I."

No one would ever know that, of course. For their own protection and privacy, no one would ever know that Darcy or Ethan had anything to do with bringing Charles Gatlin's little ring of traitors and terrorists down.

"What happens now?" Darcy asked as the secretary walked them to the door.

"The two men we took into custody have already given up their contacts. We were able to apprehend them within twelve hours. It didn't take them long to roll over, either."

He paused, smiled. "Gatlin's cohorts are bailing like rats from a sinking ship. And for the time being, at least, there will be no exchange of enriched uranium in the Middle East.

"The depth and breadth of Gatlin's sphere of influence is staggering," he went on grimly. "I can't give you specifics, of course, but as we speak, there are a number of individuals being systematically apprehended and taken into custody. Once Gatlin rolls over, there will, no doubt, be more."

"Why would he talk?" Darcy asked as they stopped by the door.

"He'll talk," Ethan explained when the secretary nodded for him to go ahead, "because he knows he has nothing left to do but try to negotiate for leniency."

"Don't worry," Morgan added, evidently reading Darcy's mind. "He'll talk, but he won't walk. What he's done, what he was about to do . . . well, the fallout for the entire free world will be stunning.

"He's going to pay. Trust me on that, Darcy. Gatlin will never see the outside of a federal prison compound."

Darcy let out a breath that was heavy with relief.

"Thank you again," Morgan said. "We'll let you know if we need anything else from you, but for now, your depositions should be more than enough to seal this up good and tight. The fact is, and don't take this wrong, but the issue of your abduction and the attempted murder will most likely never become a part of the state's case."

"Small potatoes compared to treason," Darcy said with a smile. "I understand. And believe me, I'm fine with never seeing that man's face up close and personal again."

"Freedom," she said, taking a deep breath of the summer air when they stepped outside. "No more ducking and running."

"Yeah. It feels good," Ethan agreed, standing on the steps beside her.

She tipped her head back, drew in another breath, free of the pinched, life-threatening tension she'd felt for the past two weeks.

"Thank you," she said, turning to this man who had risked his life for her. It said so much about him. And yet here they stood. Quiet suddenly.

"So," he said after a long moment, "where do you go from here?"

An unreasonable disappointment swamped her.

He hadn't asked, *Where do* we *go from here?* He wanted to know where *she* went from here.

And it reminded her that nothing had really changed between them.

"Home," she said, and meant it with everything in her. "I want to go home."

28

DARCY SAT ON THE FRONT PORCH OF THE old house she'd called home for the first eighteen years of her life. She leaned back against a porch post, feeling lazy and a little lost, and watched the sporadic late afternoon traffic shuttle by on the quiet street.

It was almost twilight and she was pleasantly saturated with the scents and sounds drifting comfortably around her. Cut grass and motor oil. The roses her grandmother had planted still climbed the trellis in the tiny flower garden beside the front steps.

Her dad had painted the porch swing just before she'd come home. Darcy could smell that, too. Along with her mom's hair spray and the lingering scent of the diner on her uniform.

A porch board creaked when Darcy's mom shifted a hip so she could face her. "So, how long before that wanderlust of yours takes hold again and we have to give you up?"

It had been a little over a week since Darcy had flown home. When she'd shown up at her parents' door, there had been a lot of crying and laughing and hugging. Her sister flew in from Chicago for a few days, too—and the crying had started all over again. It had been wonderful. And exactly what Darcy had needed.

Darcy looked into her mother's beautiful green eyes, framed now by fine lines of fatigue and time.

"I'm not so sure wanderlust is the issue that it once was for me, Mom."

Her mother was wise. Wise enough not to dig or pry into what had happened to change Darcy's mind. And when a cab pulled up and they could both very clearly see the tall, ruggedly handsome man climb out of the backseat, Darcy's mother was also wise enough to make herself scarce.

Ethan.

More than surprise made Darcy's pulse jump.

Her mother stood, then squeezed her shoulder. "I'll just go see what your father's up to in the backyard."

If Darcy were as wise as her mother, she'd follow her into the house, then right on out the back door.

But Darcy wasn't wise. And she didn't follow. She just sat there. And watched with an unreasonable hope expanding in her chest as Ethan walked up the cracked sidewalk toward her.

He was wearing a pair of snug, worn jeans, the kind that came off the stacks in department stores but looked like designer originals on him. His arms were strong and tan below the short sleeves of a shirt the color of his eyes.

Blue eyes. Amazing eyes that never left her face as he stopped on the walk in front of her.

"Hi," he said in that low and lush voice that always prompted the beginning of a meltdown.

Up close, he looked tired. No. Make that weary. A

world-worn weary that made her want to reach out to him.

She folded her hands on her lap and resisted the urge. "Hi."

"You look good," he said, and finally looked away, his attention landing on the porch roof, then wandering to the windows, the little flower garden, none of which he'd ever seen.

"Nice place. Homey," he added of the regal old house that had been built by her grandfather and cared for over the years with much love.

"Yeah," she agreed. "It's a great place."

Then she willed herself to . . . to what? Breathe, for one thing.

She didn't know what to do. What to say. She wasn't even sure what she was feeling.

Or maybe she just didn't trust what she was feeling. She loved this man. Would always love this man. But she couldn't recommit her life to someone who, in the final windup, was incapable of sharing what mattered most. His life. Both the good and the bad.

Okay. No one had said anything about recommitting. And yet . . . he was here.

"You doing okay?" she finally asked, because he seemed so *uncertain* standing there and because *uncertain* was a word she had never associated with Ethan Garrett.

"Yeah. I'm good. Fine. Um . . ." He lifted a hand. "Can I sit?"

"Oh, sure. Of course. I'm sorry." She scooted over to make room, annoyed with herself for making him stand there so long. "How's your leg?"

"Good. It's good."

He propped his feet on a lower step and his elbows on his knees. Then he stared at the hands he clasped between them. "I hope it's okay. That I came, I mean. Without calling."

She studied the slash of his dark brow, the firm line of his jaw, the slight hollow of his cheek that defined his intensely handsome features, and felt an ache of loss so sharp and deep it made her dizzy.

"Why are you here, Ethan?" He hadn't come all the way to Ohio just to sit on her parents' front porch. And she couldn't stand this strained politeness a moment longer.

Behind her, she heard the back door open, then close.

He glanced over his shoulder, then back at her. "Maybe we should walk."

When he stood, she hesitated for a long moment, mesmerized by the hand he held out to her—the strength of it, the scars, the short, neat nails and healthy veins running beneath tanned skin.

Finally, she took it. With an ache in her heart. And that damn unreasonable hope still clogging her throat.

Ethan had taken Nolan's advice. When he returned to West Palm a week ago, he'd spent that week aboard the *EDEN,* the boat the old man had bought and restored when Ethan had still been a kid.

"There's something about being aboard her," Nolan had said, working to convince Ethan. "I don't know what it is. Just you, the water, the boat. Helps you think. Maybe it's more that it *lets* you think."

Nolan ought to know. Last year, he'd lived on the fifty-six-footer for almost three months after he'd separated from the Rangers. He'd needed time to get his head back together and out of the scotch. Of course, Jillian was, in part, responsible for helping Nolan make that transition.

But the *EDEN*—well, as it turned out, she'd been responsible for Ethan getting his head on straight, too.

"It's very possible that I'm going to blow this big-time," he said as they walked toward the end of the block in the quiet, older neighborhood.

"Just say what's on your mind."

"Right," he said, regrouping and decided to just blurt it out. "The thing is, you were right."

Beside him, her hands tucked in the back pockets of her jean shorts, Darcy walked with her head down. She didn't break stride or look up from what appeared to be rapt fascination with the cracks in the sidewalks. "What was I right about?"

"About me blaming you. For Tel Aviv."

Her steps faltered, then stopped altogether. She tipped her face up to his. God, he loved that face. And those eyes that could dance with intelligence or fire or laughter. There was no laughter now. Now there were questions. And, thank you God, there was hope.

He started walking again, his eyes fixed dead ahead of them. He could smell hickory from backyard grills being fired up for dinner. A kid—maybe ten, maybe twelve—sailed by on the opposite side of the street, working his skateboard for all he was worth.

"I blamed you and didn't even know that's what I was doing until you pointed it out to me in D.C." He pushed out a sound of self-disgust. "And even then, I told myself you were way off base."

She had questions. He knew she had questions, but she let him tell this his own way.

"It took last week to figure out that you were right. That I *did* blame you. And as for the reason why . . . well, it's pretty screwed up.

"The God's honest truth," he hurried on even though his explanation made him sound like a head case, "is that it was just easier that way. *Much* easier to blame you than to accept it was *my* fault because . . . well, hell, if I took the blame, then I'd have had to actually *deal* with it, wouldn't I? And if I'd had to deal with one death, then I'd have to deal with . . . all the others."

The others. God, there had been so many others.

Beside him, she was silent. But she was listening. If her heart was beating as hard as his, they were both in trouble.

"Look," he continued, still groping for the right way to get this out. "The reason I badgered you to go back to the states was just like I said. I wanted you safe. But what I didn't say was that even more, I wanted you someplace where who I was . . . what I did, would never touch you."

"You were a soldier, Ethan. What you did was your job."

"Yeah. My job. 'Join the Army. See the world. Kill the bad guys.' It . . . it all sounded so noble, you know?"

"It *is* noble," she said softly.

"Yeah. Yeah . . . it's noble as hell. Until you live it. And then it's just . . . real."

Her hand touched his arm, soft, caring. "Ethan—"

He shook his head. Stopped her. Now that he'd started talking, he didn't seem to be able to stop. "I'd killed so much. I'd never realized how . . . I don't know . . . how dead it had made me inside. But it's how all of us guys dealt with it, you know? I mean, how else could you live with something like that? You couldn't think about it. It would drive you crazy. So you pushed it away. You buried it deep. And you pretended it wasn't a part of who you really were while you prepared to kill again."

He swallowed hard. Thinking about this and sorting it out by himself had been one thing. Saying the words aloud to the one person he needed to understand was another. And remembering . . . actually forcing himself to remember felt like a bloodletting.

"It was my job," he said, ashamed when his voice broke, ashamed of the need to defend what he'd done. "Killing the bad guys."

He drew an unsteady breath. "And then you came along. And for the first time in longer than I could remember, you reminded me what it was like to be a man. Just a man. Not a killer.

"And that's what I was, Darcy. Whether I was doing it in the name of patriotism or democracy or God, I was still a killer."

A killer. A killer. A killer.

Oh God. Oh Jesus. He was losing it. He'd come to confess to her. And all of a sudden, he was losing it. He felt the sting of tears. Clenched his jaw against the sudden need to bawl like a goddamn baby. His hands were shaking when he dragged them over his face.

And then she was there. Her soft warmth pressed against him. Her sweet, giving arms wrapped around him. He lowered his head to her hair. Breathed in the wonderful, familiar scent of her and held on.

"Christ, Darcy, the first time I saw you . . . I knew I'd kill for you if I had to. But I never thought it would happen. I never wanted it to happen. You were the one thing, *the one thing* that was good and sweet and pure and important . . . and you were never supposed to be touched by that part of my life."

In the middle of this sleepy street that epitomized all America stood for, he was back in Israel.

"When I took that guy out in Tel Aviv . . ." His voice broke again. His thoughts scattered. "Afterward. The way you looked at me . . . like I was some kind of a monster. It killed me. Ate at me like jungle rot."

She pulled back, made him look at her. "Ethan. I never thought you were a monster. Driven by them, yes. But never a monster. You were my husband. I wanted to help you. I needed to help you. But you always shut me out."

"I know that. I know that now. But back then I told myself I was protecting you. Truth was I couldn't talk about it then." He pushed out a dark laugh. "Hell. I can't talk about it now. It makes me crazy to think about it."

She leaned into him, wrapped her arms tighter around his waist, and held on.

"I still see them. I still . . . see their faces."

He lowered his face to her hair and held on to the one thing he needed to make him whole.

"I don't want to see them anymore."

Darcy didn't know how long they stayed that way. Several cars went by. She heard a baby crying and a mother calling her kids in to supper.

But she stood there. And she held on to her man. And he was hers now. In ways he'd never been before.

"Come on," she said after she felt his big body

steady. "Let's go in the house. I have a feeling there's an extra place set for you at the table."

He rubbed his cheek against her hair before lifting his head. His eyes were damp when they searched hers. "And how do you feel about that?"

She brought her hands to his face. "I feel like it's been way too long since you found your way home."

"Feels a little naughty, doesn't it?" Ethan rolled to his back and took Darcy with him. "Doing what we're doing in your parents' house, in their little girl's bedroom."

Yeah, it felt a little naughty. But it felt nice, too. So had the past few days Darcy and Ethan had spent getting to know each other again. Just lying back, letting it come, letting him talk.

They'd both done some healing. But healing wasn't on her mind at the moment. The way he made her shiver was.

He felt warm and naked and wonderful beneath her. And she wanted him inside of her so badly she ached with it.

"Come on, sweetheart. Work with me," he said with a grin spawned by the devil as he caressed her naked butt, then parted her thighs and started a little deep-tissue massage. "Tell me it feels naughty. Fulfill my fantasy."

She moaned when he touched her. "What it feels is good. Sooo gooood," she said on a deep, blissful sigh when he found a particularly sensitive spot.

"There are definite advantages to single beds." He sat up abruptly and arranged her legs around his waist. "Makes cuddling mandatory."

When he reached between them and lifted her, pushing inside her with just the tip of his penis, she gasped.

"Makes—"

"Ethan," she groaned, cutting him off. "Stop talking. Just . . . oh God . . . just stop talking."

"And do what?" he murmured against her mouth.

"What you're doing."

His chuckle was deep and smug as, still holding her hips between his palms, he lowered her another fraction of an inch. "You mean this?"

"Yesss." It came out as a plea as she tried to initiate more contact.

He wouldn't let her. He kissed her hard and deep, moving his tongue in and out of her mouth like she wanted him moving in and out of her body.

"Pleasseee," she begged. He was killing her.

"There it is." He sounded way too pleased with himself. "I love it when you beg."

"Will you quit joking around and get serious?"

"With pleasure."

He plunged her down onto him, filling her so full, then moving so hard and fast that she came in a blinding rush.

She hadn't even realized she'd screamed until he covered her mouth with his hand. She sagged against him, gasping for breath.

He stroked her back, stroked her hair. "How was that for serious?"

She smiled against his chest. "It'll work."

"And how's this for serious? Marry me."

She lifted her head. His eyes were glittering and dark when he searched hers. All the teasing and playing was gone. "Marry me again."

Darcy felt the love she'd been keeping penned up in the dark all these years dance with the joy of release.

And just as she had the first time he'd asked, she answered without hesitation. "Yes."

He hugged her hard. "I love you. My life is so much better with you in it than out of it."

Her heart nearly burst with love for him. "You just stole my lines."

"I won't blow it this time," he promised. "I'll make it work."

"*We'll* make it work," she said. "And this time I'll fight instead of run."

"This time, I won't give you a reason to do either."

EPILOGUE

**WEST PALM BEACH
THREE WEEKS LATER**

"ARE THEY ALWAYS THIS COMPETITIVE?" Darcy watched Ethan's sister and her hunky hubby try to beat the heck out of each other on the croquet court set up in Wes and Susan Garrett's backyard.

Ethan gauged the distance to the next hoop, then made his shot. His ball landed in perfect alignment with the center hoop. "Eve and Mac have been trying to best each other since they met up about a year ago— I believe she was holding a gun on him at the time.

"Don't worry about it." He slung an arm over Darcy's shoulders. "They seem to thrive on it."

Darcy couldn't argue with his take on it as she watched Eve knock Mac's ball off the court, then shoot him a gloating grin and polish her nails on her shoulder in acknowledgment of a job well done.

"That's it," Mac sputtered. "I'm cutting you off. No *sugar* for you for a month, cupcake."

Eve snorted. "Right, McClain. Like you could hold out for a month."

Mac, who could have passed for a Garrett with his tall, dark good looks, spun his spunky blond wife—who was going to look exactly like her mother when she was Susan Garrett's age—into his arms. "Oh, believe me, I can. You're the one who'll be begging. She loves her M&M's," Mac said in an aside, and made Darcy laugh.

"We're talking about M&M's, are we?"

"Might even kill for them," Eve agreed with an evil grin at Mac, who grunted, set her aside, and went in search of his ball.

"Mac seems to fit in just fine with the Garrett clan."

"Water seeks its own level," Ethan agreed. "At the risk of sounding pushy, are you planning to hit that ball or just admire it all afternoon?"

"Your mother told me you all took your croquet seriously."

"It's sacred," he said, deadpan.

Apparently, he was only half-joking. Once a month, rain or shine, the Garretts got together for cutthroat croquet and a backyard barbecue. Their father grilled and grinned and their mother beamed and fussed over her family of rabble-rousers.

"So if the game is sacred, why isn't Nolan worshipping at the altar?"

Ethan's scowl made her smile. "His priorities are a little skewed right now."

Even though he was grousing, when he cut a glance at Nolan, who was hovering around a very pregnant Jillian and catering to her every whim, Darcy could tell that Ethan was totally okay with Nolan's new priorities. Which didn't appear to be nearly as many as Nolan seemed to think there were.

It was fun watching him and Jillian together.

It was fun watching all the Garretts.

"Um . . . Darcy . . . At the risk of sounding surly—"

"I know. I know. Hit the ball."

She gave it her all. And the ball dribbled all of three feet forward.

"Oops."

"Your woman may be a looker, but she's pathetic with a mallet," Dallas said, taking his turn behind her.

"Don't pay any attention to him. You just need a little practice. Then you'll whip his whiny ass." Ethan drew her into his arms. His eyes lit with an intimate and smoldering heat. "In the meantime, you're good at so many other things."

"Yeah. And I'm a fast learner."

"Won't get any argument from me on that count."

Darcy felt her cheeks heat. She knew he was thinking about what they'd done in bed last night. He was always inventive, this man she would marry in three months.

They were doing it right this time. A church wedding with all their family and friends in attendance to witness their love for each other.

"You know something else I love about you?" Ethan dropped a kiss on her nose and offered her a Life Saver. "You work cheap."

It had become a standing joke between them. Whenever he was feeling romantic, he dangled a cherry Life Saver in front of her like a carrot.

What could she say? She was a sucker for his candy. And she was a sucker for this beautiful man who had done more than make promises not to let her down this time.

He wasn't letting himself down, either. He was seeing someone. A psychiatrist at the VA center was helping Ethan work through the guilt he'd bottled up for years.

The sessions were hard sometimes. For both Darcy and Ethan. But they were also healing. And Darcy wanted that for him more, even, than she wanted it for them.

"Ha!" Eve's ball sailed through the last set of hoops and hit the stake with a crack. "You're looking at the winner and new *champion*."

She did a little victory dance. "Pay up, chumps. I'll take it in chocolate."

Dallas shook his head. "She's gonna gloat all week."

"Damn straight," Eve crowed.

And while her brothers all grumbled, the love they felt for their sister was apparent.

"I swear, Eve. I never taught you to behave like that."

"Don't worry, Mom." Mac hooked an arm around Eve's neck and tipped her face up to his. "I know how to shut her up."

Then he kissed her, long and loud and noisy. Eve's eyes were a little glazed when he finished with her.

"You kids go on in and wash up now," Susan said, shaking her head. "Those burgers are about done, right, Wes?"

"If you like 'em medium well"—Wes, who was an older version of his boys, checked his wristwatch— "you've got about two minutes."

Darcy and Ethan hung back while Eve and Mac, followed by Dallas, trooped into the house.

"Dallas seems a little quiet, sometimes."

Ethan glanced at his brother. "Sometimes, yeah."

"No word from Amy?"

Ethan shook his head. "Guess not."

"She went through a lot. Maybe she just needs some time to sort things out."

"Yeah, well, we may never know. I didn't see it anyway. Amy Walker just didn't seem like Dallas's type. You, however," he said, his smile returning, "are definitely mine."

"Damn straight," she said, echoing Eve's crowing tone and accomplishing what she'd set out to do.

He laughed and pulled her into his arms. "Warning: do not take lessons on sass from my sister. It'll land you in big trouble."

She snuggled up next to him. "I've had enough trouble lately to last me a lifetime. But then again," she said, reconsidering, "there have been certain benefits."

"Like?"

"Like a lifetime supply of Life Savers and my own personal candy man."

"Whatever it takes, babe. Whatever it takes."

Darcy was sound asleep and tucked against Ethan's side in bed when the news report came on at eleven.

"Sources close to the State Department have confirmed that former U.S. ambassador to the Philippines Charles Gatlin, who was removed from his post last month, is dead, his death the result of a self-inflicted wound.

"As we first reported, Gatlin, a well-known industrialist who had gained his ambassadorship several years ago, was charged with several counts of embezzlement, fraud, and illegal brokering of weaponry.

"While never confirmed, it has been reported by an unidentified source that the former ambassador was believed to have been involved in a corporate espionage scam that had the potential to place the national security of the United States and other nations committed to democracy in jeopardy. The State Department has made no comment on the accuracy of those rumors.

"Secretary of State Hugh Morgan expressed condolences to the Gatlin family today along with regret over the circumstances of both Gatlin's removal from office and the charges that were filed.

"Morgan further stated—and this is a direct quote— 'While the former ambassador's death is regrettable, it would appear that justice has been served.'

"Moving on to other news . . ."

Ethan didn't hear a word after the report on Gatlin. He was too busy feeling relief.

Darcy's ordeal was officially over.

Finally.

He picked up the remote and hit the power button.

Then he turned off the light and drew his woman— his life—closer against his side.

She murmured in her sleep and nestled her cheek on his shoulder.

She thought he'd saved her life when he'd found her in the jungles of Jolo.

Ethan knew better. He knew exactly who had done the saving.

And he knew exactly who had been saved.

Don't miss the next novel in
the heart-stopping Bodyguards series from
USA Today bestselling author

CINDY GERARD

INTO THE DARK

[ISBN: 0-312-98118-X]

He's bound by duty . . . and unleashed by desire.

Amy Walker endured unspeakable horrors while
being held as a hostage before she was rescued by
Dallas Garrett and his brothers from E.D.E.N.,
Inc. But now that Amy has received Dallas's
sworn protection, will she accept his heart?

Coming in June 2007 from St. Martin's Paperbacks

www.cindygerard.com